So Far Gone

ALSO BY JESS WALTER

Fiction

The Angel of Rome

The Cold Millions

We Live in Water

Beautiful Ruins

The Financial Lives of the Poets

The Zero

Citizen Vince

Land of the Blind

Over Tumbled Graves

Nonfiction

Ruby Ridge (previously released as *Every Knee Shall Bow*)

SO FAR GONE

A Novel

Jess Walter

HARPER

An Imprint of HarperCollinsPublishers

HarperCollins books may be purchased for educational, business, or sales promotional use. For information, please email the Special Markets Department at SPsales@harpercollins.com.

FIRST EDITION

Designed by Michele Cameron

Library of Congress Cataloging-in-Publication Data
Names: Walter, Jess, 1965– author.
Title: So far gone: a novel / Jess Walter.
Description: First edition. | New York, NY: Harper, 2025.
Identifiers: LCCN 2024043225 (print) | LCCN 2024043226 (ebook) |
ISBN 9780062868145 (hardcover) | ISBN 9780062868169 (ebook)
Subjects: LCGFT: Novels.
Classification: LCC PS3573.A4722834 S64 2025 (print) |
LCC PS3573.A4722834 (ebook) | DDC 813/.6—dc23/eng/20240920
LC record available at https://lccn.loc.gov/2024043225
LC ebook record available at https://lccn.loc.gov/2024043226

25 26 27 28 29 LBC 5 4 3 2 1

To my family

Not till we are lost . . . till we have lost the world,
do we begin to find ourselves.

—HENRY DAVID THOREAU

So Far Gone

ONE

What Happened to Kinnick

A prim girl stood still as a fencepost on Rhys Kinnick's front porch. Next to her, a cowlicked boy shifted his weight from snow boot to snow boot. Both kids wore backpacks. On the stairs below them, a woman held an umbrella against the pattering rain.

It was the little girl who'd knocked. Kinnick cracked the door. He rasped through the dirty screen: "Magazines or chocolate bars?"

The girl, who looked to be about ten, squinted. "What did you say?"

Had he misspoken? How long since Kinnick had talked to anyone? "I said, what are you fine young capitalists selling? Magazines or chocolate bars?"

"We aren't selling anything," said the boy. He appeared to be about six. "We're your grandchildren."

A sound came from Kinnick's throat then—a gasp, he might have written it, back when he wrote for a living. *Of course* they were his grandchildren. He hadn't really looked at their faces. And this strange woman on the steps had thrown him. But now that he did look, he saw family there, in the pronounced upper lip, and the deep-set, searching eyes. No, clearly this was Leah and Asher. Christ! When had he seen them last? He tried to remember, straining to apply an increasingly muddled concept: time. His daughter had brought them up here for a short visit one afternoon. When was that, three years ago? Four?

Either way, these were *not* strangers selling candy for their school. These were his *grandkids*, flesh and blood of Rhys Kinnick's flesh and blood, his only child, Bethany. But older than six and ten. More muddled time work was required to figure out how much.

"Mr. Kinnick?" The woman with the umbrella was speaking now.

"Yes," he said. "I'm Kinnick." He addressed the kids again. "Is . . . is everything . . . Are you . . ." The thoughts came too quickly for his mouth to form around them. He opened the door wider. "Where's your mother?"

"We're not sure," Leah said. "Mom left a couple of days ago. She said she'd be back in a week. Shane left yesterday to find her." This was *thirteen*-year-old Leah. Her father was Bethany's old boyfriend Sluggish Doug, long out of the picture.

The boy, eight, no *nine*! Nine-year-old Asher was Shithead Shane's kid.

Oh, the riddle of time—and of Bethany's taste in men.

Kinnick looked at the woman behind his grandchildren. She was Black, with big round glasses, in her thirties, if he had to guess, roughly his daughter's age. She climbed the last step onto the porch.

"I'm Anna Gaines," the woman said. "My husband and I live in the same apartment complex as Bethany and Shane. This morning, Leah came over with this." She held out an envelope. On it, written in Sharpie in Bethany's handwriting: "FOR ANNA." Below that: "in case of emergency."

"Mom left it in the closet," Leah said, "in one of my snow boots."

Kinnick opened the front screen, came out, and took the envelope. He removed a single sheet of paper, handwritten on both sides in Bethany's neat, backward-leaning script. He patted his shirt pocket for his readers, then squinted to make out the note:

> Dear Anna. If you're reading this, I had to leave in a hurry. I know this is a lot to ask but can you take the kids to my father, Rhys Kinnick. He is a recluse . . .

Kinnick looked up. "I am not a recluse." He looked down and began reading again.

> Dear Anna. If you're reading this, I had to leave in a hurry. I
> know this is a lot to ask but can you take the kids to my father,
> Rhys Kinnick. He is a recluse who cut off contact with our
> family . . .

"I did not 'cut off contact.' It was—" Rhys felt his blood rising. "Complicated." But his grandchildren just stared at him, apparently as uninterested in nuance and complexity as everyone else in the world. Kinnick grunted again and went back to reading.

> Dear Anna. If you're reading this, I had to leave in a hurry. I
> know this is a lot to ask but can you take the kids to my father,
> Rhys Kinnick. He is a recluse who cut off contact with our
> family and now lives in squalor . . .

"Squalor?" Kinnick looked around his covered front porch. "Squalor?" In one corner, a broken old refrigerator stood next to a stack of used boat and car batteries and a burned-out inverter generator; in the other corner was his old wringer washing machine and a single clothesline, from which hung a pair of jeans and a sweatshirt. "What is this? *In case of emergency, go find my father and make him feel terrible about himself?*"

His grandchildren continued to stare. Kinnick groaned again, then resumed reading, vowing to make it through the whole letter this time.

> Dear Anna. If you're reading this, I had to leave in a hurry. I
> know this is a lot to ask but can you take the kids to my father,
> Rhys Kinnick. He is a recluse who cut off contact with our
> family and now lives in squalor in a cabin north of Spokane, in
> Stevens County. He lives off the grid and doesn't have email or

phone. Go north out of Spokane on Highway 395 for thirty-five
miles. At Loon Lake, turn onto Highway 292. Drive five miles,
and at the T, go right, in the opposite direction of the Spokane
Indian Reservation. Go through the little town of Springdale,
then turn left onto Hunters Road, and drive ten miles. You'll
come to another dirt road on the left that crosses a small bridge,
drive another quarter mile until you see a culvert and two tire
tracks cutting through a stand of birch trees on your left. This
is Dad's driveway. It is unmarked. Drive up a small rise and
you'll see his gray, cinder block house at the base of a hill above
a stream. A warning, my father can be rather acerbic—

"Acerbic?" He let the letter fall to his side. "Seriously, who asks for
help this way?" Still, in a flash of pride, he admired the rich language—
recluse, squalor, acerbic—Bethany still had a way with words. At one
time, he had thought maybe she'd become a writer, like he used to be,
but she lacked the patience, he supposed. Or maybe the confidence.

Then something else occurred to him, and he looked down at the
girl. "What about your grandmother?" But, as soon as he said it—

"Grandma Celia died," Leah said.

Asher nodded.

"Oh, no," Kinnick said. "When?"

"A month ago," Leah said.

"Oh, Celia." She'd always exuded a sort of frailty, as if she didn't
belong on this plane of existence. Kinnick fell against the doorframe,
his side cramping. No wonder Bethany had run off. Her mother had
been the closest thing she'd had to a compass.

"Grandma got lymphoma," Asher said. So strange, such a big word
coming from such a small mouth. Reminded him of Bethany when
she was little.

"Oh, Celia," Kinnick said again, and his eyes got bleary. He pictured
her as she'd been when they'd first met, at the University of Oregon

library, forty years ago, her long hair swishing side to side like a show-horse's tail. He was studying botany and natural sciences; she wanted to be a nurse. He remembered her asleep, turned away from him, the high curve of her cheekbone. Had anyone ever slept so peacefully? He used to put a hand in front of her mouth, just to feel her breath, make sure she was still there. They married a year after meeting, then finished grad school, welcomed Bethany into the world, and started their life together—until that life, like everything else decent and worthwhile, began to crack.

"I'll bet she was a wonderful grandmother," Kinnick said.

"Yes," said Leah, her brother nodding at her side.

Oh, poor Celia, Kinnick thought. And poor Bethany. He didn't picture her as she was now, lost mother to these two kids, but as his big-eyed baby girl, lying awake in bed every night, waiting for a story from her dad. And now, that girl, that woman, that mother, was without a mother. Oh, poor Bethany. And these poor kids, grandchildren he hasn't seen in years, that he hadn't even recognized on his front porch.

Rhys Kinnick nearly doubled over with a previously undiagnosed condition: regret. And this single, overwhelming thought: *What have I done?*

He cleared his throat. "Come in," he said to his grandkids. He opened the door wider. "Please, come in."

- - -

THE DAM BURST seven and a half years earlier, in Grants Pass, Oregon, 2016, forty minutes before Thanksgiving dinner, when Rhys Kinnick realized there was no place left for him in this risible world. It happened during a televised football game, of all things, Kinnick's son-in-law, Shane, running the remote, along with his mouth. Celia's new (old) husband, Cortland, snoring away in a recliner. Rhys sat helplessly between the dim husbands of daughter and ex-wife, quietly nursing his fourth beer. He was a terrible nurse. This patient wasn't likely to make it, either.

Kinnick had agreed to drive ten hours from Spokane to Grants Pass for one more attempt at a calm, blended family holiday. "No politics," Bethany had proposed, or maybe pleaded, Kinnick quickly agreeing to terms. He was the first to admit that he could get worked up talking with Shane about the recently decided dumpster fire of an election, and that, in Shane's words, he was still "butt hurt."

"I told Shane the same thing," Bethany said. "No religion. No politics. Let's just try to be a normal family."

Normal. Sure. Family. Right. And the first two hours were fine. Leah colored, Asher toddled, small-talking adults small-talked. So far so—

Then Asher went down for a nap, Leah went off to play dolls, Celia and Bethany drifted into the kitchen to cook dinner, and Shane immediately launched into his nutty Christian nationalism rap: "It might make you feel better, Rhys, to know that this was all prophesied in the Book of Daniel—"

—it did not make Rhys feel better—

"—that a king would rise up in the West to make his nation great again," Shane said, cracking a pistachio shell and eating the nut.

"Two thousand years ago," Kinnick said into his beer. *And*, he thought, *spoiler alert: Didn't happen then, either.*

"The Bible speaks to us in *our* time, in every time," Shane said. "Revelations 22:10: *'Seal not the sayings of the prophecy of this book: for the time is at hand.'*"

Rhys had promised Bethany and Celia he wouldn't make trouble, so he merely thought his answer: *Yes, Shane, you know-nothing know-it-all, the time IS at hand, present tense, meaning 95 AD, when some long-dead author wrote that allegorical nonsense about the brutal reign of the Roman emperor Domitian, not about immigration or the deep state or whatever bullshit you're confused about today.*

Next to him, Cortland—fifteen years older than Celia and as political as a tree stump—hummed in his sleep. Rhys looked around Shane and Bethany's tidy living room, with its cursive needlepoint (*Bless the Lord, O, my soul*) and framed Jesus-at-Sunset posters (*Praise Him, ye heavens of heavens, and ye waters that be above the heavens*).

He glanced back at Shane, all self-satisfaction and mudflap mustache, chomping pistachios. It was blissfully quiet for a moment, and Kinnick thought the worst might be over. Then, on TV, a pass interference call went against the Green Bay Packers, and Shane leaned across the recliners and confided to Kinnick: "They're in on it, too, you know."

It, Rhys knew by now, was the elaborate and all-encompassing conspiracy to indoctrinate Americans into a Satanic liberal orthodoxy whose end goal was to subsume good Christians like Shane into an immoral, one-world socialist nightmare in which people pooped in the wrong bathrooms.

Kinnick urged himself to stay quiet. To not ask questions. If you didn't ask Shane for more information, he sometimes just muttered off into silence. Rhys checked his watch. Thirty-five minutes to turkey. He could make that. Surely, he could be quiet for thirty-five—

"Who?" he heard himself ask. "The officials? You're saying the refs are in on it?"

Shane turned his head. "Refs? Come on, Rhys. You think the refs have that kind of power? Think for a minute: Who pays the refs?"

"Okay. So—" Rhys tried to keep it casual, asking over the rim of his beer, "you're saying the National Football League is engaged in a massive conspiracy . . . whose sole purpose is to deny victory to the teams you happen to like?"

"It's got nothing to do with me," Shane said. "It's common knowledge that politics and professional football were rigged the same year—2008. That's when the globalists put forward the final part of their plan: they'd already taken over universities, schools, every level of government, and they were about to give us a certain foreign president whose name I will not say out loud, but whose middle name is Hussein. The final push. They were starting to control sports, too. Don't forget who won the Super Bowl that year."

"No idea," Kinnick said.

"Two thousand eight? The New York Giants? Beat the New England Patriots? Think about it for just a second, Rhys. The *Patriots*? As in the real Americans? Losing to the *Giants*? Of New York? Giants as in the beast that rises out of the sea with seven heads and ten horns? As in the ten media companies and the seven boroughs of New York City? Come on, Rhys, you're a smart man. You think this is all a coincidence?"

"There are five boroughs in New York, Shane. And thousands of media companies."

"Then it's seven million people. I get the numbers mixed up."

"There are eight million people, and I seriously doubt that many lived in New York when Revelations was written."

"I told you: that's not how the Bible works, Rhys. It's a living document."

"It's not, Shane."

"Believe what you want." Shane was getting red-faced. "But I saw a thing on-line that explained the whole deal." He was always seeing things on-line that explained the whole deal. Or deals on-line that explained the whole thing.

"Wait a second," Kinnick said, convincing himself that logic might still matter with Shane. "But the Patriots won the Super Bowl *last year*!"

This, somehow, excited Shane even more, and he leaned in toward Kinnick and confided in him. "I know! That was *awesome*, a sign of the coming triumph, a clarion call for patriots to rise up and prepare for the final fight. See, New England wasn't *supposed* to win. The secular globalists picked Seattle to repeat as champions. But Brady and the Patriots wouldn't allow it. See? They broke the script. Stole that game at the goal line! Said, 'We will fight rather than surrender to the New

World Order!' That's why the NFL had to start the whole deflate-gate controversy. To go after New England. As a warning."

This was the danger of winding up a toy like Shane. He could go on for hours like this, weaving every loose strand into a blanket of conspiratorial idiocy as he explained how, at the beginning of every season, NFL officials and team owners got together with TV execs, who handed out scripts for the season. But in the 2015 Super Bowl, Brady, Belichick, and the brave Patriots refused to go along with the globalist-satanist-liberalist-trafficker agenda, and they struck a blow for the original America! New England! Patriots! Thirteen original colonies!

It was the sort of logic hash that Kinnick had encountered when dealing with conspiracy theorists in his old job as a newspaper reporter, like the logger who once explained to him that some of the forest had been replaced with fake trees that were in fact surveillance devices. Gibberenglish, Rhys used to call it.

"New England's victory was a sign to all patriots," Shane said. "We've been waiting for a king to arise, and now, he was on his way. This election would be our Valley Forge."

"I'm pretty sure at Valley Forge, they were fighting *against* having a king, Shane."

"I'm just saying the call went out," the undaunted Shane said, "and true patriots have answered, and our time is nigh."

"You know what? I got a thing at nigh." Rhys pretended to look at his watch. "Can we do it at nigh thirty? Maybe quarter to rapture?" Rhys glanced over at Celia's husband, a retired high school math teacher— *Are you hearing this?*—but Cortland was snoring away.

It was quiet for a few more minutes, Shane pouting at being teased, Kinnick doing his best to let it go. He would eventually tell Bethany that: *I tried to let it go.*

You egged him on, Bethany would say.

I tried to steer us back to football! Rhys would insist.

"So, they script every play?" he asked Shane. "Or just the final score?"

"I mean, they leave room for ad-libbing, but yeah, everyone basically knows who will win before the game starts. It's been scripted since 2008." Shane leaned across the arm of his recliner. "Think about it for a second, Rhys. There's literally billions of dollars at stake. You think they're just gonna leave that to chance?"

"Right," Kinnick said. "So, the owners get together and decide before the season who's going to blow a knee, who's going to fire a coach, who's going to win the Super Bowl?"

"Owners?" Shane scoffed. "You think the *owners* run the league? Owners are patsies, Rhys! Wake up! You gotta follow the money on a deal like this."

After getting a degree in natural sciences Kinnick had been an environmental journalist for thirty years, at a paper in Oregon, at a Portland magazine that went under, and finally, in Spokane, where the foundering newspaper "offered" him a buyout in 2015. And now, what could be more depressing than his carpet-laying, truck-driving, recovering-addict son-in-law lecturing *him* to *follow the money*?

"This"—Shane held up the remote—"is where the money is."

"Remote controls? Sure." Kinnick leaned in. "So, who's behind it all? Best Buy? RadioShack?"

"Think for a minute, Rhys!" Shane tapped his own head with the remote. "I'm talking about . . . the *media*." Or *me-juh*, as Shane pronounced it, that word being one of the four—*elites*, *liberals*, and *socialists* were the others—that found its way into every Shane Collins conspiracy theory. "And I don't need to tell you who controls the media."

"No, you don't."

"The so-called—" Shane said.

"Please don't say it." Rhys pointed with his beer bottle. And, for a moment, Rhys thought maybe the worst was over, that they'd make it to dinner after all without a problem.

But then Shane added, "I mean, they don't call it *Jew* York for nothing."

"I wish you wouldn't say stuff like that, Shane."

"Hey, I'm pro-Israel! No one loves the Jews more than me. The real Jews, I mean. Jesus was a real Jew."

In his defense, Rhys would later think, he had endured four years of such nonsense, ever since Shane had traded his mild drug habit for a Jesus-and-AM radio addiction—"real Jews" and "real patriots" and "Black-on-white crime" and "owning the libs" and the "lame-stream media" and the "vast conspiracy" perpetrated on "real Americans," by which Shane always meant people like him.

This raw sewage had been seeping into American drinking water for years, until it eventually contaminated the mainstream, and won over enough Shanes to convince the chattering TV heads and Twitter-taters that such half-assed conspiracies were a legitimate part of the body politic, that somehow, they had to do with white, working-class people getting the short end of some imaginary economic stick.

But fine. Shane could believe whatever he wanted.

It was Bethany who broke his heart. Once-brilliant Bethany who should've known better, but who pretended, maybe for her marriage's sake, or her kids' sake, that this was all okay. Bethany who practiced a quiet, metaphoric faith, but who kept the peace by going along with Shane's crazy eagle four-wheel-drive oppo-Christian patriotism, watching quietly as he chased blue-eyed salvation with the zeal he'd once chased meth, venturing ever further into the paranoid exurbs of American fundamentalism.

But how far would they go? How far would the country go? A familiar feeling of grim hopelessness washed over Kinnick, the sense that, just when he thought it couldn't get worse, it not only got worse, but exponentially more insane. Some days, reading the news felt like being on a plane piloted by a lunatic, hurdling toward the ground.

And to have his daughter *not see* this, to have her decide that, in fact, it was Kinnick and his reaction that were the problem—*No religion! No politics!*—made him feel so disoriented, so alone, so . . . bereft.

It was while thinking of Bethany, and how close Kinnick had been to her when she was little—that these four, unfortunate words slipped from Rhys's mouth: "Daughter married an idiot."

Shane sat up. "What did you say?"

"Nothing. I was talking to myself."

"Did you call me—"

"I'm sorry."

"You come into my house and call me names?"

"I shouldn't have said that." Kinnick stood. "I just need some air."

He started for the door, but Shane leaped out of his recliner and blocked his father-in-law's path. "Why do you get so bent out of shape, Rhys? Is it maybe because I'm getting close to the truth?"

"Yeah, you got the truth surrounded, Shane. Now, please, I need some air."

Shane grabbed Rhys's arm and lowered his voice. "Sit down, Rhys."

"Let go of my arm, Shane."

"Please." His grip tightened. "Bethany's gonna get mad at us both."

Rhys yanked his arm away. "Get out of my way, Shane!"

Their raised voices brought Bethany from the kitchen. "Dad, what's the matter?"

"Nothing." Rhys pulled away. "I just need some air."

"Your father called me an idiot!"

"Dad!" Bethany said.

Rhys put his hands out. "I can't do it anymore, Beth! It's like talking to a belt buckle!"

"I begged you both," Bethany said. "No politics."

"I wasn't talking politics!" Shane said. "I can't even talk about football without your dad losing it!"

Celia came in from the kitchen, too, still holding the turkey baster, long gray hair piled and pinned atop her lovely head. "What did you do,

Rhys?" His ex-wife and daughter stood there, at the edge of the TV room, staring at him accusingly, Shane blocking the door, Kinnick breathing heavily, looking for a way out, and on the wall next to the door and his escape, more framed needlework: *This is the house the Lord has made.*

"Time to eat?" Cortland stirred in his recliner.

Kinnick could feel his chest tightening, his pulse racing. He was surrounded, smothered, claustrophobic. "Really, I just . . . need some air. Let me go outside for five minutes and—"

Bethany crossed her arms. "Dad, do not leave this house—"

"I'll be back. I just—" Rhys tried to edge past his son-in-law.

But Shane grabbed his arm again, leaned forward, and hissed, "Don't be such a snowflake, Rhys."

He hadn't hit another human being in thirty years.

And then, in a flash that would replay over and over in his mind, he had.

It was a streak that ended satisfyingly at first, and then—not so much.

- - -

LEAH STOOD JUST inside Kinnick's front door, looking around her grandfather's little house in the woods. A fire crackled in the old-fashioned woodstove at the center of the room. A dented tin coffeepot percolated on one of the burners. As she'd heard from her mother, the only electricity in the house came from car and boat batteries that Grandpa Rhys charged with rigged-up solar panels and propane tanks. But it wasn't neat and futuristic, like she'd imagined. It seemed dirty and half-finished. Decrepit. He had no television or computer. He didn't even have a phone. This was what it meant to live *off the grid*. There was a bathroom, the tap water and small handheld showerhead coming from a tank hooked to an electric pump powered by one of the marine batteries he had sitting around. But if you had to use the toilet, you went outside to an outhouse. Like in olden times. Like in the Bible. There were candles and battery-powered lanterns all about the room. A small refrigerator was plugged into a portable generator. There were no pictures or art on the cinder block walls. Instead, the house seemed to be bursting with words, bookshelves covering every wall and blocking two of the windows. Books were double- and triple-stacked next to piles of magazines and spiral notebooks. Books covered every available surface and much of the floor. Leah loved books more than she loved anything in the world, but this . . . this seemed like a sickness, like an infestation of words.

"Are these all yours?" Leah asked, picking up a hardcover book called *Vitruvius: The Ten Books on Architecture*.

"Yes." Kinnick scratched his head, as if the very idea made him uncomfortable. "I mean, as much as we can own books. I get them from libraries and yard sales, but they aren't technically *mine*. They pass through me." He looked down then. Laughed at himself. "Forgive me. I'm rambling, I'm not used to— My thoughts are—"

He turned to Mrs. Gaines and cleared his throat. "—discordant. Would you like some coffee, Mrs.—"

"Gaines," she said. "No, thank you." She was looking around, too, at the ancient coffeepot, at the books, at a corroded battery sitting on the floor next to a 1950s hi-fi, also covered in books. Her hands curled up like she was afraid to touch anything.

The smell was something Leah hadn't been prepared for— woodsmoke and musty books and what she thought must be Grandpa Rhys himself, some mixture of sweat and dirt and coffee and age.

Kinnick kept looking from Leah to Asher and back, muttering. "Kids don't drink coffee, right? No, of course not. I have bottled water. You want water? Or dried berries? Beef jerky?" He started clearing space on the two reading chairs, the only real furniture in the room, other than the hi-fi and the library table, which was also covered with piles of reading material.

"Please," Kinnick said, when he'd carved two hollows in the grove of literature. "Sit down, sit down." One of the stacks began to list and Kinnick righted it. "Sorry about the— Obviously, I wasn't expecting— It's a little—" The stack fell in the other direction, and Kinnick watched it helplessly. "Bestrewn," he said.

Oh, what words! Leah couldn't help but smile. *Discordant! Bestrewn!* This was the mysterious grandfather she'd imagined, back when her only real impression of him was the smart-looking photo on the back of his book, *From River to Rimrock*, which for years had been filed on their mother's bookshelf back home in Oregon, in the *K*'s, as if her father were just any other author. (It was what Leah wanted, as well, to be a writer one day, to create a series of fictional stories about two young Christian heroes living and adventuring and ultimately falling in love in the end-times.)

"What's Grandpa Rhys's book about?" Leah had asked her mother once, when she was younger. When Bethany responded that it was a book of essays, Leah had asked, "What are essays?"

"Well," her mother had said, "essays are stories for readers who care more about ideas than they do people."

Leah remembered the crisp judgment of that description, and she remembered the last time they had come up here, to see Grandpa Rhys, almost four years ago now, at the beginning of the pandemic. As she recalled, the drive had seemed to take forever, and then, when they got here, they hadn't even come inside. Instead, they'd walked along a stream, throwing rocks into the water while her mother talked in hushed tones to Grandpa Rhys. She could tell something was wrong. After an hour, they said their goodbyes, and she and Asher and their mom had gotten in the car and driven back to Spokane to see Grandma Celia, her mom stifling tears as she drove. *He's so far gone.* This was the report she'd heard her mother give Grandma Celia: *so far gone.* Still, she'd imagined some hope in that phrase: *so far . . .*

But this craggy, bushy-haired, bearded grandfather didn't look much like the tall, trim, dignified man she recalled from that earlier trip, and certainly not like his square-jawed author photo from twenty years ago. He wore a heavy flannel shirt over what appeared to be a lighter flannel shirt over what appeared to be a once-white T-shirt, now a dirty beige-gray color that Leah might have called *twice-plowed snow*. (It was a hobby of hers, naming new colors. Shane once said she should go to work for the big paint companies.) Kinnick's face was gaunt and his long, unkempt brown hair was streaked with gray (*hash browns and country gravy*) while his shaggy beard was dusky white (*high winter clouds*). Whiskers migrated down his neck nearly to his chest and up his cheeks, nearly to his *regret-to-inform-you* blue eyes.

"So, Leah, your grandmother—" Kinnick's voice cracked. "Was she sick a long time?"

"No, not very long," Leah said.

"And Cortland, he was with her?"

"Grandpa Cort's in a nursing home," Leah said.

"When we visit, he thinks we're his brother and his sister," Asher added. "He plays with dolls. It's called regressing."

"I'm sorry to hear that," Kinnick said.

Leah nodded. "Mom was planning to come up here and tell you when Grandma got sick, but she asked Mom to wait until she was done with her treatment and then—"

"And then she died," Asher said.

"It happened fast," Leah agreed. "We moved up here from Oregon so Mom could take care of her and a few months later—"

"She didn't want a funeral," Asher said. "She got cremated." Then, he leaned forward, as if confiding in his grandfather. "That means turned into ashes."

Kinnick wanted to go back a few steps. "So, wait, you've been in Spokane . . . this whole time?"

"For about five months," Leah said. "Mom wants to go back to Grants

Pass now. But Shane has been wanting us to move here for a long time. He says it's safer up here. Because of the redoubt."

"The—" Kinnick cocked his head.

"Redoubt," Asher said. "The safe zone for Christians."

"It's different places in the mountains of Washington, Oregon, Idaho, and Montana," Leah added helpfully. "Like a fortress built in a bunch of different places."

"It's where the Rampart is," Asher said.

"The Rampart?"

Before they could explain, Anna Gaines stepped in. "Mr. Kinnick, I have to ask, are you . . ." She looked around the house. "I mean, can you take care of the kids for a while? Until Bethany comes back?"

"Tell him about my tournament," Asher said from one of the chairs, his legs pressed together, big snow boots swinging above the floor.

Mrs. Gaines looked pained. "Asher has a chess tournament tonight."

"Tonight?" Rhys ran his hand through his hair.

"Yes. At six p.m.," Asher said. "I was the number-five ranked player in Southern Oregon. This will be my first tournament in Spokane. Mom registered me for it."

Anna said, "He's very worried about missing it."

"I'm a prodigy," the boy said.

Leah sought out her grandfather's eyes and gave him a small shake of the head meant to convey, *No. He's not.* Asher had, indeed, been the fifth-ranked eight-year-old in the Southern Oregon Chess Club. But that was among the seven eight-year-olds who had qualified for ranking.

"Dad and Pastor Gallen are praying about whether chess is a Godly endeavor," Asher said. "It comes from the Arabs, which Pastor Gallen says is bad, and Dad is worried the board represents the illuminati and has graven images. But Mom says I can keep playing while they're discerning."

"Discerning." Kinnick closed his eyes, overwhelmed by all of it: re-doubt and Rampart and the illuminati and discerning whether chess was a Godly endeavor. He breathed in heavily, and back out of his nose.

As she watched him, Leah remembered her mom describing Rhys as "eccentric," "half as smart as he thinks he is," and "twice as antisocial." She wondered how long it had been since he'd talked to other human beings.

Finally, he opened his eyes. "Wait. Can we back up? Your grandma got sick and a few months ago, you moved up here from Oregon with your mom?"

"Yes," Leah said.

"And you live in Spokane?"

"Shane wants us to move to Idaho once our lease is up," Leah said. "He's been bringing us there for church summer camp and tent revivals the last two summers. To the Church of the Blessed Fire."

Asher picked up the story now: "Dad's a member of their men's group, the Army of the Lord. They train out at the Rampart."

"Blessed Fire? Rampart? Army of—" Rhys kept repeating details, as if saying them out loud would make them make sense. He turned from Asher to Leah. "And you don't . . . you don't have any idea where Beth—where your mom went?"

"Shane thinks she might have gone back to Grants Pass," Leah said carefully. "She has a lot of friends there. We all do."

"Or maybe Dad killed her," Asher said.

The air seemed to leave the room, Kinnick steadying himself on the table. Leah spun on her little brother. "Why do you say things like that?"

Asher shrugged, looked at Rhys, at Anna Gaines, then at the ground.

Anna put a hand on Asher's shoulder. "I'm sure that isn't what hap-pened, Asher." Then she looked at Kinnick. "We've been worried, even before Shane left. Bethany has confided some things to me . . . she's been depressed since her mom died. And she's worried about Shane and this new church." She leaned in. "My husband and I aren't exactly Shane's biggest fans. He can be kind of—"

"Racist?" Kinnick asked.

"No, not that." Mrs. Gaines gave a thin smile. "I was going to say opinionated."

"Mom and Shane have been arguing about the new church." Leah took a deep breath, her lips pursed. "Mom thinks the new church is too radical. Shane just keeps saying that Mom isn't whole with the Lord, yet."

"Tell the rest of it, honey," Anna Gaines said.

Leah chewed her bottom lip.

"Do you want me to tell it?" Anna asked her.

Leah sighed. Fine. She would say it. "Shane wants to betroth me."

Kinnick cocked his head. "He wants to *what*?"

"Betroth me. To the pastor's son. David Jr. It's not as big a deal as it sounds, but when Mom found out, she got really mad."

"*Betroth* you?" Rhys repeated.

"It's not like that," Leah said. So much about the new church she thought was misguided, but why did they have to talk so much about *this* part. "It's just a thing they do at this new church when two young people like each other, that's all. It's supposed to be joyful. It's like . . . a plan is all. That I *might* marry David Jr.? Like . . . when I'm older? And it wouldn't even be for sure. Just . . . you know . . . if we both still want to. When I'm older." She could feel her face heating up.

"When you're older," Kinnick repeated. "Sure."

She sighed again, angry to have to explain this. She and Davy weren't freaked-out about it, why did other people have to be? "See, in our new church, if a boy likes a girl they aren't supposed to hide it. They announce it during services, and then, if the apostolic council approves, then the congregation prays over us, and eventually, when I turn fifteen, we could have supervised dates. And, if we still liked each other after I turned sixteen, we could go to Idaho and get married. If we wanted to. Since we'd already be betrothed. That's all."

The room was quiet.

"But it would probably be after I'm sixteen. Like . . . when I'm eighteen."

The room was quiet.

"I would get a promise ring now," Leah said. "And then, if we *don't* get married, I just give the ring back. But like I said, that's a long ways off, so—" She smiled as if—*see, no big deal*.

"You can get married younger in Idaho than you can in Washington or Oregon," Asher added helpfully.

Leah shot him another glare and Asher shrugged again.

Kinnick made eye contact with Anna Gaines, and they held it for a long time. "How old is the pastor's son?" he asked finally.

"That's not—" Now Leah's face was burning. "He's nineteen, but—" She sighed. "It's not like—" She knew how bad this all sounded, but Davy had *just* turned nineteen and she was *almost* fourteen and— "He's not— We haven't even—"

She let out a deep breath. To her mother's point, no, she didn't necessarily *want* to get married at *sixteen*, but she didn't see the harm in getting a promise ring from a nice boy like David Jr., who was smart and sensitive, and a reader like her, and who had bright green eyes the color of the outside feathers on a peacock. They'd met at Bible Camp last summer, when she'd talked about the book she wanted to write, and they had spoken again this winter, when he came home from Covenant College, in Tacoma, where he was a sophomore studying theology. And, unbeknownst to her mom and Shane, they wrote emails back and forth, talking about books and the college classes he was taking and her future post-Apocalyptic novel. They *liked* each other. That's all. Why did everyone have to make such a big, gross deal about it? Sometimes, Leah felt like the whole world was a shirt she'd outgrown, squeezing tight around her chest.

There was no sound in the old house except the faint whistle of firewood burning in the stove. Suddenly, Leah spun toward her little brother. "Shane did not kill Mom! Why would you say that? That's a terrible thing to say! And it's not true!"

Asher looked at his grandfather and shrugged once more.

- - -

ASHER WAS RELIEVED as they walked Mrs. Gaines to her car and watched her drive away, a wake of dust rising on the driveway behind her. He liked Mr. and Mrs. Gaines, but the way they talked about Asher's dad, like he was a dangerous kook, made Asher nervous. And when Asher felt nervous, he couldn't stop talking, and he said dumb things like the thing about his dad murdering their mom, which wasn't at all what he thought had happened, but what he thought *other* people might think had happened, and sometimes, when he got *really* nervous, other people's thoughts seemed to rush into Asher's mouth, and he felt the urge to say what he thought people were thinking before they said it.

Asher knew that his father's beliefs upset people, like thinking they needed to move to the mountain redoubt to prepare for the coming holy war, and that God had commanded Shane to be the master of his wife, and that Shane should not spare the rod to his children and that Earth might be flat and that chess came from the Arabs or from a secret Satanic society. But the rest of the family just let him talk and it mostly didn't affect them. And his dad didn't seem to mind that they believed other things. He didn't say anything when Asher read books about dinosaurs, or when he made a book report saying volcanos were millions of years old, and a lot of what Shane talked about, he didn't even do—like not sparing the rod? He'd never hit Asher. Some of the other kids from Bible Study got hit a lot, but his dad hardly ever even spanked him, only one time that Asher could remember, when Asher was interrupting, and it wasn't even very hard, more like a swat so that Shane could tell the other guys at church that he'd done it.

But none of that was what Asher worried about. The thing Asher worried about was the sort of trouble they'd had last year in Grants Pass, when his dad got upset that they were teaching about sex in Leah's science and health class and he made a big fuss at school, and tried to pray in her classroom, and the teacher said she felt threatened, and after that, they'd had to get homeschooled.

Asher didn't like home school as much as he liked school school.

They watched Mrs. Gaines's car disappear through the stand of spotted white birches. "Those trees look like the legs of tall, skinny Dalmatians," Leah said. It was true, Asher thought. His sister really did have a way of describing things.

They listened to the sound of Mrs. Gaines's car engine accelerate onto the dirt road beyond, fading toward the highway. The rain had stopped and beams of sunlight appeared on the misty droplets of low, lingering clouds.

They all turned to face each other, Asher and Leah and their grandfather. "I wonder," Asher said, "if you might have a chessboard."

"I don't. I'm sorry," Rhys said. "No one to play up here."

"I play games by myself sometimes."

"I've heard people do that," Rhys said.

Asher nodded. "I usually open with the Ruy-Lopez. Or the Sicilian Defense. I can only play a few moves in my mind. After four or five, I either need a board or pen and paper to keep track. I'm not very good at notation. Eventually, I'll be able to play entire games in my mind, though. All the best players can."

"Well, until then, I have plenty of pens and lots of scratch paper," Rhys said.

"What's scratch paper?"

"It's paper with something on the other side."

"What's on the other side?"

"Various things. Reports. Bills. It's just a way to use paper twice."

"Oh. That's smart. Can I use your bathroom?"

Kinnick scratched his head. "Well, about that . . . I have a composting toilet, but I've been having trouble installing it and I ordered the wrong chemicals, so it still isn't working."

"What does that mean?"

"Oh. Right. It means you can either go outside or try the big drop."

"What's the big drop?"

Rhys started toward the outhouse. "Come on, I'll show you." He unlatched the door and opened it. "I apologize for the smell."

Asher walked over and stuck his head in. "It doesn't stink too bad," he said.

"I sprinkle wood ash to help with that."

"What's wood ash?"

"Ash from the fire."

"Oh. Right." Asher came in farther and looked around. It was a toilet seat over a dark, scary hole in the ground. "How far down does it go?"

"Six feet."

Asher went all the way into the outhouse, closed the door, unzipped, and gave it a go, dappled sunlight coming from screened openings on either side of the tiny building. He liked the way his pee disappeared into the dark hole, and he liked the deep trickling sound of it hitting water down below, but then he started imagining what might be living down there and the stream immediately stopped. There was nowhere to wash his hands, so he just zipped his pants and left the outhouse.

It was quiet outside. Leah and Grandpa Rhys were standing there, hands in their pockets. The three of them made an awkward triangle near the back of the house, each waiting expectantly for the next move. Who knew quiet had its own sound? Wind running fingers through the trees, the burble of nearby water, even the ground seemed to make tiny crackling sounds. Asher looked all around his grandfather's place, the sad house on this knob, and the two outbuildings, the hillside behind the house covered with mountain grasses and thin, scraggly pine trees, mostly green, with a few reddish and yellowish ones thrown in.

"The trees with the orange needles," Asher finally asked, "are those sick?"

Kinnick turned and looked up at the hillside. "No. They're mostly tamaracks. Larches."

"They look like candles," Leah said.

"They do, don't they?" Kinnick smiled at Leah's keen observation. "Like lit matches surrounded by all that green." He squinted one eye. "They make good firewood, too, if you catch them at the right time. Just after they've died, before the bugs and rot set in."

"Didn't you used to have a barn?" Leah asked.

"Yes," Kinnick said. "Good memory, Leah. I took it down. I'm trying to take it all down, one building at a time. The outhouse is next. If I ever get that toilet installed."

"Why are you taking it all down?"

"Well." Kinnick rubbed his head again. "This was my grandfather's land. He bought it from a guy who'd built it ten years earlier. Before that, it was pretty much wild out here. A few years ago, I had the idea to erase my presence here, slowly return it to its natural state."

Asher looked all around, trying to imagine it all gone.

Beneath a single row of solar panels, the roof of Grandpa Rhys's house was rusted metal, brown streaks staining the gray cinder block where water had run off. Across the driveway was the narrow wooden outhouse with the quarter-moon on the door, and, beyond that, a pump house. An old rusty flatbed pickup was parked next to it, cracks spiderwebbing the windshield, two flat front tires settled in the dirt. A small stream ran through the grassy field beyond the house.

Asher asked: "Can I look at your stream?"

"The creek?" Kinnick asked. "Sure."

Asher clomped toward it in his boots.

"When I was a kid," Kinnick said, "that creek ran year-round. We used to visit my grandfather up here and it ran like a small river this time of year. Probably had three times as much water as it does now."

Asher turned back. "What happened to the water?"

Kinnick explained that years of logging, drought, and development, along with decreased snowfall each winter, had reduced the creek to a spritz of spring runoff—five or six inches in its deepest spot—a flat series of esses that flowed past the house to the gully below, where it joined the larger Tshimakain Creek, which ran along the highway back toward town and the reservation, and eventually, to the Columbia River.

"What's a reservation?" Asher asked.

"It's the land where the Spokane Tribe lives."

"An Indian tribe?"

"Yes, that's right."

"And this water goes there?"

"Well, it passes through. On its way to the ocean. Where all water goes."

Asher looked back down at the babbling stream. "Do you think I could jump over it?"

Rhys walked over and stood next to his grandson. "Do you mean would I *allow* you to jump over the creek, or do I think you are *capable* of jumping over the creek?"

"Both, I guess."

"Then I'd say yes to both."

"Don't do it, Asher," Leah said. Then to Rhys: "He's not very good at things like jumping." She hadn't followed them the twenty paces to the creek and now stood sternly with her arms crossed near the back of the house. It drove Asher crazy: whenever Mom wasn't around, Leah acted like Professor Expert about everything.

Kinnick crouched next to the boy. "You can jump over if you want, Asher. But here's a little tip." He pointed to the banks. "A creek tends to be narrower but deeper in the straight part. See? And on the corners, there are two sides to a creek. There's the cutbank and the point bar. Cutbank is the outside corner. Do you see how water cuts against the bank and makes that little cliff? Water runs deeper there. Other side is the point bar. It's shallower and flatter. So, before making a daredevil jump like this, I'd scout out a place to jump from cutbank to point bar, not the other way around. That way you won't cave in the bank or come up short and fall into the deeper water. See? If you land on an inside corner, it's easier."

"Cool," Asher said. It was a word he'd been thinking of trying out. "Cool," he said again. Yes, he liked the sound of it. And he liked the idea of *scouting* out a place to jump. Like an Indian scout exploring the other side. *Very cool.*

"Asher," Leah said.

He waved his sister off without looking at her. "Watch this."

- - -

KINNICK WASN'T QUITE sure what he'd just seen. It was like watching a bird try to fly with one wing. His grandson had jumped with only his left foot, the right boot dragging behind. Or maybe he'd changed his mind before the command to *jump* had reached his second foot, but whatever it was, he'd made a half-step-leap-fall-stagger, and then had simply fallen, face-first, into the creek, getting far wetter than Rhys could've imagined was possible in four inches of mountain runoff.

Leah's assessment was even harsher, a sigh followed by: "That's why you don't jump in snow boots, Asher." Then to Kinnick: "He wears those stupid boots year-round."

Rhys stoked the fire in the woodstove and hung the kid's shirt, pants, and socks on the winter clothesline he'd strung in the kitchen. Asher was all bony edges: clavicles and neck vertebrae jutting out of the long johns Kinnick had loaned the boy until his clothes were dry enough to put back on. Thankfully, his nose had stopped bleeding. He sat there staring at the fire, his light brown hair a collection of cowlicks too unruly to be called curls.

"This fire is warm," he said.

"Warm fires are my specialty."

While her grandfather put the clothes on the line, Leah picked up one of the spiral notebooks that were spread around everywhere. Written on the covers were what appeared to be chapter numbers and short descriptions. This one read: "Ch. 47—Vulgar Errors." She flipped through the notebook. It appeared to be Grandpa Rhys's thoughts on books he was reading. On the first page, she read, in his block hand-writing:

> In *Pseudodoxia Epidemica* (1646, rev 5X, 1672) Browne sought to identify the "vulgar errors" of his times. This chapter proposes a new era of rational vulgarity based on our humanistic view of the environment, i.e., how philosophy, morality, wisdom, et al. failed to keep pace with scientific discovery, reflected, for instance, in Kant's separation of nature and human experience in *Critique of Practical Reason*: "Two things fill the mind with ever new and increasing admiration and awe, the more often and steadily we reflect upon them: the starry heavens above me and the moral law within me." (See also Ch. 36, ontological failures of Cartesian substance dualism.)

Kinnick finished hanging the clothes and looked back to see Leah reading one of his notebooks, her dark eyebrows knit with concentration. "Oh, those are . . . It's just . . . That's not . . ." He shifted his weight nervously. "That's kind of a work in progress. Or"—he chuckled a little at himself—"a work in nonprogress."

Leah set the notebook down and picked up an old hardcover book near it, whose dust jacket read: *The Ethics of Ambiguity*, Simone de Beauvoir. "Is this good? Simone . . ."

"De Beauvoir. Yes, it's very good."

"*Boovwah.*" Leah repeated it the way Rhys had pronounced it. She liked the cover, the title, and *Simone de Beauvoir* stripped across four banana-Popsicle panels, between them, a small black-and-white photo of a serious-looking woman in profile. (Perhaps she would put her picture on her own books one day.) Leah opened the book, and read a little bit, but it seemed even more technical than her grandfather's notebook, so she closed it. "Do you have the *Wraith of the Kingdom* series?"

"Probably not."

"I like to read whole series. If there's just one book, it makes me sad when it's over."

"That's reasonable."

"How about Valerie Godwin? Do you have her books?"

"Is Valerie Godwin alive?"

"Yes. She writes about young people who are called to do special tasks by a council of elven elders."

"Hmm . . . I don't think I have that one." Rhys gestured toward the packed shelves and tables. "These books are mostly by dead authors. Of course, they weren't dead when they wrote them."

"We used to have your book at home," Asher said, looking up from the fire.

"I wasn't dead when I wrote mine, either," Kinnick said. And then he noted the boy's tense. "Wait, did you say you *used* to have my book? What happened to it?"

"Shane got rid of most of our books," Leah said. "Just before we moved."

"Your mother let him get rid of *my* book?"

Leah set Simone de Beauvoir back on the stack. "There was a committee at our new church, and they sent out a list of approved and recommended titles," she said. "We got rid of some books then. And when we moved, we just didn't have room for a lot of our other books. I think that's when we got rid of yours."

His one book, *From River to Rimrock*, had taken him twelve years to write. It was a series of essays about environmental degradation in the

Inland Northwest in the twentieth century. Published by a university press, he'd written it as a gentle call for small-scale local change, but maybe it had been too gentle, too small, too local. He'd worked on it during weekends and holidays, and its publication had been—briefly—his proudest professional moment. He did a few readings around the Northwest, and at a couple of colleges. But the thing sold all of eight hundred copies and promptly went out of print. He wondered how many even still existed.

He used to imagine that, when the last copy of his book was gone, Kinnick would be gone, too, wiped from the earth. This felt like a relief at times. The world had no use for him, or for his curious little book (and, more than likely, would have even less use for the unwieldy second book he was writing, should he ever finish it). It was a kind of delusional self-centeredness, connecting his failure as a writer to the culture's growing rejection of science, philosophy, and reason, of basic common sense. But, of course, when he was moping around, thinking about his slim foothold in the publishing world, he didn't consider that his daughter and his grandchildren would surely outlive his little book, that Leah and Asher might be around longer, than, say, his research on the decline of native trout populations in Inland Northwest streams, or the shortage of huckleberries in the once-purple Selkirk Mountains.

Right, he thought. *We live only as long as someone remembers us. Only as long as someone cares.*

A shiver went through him then, the same wave of ruefulness and contrition he'd felt before, standing on the porch, staring at these kids whom he hadn't recognized at first, finding out that his daughter had run away, that his ex-wife was dead: *What have I done?* His eyes welled, and his voice cracked when he spoke: "I'm gonna go check on the car." The kids looked up from the fire. Did they hear that break in his voice? "Make sure it starts," he added, "so we can get to that chess tournament on time."

Kinnick started for the door. He'd used the old '59 Ford flatbed for a while, but it gave up the ghost six months ago, so he was back to using his car to get supplies. He'd tried to start the car two days ago and found the battery dead, so he'd dragged an extension cord down and connected a charger to the car battery posts. Rhys went outside, buttoning his chore coat as he stepped off the back porch, to where a two-track driveway curled around the house and down into two wooden doors cut into the hillside and the concrete foundation below his floor. He unlocked the padlock and swung the short doors open, revealing a five-foot-high crawl space where his old lime-green car was parked in the half-basement garage that he'd shoveled out and fortified with cinder blocks.

"What is that?"

Kinnick turned and saw Leah looking down on him, over the bank of the driveway.

"That?" Rhys turned to the car. "Is a 1978 Audi 100 GLS," Rhys said. "Arguably, the low point in a long, proud tradition of German automotive excellence."

"Is it a hybrid?"

"It is, actually—half car, half garbage. Carbage." Kinnick could feel the give-and-take of spoken language coming back to him, filling his chest, like he'd come up from diving and was breathing again. And Leah—so smart, so observant, she reminded him of Bethany at that age—was already a fine conversational foil. "Has almost three hundred thousand miles on it."

"Is that good?"

"Not for the car it isn't." Kinnick bent down and edged into the dark crawl space. He unhooked the charger from the battery and set it on a cluttered shelf. He opened the car door—the light went on, that was good—slipped into the driver's seat, closed his eyes, and turned the key. It shuddered and clunked—those metal-on-metal sounds did not bode well—and then, it caught! It sounded like a handful of wrenches in a dryer, but after a belch of green-black smoke—unmitigated success!

As the car warmed up, Kinnick cleared magazines and books off the backseat, throwing them into a pile among the other piles of magazines and books in the small, dirt-floored crawl space.

He emerged from his little Hobbit garage and stood up straight. "See that? First try."

"Why did you drop out?"

Kinnick looked up at his granddaughter, gazing over the edge of the sunken driveway. "Is that what your mom said? That I dropped out?" How had he not recognized this girl on the porch? She *was* her mother at thirteen, the age when Bethany and he were the closest. Before the trouble. Same insistent, dark, almond-shaped eyes. Same long brown hair. Same direct way of speaking.

"Yes. Mom said you dropped out."

"Well." It was funny she would use that phrase. By the time Bethany was a senior in high school, Kinnick worried constantly about her quitting school. The fear of every parent: having your kid drop out. Bethany was a strong candidate, too: she'd found her way to drugs—pot, mostly—harder stuff later on. And she'd always had problems with authority, watching teachers and principals (and parents) for any sign that they were hypocrites, which, being human beings, of course they were. As Celia always said, their daughter was "allergic to conformity." But, even with her parents beginning to talk about divorce, and Bethany in full sullen weed-smoking seventeen-year-old slackery, she had *not* dropped out. In fact, she'd finished high school, and then college and now, look—it was her father who was the dropout. He wondered if Bethany saw the irony, too.

"At the time, it didn't feel like I was dropping out," Kinnick told Leah. "It felt more like I was . . . stepping aside." Did that explain it? Should he say more than that? He was so rusty at communication. Yes, he thought, he should probably say more. "It certainly wasn't about your mom. Or your grandma. Or Shane. And it sure wasn't about you and Asher. I hope you know that. And I hope Beth—I hope your mom knows that. It was about me. I felt like the world was drifting in one direction and I was going the other way."

And still his granddaughter stared. How to explain self-exile? Part of it *had been* the fight with Shane. And Bethany's reaction. It symbolized the dark, sour turn the whole country had taken. As a journalist, as an American, as a rationalist, Kinnick had come to terms with the fact that 20 percent of his countrymen were greedy assholes. But then, in 2016, the greedy assholes joined with the idiot assholes and the paranoid assholes in what turned out to be an unbeatable constituency, Kinnick realizing that the asshole ceiling was much higher than he'd thought, perhaps half the country. Whatever the number, it was more than he could bear. Especially when they were in his own family.

But, if he was being honest, it wasn't those people, his fellow Americans, many of whom had probably always been as distracted or as scared or as cynical as they revealed themselves to be by electing a ridiculous racist con man. No, *they* weren't really the problem. Most of them probably just wanted lower taxes, or liked bad television, or, like Shane, had fallen into the fake-Christian faux-conservative Nationalist cesspool; or maybe they were just burned-out and believed that corruption had rotted everything, that one party was as bad as the next; or maybe they really did long for some nonexistent past.

Whatever *their* motivation, for Kinnick, it was all just part of a long sad cultural slide that he'd had the misfortune of witnessing firsthand (celebrity entertainment bleeding into government, cable TV eroding newspapers, information collapsing into a huge Internet-size black hole of bad ideas, bald-faced lies, and bullshit, until the literal *worst* person in America got elected president). There was inside of Kinnick an emptiness that felt like depression. Probably no coincidence that this bone-deep sorrow arrived as his relationship with his then-girlfriend, Lucy, was ending, as his newspaper was laying him off, as he lost a career that he'd believed was not only vital for him but also for his community, and, perhaps, naively, for democracy.

No, it was *he* who had failed, *he* who couldn't adjust, *he* who couldn't deal with this banal, brutal idiocracy, *he* who couldn't admit *this* was the world now. And so . . . he'd stepped aside. Moved to the last sliver of land once owned by his wannabe sheep-rancher grandfather. But once he began withdrawing, erasing himself, he couldn't stop. Until now, when Kinnick saw that he'd been living entirely in his own head for a year now, and had inexplicably reached a place where he didn't even recognize his own grandchildren.

"'I find it wholesome to be alone the greater part of the time,'" Kinnick finally said to his inquisitive granddaughter. "'To be in company, even with the best, is soon wearisome and dissipating.'"

She stared at him.

"I don't suppose Thoreau's *Walden* was on your church's list of approved titles."

"I don't think so," Leah said.

"No, probably not." Rhys Kinnick tried his best grandfatherly smile, and he thought again: *Oh, Celia. Oh, Bethany. I'm sorry.*

"Well then." Kinnick cleared his throat. "What do you say we go get your wet, prodigy of a brother and get him to his chess tournament." He started to walk, but Leah didn't move.

"I should tell you . . ." She scrunched up her face. "He plays chess about as well as he jumps over creeks."

Kinnick smiled. "Well, you know what? I kind of want to see that."

- - -

THANKSGIVING DAY 2016 Kinnick drove away from his daughter's house with no idea where he might be going. His right hand throbbed below the ring finger knuckle, where he'd broken one of the small bird bones in the back of his hand punching Shane's thick head. He almost wished

Shane had punched him back, but for all his bluster, Shane wasn't really a violent sort. Kinnick had to give him that. He sped north on I-5, through patches of fog, his cell phone in the passenger seat like a disapproving friend, alternating buzzing and ringing. He reached over for it and read the text messages as he drove, glancing back and forth from road to screen and back. Celia's were of the Just turn around, you made your point variety, Bethany's more Don't bother coming back.

He should call Bethany and apologize, call Celia and explain, maybe call his old flame, Lucy, in Spokane, and ask her to talk him down. This last call was the most appealing, frankly, but Lucy had been clear about ending the affair with Kinnick. (*I don't want to fucking see you ever again.*) God bless Lucy Park and her profane lack of ambivalence. Still, technically, talking on the phone with someone *wasn't seeing them*.

But no. If he was going to call anyone, it should be Bethany. That was the right thing to do. She had left two voicemails, and she was the one he owed an apology to. All he had to do was press her name on the screen, and boom—even speeding away at eighty miles per hour, technology would put her right here next to him, in his ear, his brilliant baby girl, as clear as if she were in the car with him. He turned his iPhone over in his hand. Remarkable. Every human connection he had left was contained inside its miniature electronic circuitry. Kinnick didn't know a single phone number by memory anymore. They were all just filaments, bits of data in this device. He could rattle off the exchange numbers of his youth (Walnut-4–9378, Keystone-6–2454 . . .), but without this $600 Pop-Tart of modern science, he had no way of reaching any other human being, and they had no way of reaching him.

But more than that! This device knew him better than anyone ever had; it knew his weaknesses (*best happy hour near me*), his tastes ('*70s soul and R&B*), his worries (*erections after fifty*), his crude, sad desires (*adventurous 40-to-50-something, dates only, not looking for a relationship*), even what socks he preferred (*athletic, white and black*), knew every place he'd ever walked and driven and—

He was surprised to be surprised to see the phone fly out the window. He had been the one to lower the window in the first place, after all, so it shouldn't have shocked him, but it was almost as if the act of flipping it out the window had preceded the idea. A quick glance in his side mirror and he saw his phone cartwheel once on the shoulder and then disappear in the weeds between lanes.

Go back! The urge was physical, intense, like he'd tossed out a baby, or his last bottle of booze. What if someone needs you? What if Shane becomes violent back there? What if there's some emergency with Bethany's kids? What if Lucy Park changes her mind? What if the *New York Times* offers you a job? What if the perfect 40-to-50-something interested only in sex and not in a relationship sends you a text message? What if you run out of socks?

Of course, he could just get another phone.

"If I do that," Kinnick muttered to himself, "I'll be lost forever."

It was quiet. In his head. Without his phone. Finally.

A sign informed him that the next town was called Riddle. "Well, there you go," Kinnick said aloud, the first of a million times he would talk to himself in the next seven years. He decided to let the car choose its course, and removed his hands, the Audi's crap-alignment drifting him off the freeway into this skid mark of a little freeway-side town.

On Riddle's Main Street he found an Irish bar, with a lit neon OPEN sign in the window. *Blessed be thy* . . . Front awning of the building was held up with the kind of posts cowboys might've once tied their horses to. After Kinnick got out of his car, he pretended to tie the old Audi to a post. "Settle down, girl," he said to the car.

The front door of the Irish bar opened with that pleasing squeal into darkness—a daytime drink always thrilled him, and he plopped onto the first stool he saw. Shamrocks, beer signs, pool tables—the place was exactly what it should be. Two other men were at the bar, bent over plastic pie-shaped bowls with draft lagers at their sides.

"Happy Thanksgiving," said a barmaid, perhaps six months pregnant, a tattoo of roses rising from her cleavage to her neck.

"You, too," Kinnick said.

She held up a microwavable turkey pot pie. "Only one left, you want it?"

"Sounds like it's all the rage."

"Six bucks."

"A bargain at half the price."

She took it out of the box and put it in the microwave.

I'll move up to the old Kinnick homestead, he thought. He'd been trying to decide what to do with the forty acres he'd inherited a decade earlier, when his father died, Kinnick's dad having inherited it from *his* dad. He could fix up the old, vacant cinder block house. Live off the grid. A simpler life. *Disappear up there. Yes.*

It *was* possible to disappear from others' lives, of course—from Lucy's, from Bethany's—but he suspected that when he woke up tomorrow, wherever he was, the person he really wanted to never see again would be staring right back in the mirror.

Maybe don't get a mirror, he thought, and this made him smile.

"What do you want to drink, smiley?" The bartender pushed the steaming turkey pot pie in front of Kinnick with a fork and a single paper napkin.

"Seeing as how this is going to be my last one for a while," he said, "dealer's choice. What do *you* like to make?"

She turned to the taps. "Bud. Bud Light . . ."

"How about a Manhattan."

"I don't know how to do that."

"It's just whiskey, sweet vermouth, and bitters."

"Of those ingredients, I got the whiskey is all."

"Then whiskey it is."

"Beam, Jameson, or Jack?"

"When in Cork—let's go with the Jameson."

"Double? Same price as a single before five."

"Lucky day," Kinnick said.

The bartender set a double whiskey next to his pot pie.

"Thanks," Kinnick said, and, looking to make polite conversation, added, "So, when are you due?"

"Do what?" the bartender asked.

"Never mind," Kinnick said.

And with that, he took a bite of microwaved turkey pot pie, toasted the other bar patrons—"Happy Thanksgiving, gents!"—and started his life over.

- - -

KINNICK DROVE LEAH and Asher away from his house in that smelly old car, down a dirt road to a two-lane highway cut between dense stands of trees, past cattle and sheep ranches, as they wound ten miles back up the twisting Hunters Road to the town of Springdale. He narrated as he drove, pointing out neighbors: "Brattons used to run a couple hundred head of Hereford till the old man's back gave out," and "That place was a commune for years, but they all eventually moved away." He explained that Springdale had been an old logging and mill town, a crossroad, a rail stop, and that his grandfather had bought a small homestead ranch up here in the late 1940s, back when there were twice as many people in the town. He slowed and turned onto the two-block Springdale Main Street, which he said had once consisted of a busy lumber railroad siding and a dozen small businesses supporting it. The railway was gone now and only two storefronts were open: a sad tavern, and a sadder little grocery store, whose prices, Rhys said, "Aren't much better than the convenience store up at the Y."

Asher and Leah made eye contact, curious about this tour they were getting. At first, their grandfather had barely seemed capable of speech, and now it seemed, a tap had opened, and he couldn't stop.

At the highway fork, they didn't turn west toward Loon Lake, the way they'd come with Anna Gaines, but drove south toward the town of Ford, past a sign that pointed to the entrance of the Spokane Tribe of Indians.

Rhys began muttering to himself. "Oh boy. I probably shouldn't. Or maybe—" He bit his lip. "And maybe they aren't even . . ." He slowed the car. "I'm sure they don't want to—" He eased the car to a crawl, craning his neck to scope out a newer double-wide trailer just off the highway, two cars parked in front.

"Well shit," he said, "they're home. I guess now is as good a time as any." He pulled off the highway into a fenced dirt yard, parking in front of the double-wide, which sat next to a large steel building with a faded sign that read: SPOKANE TRIBAL SURPLUS. There were also home-made signs on the fence that read: MIDNITE MINE KILLS! And: CLEAN UP DAWN URANIUM. And: DOE LIES!

"Okay, kids." Rhys took a deep breath. "I apologize in advance for any language you are about to hear, but this will be a good lesson for us all. Don't put things off. And don't drink wine in the afternoon."

"Whose house is this?" Leah asked.

"It belongs to my friends Brian and—"

Before he could finish the sentence, a German shepherd came out of the house and began barking, followed by a top-heavy Native Amer-ican man in gray sweatpants, fuzzy slippers, and an Oakland Raiders sweatshirt, who burst out of the double-wide's doors and down two steps. "Kinnick, what the actual fu—" But the man caught himself when he saw the children in Kinnick's car. "What do you think you're doing?"

Rhys climbed out of the car and showed his hands. "Brian. I'm sorry. I would've called first, but I just realized I don't have a phone."

"I don't believe it. You just show up like this?"

The dog continued to bark but stayed on the porch. A woman, also top-heavy, came out next. "Okay, Billy," she said, and the dog went back in the house. The woman was thick and pretty, lighter-skinned than the man, with short, gray, spiky hair. "Rhys, are these your grand-children?"

"Allegedly. Hello, Joanie. How are you?"

"Fine. Just fine." There was a swirl of activity then. The men stepped in close and talked quietly to each other through gritted teeth. The woman, Joanie, hustled over and pulled the kids out of the car and brought them into the house, and somehow, had cocoa and maple cookies ready to go before they got out of their shoes and raincoats. It was a warm place, with shag carpet and a big-screen television facing two leather recliners beneath old Native ledger paintings of warriors on horses. The dog fell onto a lumpy bed in front of the TV. Joanie put the kids at a small bar with their cookies and hot chocolate, which were delicious.

"Have more," Joanie said, and pushed the package of maple cookies their way.

"Do you have an indoor toilet?" Asher asked.

"Of course we do," Joanie said, "just down the hall."

They watched out the window as, in the dirt lawn in front of the double-wide, Brian pointed and yelled at Kinnick, who stood sheep-ishly, hands in his pockets, nodding along.

"What's he so angry about?" asked Leah.

Joanie looked them over and must have decided they were old enough to hear. Either that or it was just too good a story not to tell.

"Well, see," she said, "one day we was up to Two Rivers boat launch, drinking wine, me and Brian and Rhys, and out of nowhere, your grandpa gets me alone and tells me that he might be in love with me . . ." Joanie didn't stop speaking, but sort of hummed a little laugh. Then, without looking away from the two men, she fell back into the story: "But that wasn't the worst of it. I would've just said 'O-o-okay,

Rhys,' and chalked it up to the wine and him living all alone like he does. But Brian comes back from taking a piss and your dumb grandfather decides he needs to tell Brian what he just told me."

"That he loves him?" Asher asked.

This caused Joanie to look away from the window and laugh with her full chest, a sound like someone barking. "He does love Brian! That is true, son. Sure more than he loves me. Them two talking politics is like watching a mating dance.

"But, no, he told Brian that he was taken with me, and that he didn't plan to do nothing about it, but that such business had caused trouble in his life before, etcetera. He said he was trying this new honesty approach or some such thing, and he didn't want nothing, it was just something that needed to be said out loud—apparently while we were all drunk on wine at the Two Rivers boat launch!" Joanie laughed again.

"When did this happen?" asked Leah, remembering Rhys saying something about not putting things off.

"Be a year in July."

"And you haven't seen him since?"

"Nope. Because your drunk grandfather starts in about how, also, while he's on the topic, maybe Brian ought to treat me better, pay more attention to me—which is true by the way—but that was a lot for Brian to take in on the same day he hears that your grandfather has taken a liking to his common-law wife, and so Brian tells Rhys that maybe he should mind his own damned business, and them two rise up and nearly come to blows! Like I told your grandfather, I was flattered, but Brian and me, we have a good life together, going to the casino, fighting the Department of Energy, all the work we done blending our families together." She waved like she was shooing a fly away. "Anyways, I'm too old for a . . . what do you call it?"

Both Leah and Asher shrugged. They had no idea what you called it.

"A throuple?" Joanie made that barking laugh sound again and the dog's ears rose. "No. Thank. You. That just sounds like twice the cooking and laundry."

Asher and Leah glanced quickly at each other, Asher mouthing, *Throuple?*

"I figured they'd need some time apart, but a few months passed, and a few more months and Brian just got angrier and . . . well . . . they can both be a little stubborn."

In the yard, Brian seemed to be winding down, no longer pointing, just leaning forward and lecturing Rhys, who continued to nod. Finally, he seemed to run out of gas. Kinnick said something, and offered his hand, and a second later, Brian took it. They shook. Clapped each other on the back. Then Rhys said something that made Brian laugh.

"About time," Joanie said. "Peace has come to the valley." She toasted the window with her coffee cup. "Don't tell your grandpa, but Brian has missed his friend something fierce."

The men came inside.

"Coffee?" Joanie asked.

"Thank you, Joanie," Rhys said. "That would be nice. I wanted to apologize to you, too. I shouldn't have—"

"No, no, no!" Joanie interrupted. "You do not get to take back what you said, Rhys Kinnick. You are on the record, my friend." She turned and winked at Leah. "Girl my age doesn't get too many confessions of love, even drunk ones. You're not taking that one back, thank you very much. You're going to have to suffer it."

"Go on," Brian said to Rhys, "ask her your other thing."

"Well," Rhys said, "Joanie, I wasn't expecting to be watching my grandkids today, and, as you can see, I'm a bit of a fright. I was wondering if I could use your shower, and after I got cleaned up if . . . maybe . . ." He fluffed his bushy graying hair. "Would you cut my hair?"

She put her hand to her chest. "Why, of course I would, Rhys."

This caused Brian to smile. "Shower's a good idea," he said to Rhys. "You've gone a few miles past stale, my friend."

Kinnick smelled his armpit.

"Are you an Indian?" Asher suddenly asked Brian.

"Asher—" Rhys began.

"Native American—" Leah corrected.

"Oh. Right. Sorry," Asher said. "Are you a Native American?"

"I am," Brian said to Asher. "Spokane and Colville."

"Do you have a different name than Brian? Like, a warrior name?"

"Sure," Brian said. "I am known to my people as Standing Water. My older sister is Flooded Basement. And my younger brother is Ruined Carpet."

"Brian," Joanie scolded. "Be nice to the boy."

Brian winked. "I am known to my people as Brian." He offered his hand. "And you?"

Asher took his hand. "I am known to my people as Asher," he said.

- - -

RHYS RAN HIS hand over his clean-shaven face, then over the short, stubbly hair on the back of his head. It reminded him of being a boy, on bath night, after his father had cut his ratty hair and his younger brother's ratty hair, with his old US Navy clippers, little Rhys tracing his hand along the soft, stiffening stubble running up from his neck.

He glanced over at his grandchildren. They could never have imagined that he was a kid like them at one time, and that, one day, they would be as old and as brittle as he was now. Of course not. No one could. He hadn't seen his grandfather or his uncles or his parents as the children they once were. They were another species, dinosaurs. "All of them gone now," Rhys said.

"What?" Leah asked.

"Nothing," Kinnick said. He had gotten so used to speaking aloud to himself, he didn't always realize when the words were coming out.

Of course, he would be gone one day, too, soon enough, like his grandfather and his father and his brother before him. Everything he did would exist only in the minds of people who recalled him. He would cease being flesh and blood, or even a book in someone's basement, as he had realized back at his house—and would be a fading memory for the few living souls who recalled him, and not nearly as warmly or vividly as the way his grandkids remembered their grandma Celia, gone now to the loopy Unitarian heaven she longed for. Or, if Kinnick was right, gone back to the earth and the simple elements that had made her. Or, if Shane was right, burning in an eternal hell-pit beneath the hooves of a dancing goat-demon for not choosing the right church, for not speaking in tongues, for not voting the right way. *Oh Celia*.

"They're nice," Leah said. "Joanie and Brian."

"Hmm?" Rhys turned. "Yes. Yes. Joanie and Brian, they *are* nice."

"Did you love her?" Leah asked.

This girl. Cutting right to it every time, the way she used to when he would come home from work and Bethany would—Kinnick laughed, realizing that he was doing it again, conflating his granddaughter with his daughter, looking at Leah and flashing back twenty-five years. Jesus. If Shithead Shane hurt a single hair on Bethany's head . . . Kinnick tried not to think about this worst possibility.

Leah was still staring at him from the passenger seat, waiting for an answer. In the rearview mirror he could see Asher, too, looking up from the chess notations he'd been writing in the notebook Rhys had given him.

"Did I love Joanie?" Rhys screwed up his mouth. "No, in hindsight, I don't think I did. Certainly, not the way I loved your grandmother." *Or Lucy*, he thought. "But I liked her a lot."

"How do you know when it's really love?" Leah asked, more quietly this time.

"Well. I'm not sure I know the answer to that. At first, I guess, it's just a feeling. That you really want to be with that person. You think about them all the time." He thought of Lucy again. "And maybe, if it's the real thing, you start to want their happiness more than your own." Kinnick looked over at his granddaughter, wondering if this wasn't more than a passing concern of hers. "It can be confusing, huh?"

Asher chimed in from the backseat: "Mom says that alcohol makes people do funny things."

Rhys laughed. "It does. Loneliness does, too." He touched the back of his neck again, remembering the feeling of Joanie's hands there. That was how he'd met her. She used to cut hair out of the shop next to their trailer and it was Brian who suggested Rhys go to "my old lady" for trims in the first place, and something about her floating above him, the feeling of her hands on his shoulders, fingers running through his hair—the care she took with him. Undoubtedly, he'd confused hair-cuts with real intimacy, which he'd mostly forsaken when he'd moved up to the woods. And this was what he considered the lowest point of his life as a recluse, when he'd gotten so rusty at human interaction that he felt like he'd lost the ability to communicate. He'd pushed his loneliness aside and convinced himself he didn't need people, but of course, once he started thinking of Joanie that way, it was as if he would die if he didn't say *something*. Add to those feelings two bottles of a flat, oaky red wine on Brian's old fishing boat, and he'd drunkenly convinced himself it was somehow a question of his integrity, and he'd chosen to tell Brian what he'd told Joanie. "Integrity," he said aloud, and scoffed at himself.

Leah glanced over again.

"Sorry. I keep thinking aloud."

He drove them through the community of Tum-Tum, tracing the

Spokane River upstream toward the city. It was as if they were moving back in time, traveling the path Brian called the Tiny Trail of Tears. It was only fifty miles from Spokane's series of waterfalls—a fish vending machine in the centuries before the river was dammed and the salmon stopped coming this far upstream—to the remote place where Brian's tribe had been exiled in 1881, the Spokane Indian Reservation, a starkly beautiful, dry-forested, uranium-rich, radon-sick landscape almost forty miles northwest of the farthest edge of Washington's second-biggest city.

Rhys had first met Brian and Joanie when he'd written a newspaper story about the cause they'd taken up, pressuring the US Department of Energy and the state Department of Ecology to clean up the old Midnite Mine, where three million tons of uranium had been scraped out of tenuous reservation ground, shipped 160 miles south to Hanford, enriched, refined, and used to test Cold War atomic bombs on various islands and sea floors, and in outer space. In 1981, exactly a hundred years after the tribe had been relocated to this place, the open pit mine was played out and abandoned, its tailings left to leach into the creeks and groundwater that laced the Spokane Reservation. Rhys had written stories about the toxic sludge and the open pit, about the high rates of cancer and multiple sclerosis among people who lived near the mine, but proving causality in environmental diseases was nearly impossible, and as with much of his journalism career, Rhys had accepted that the stories he'd written had changed nothing.

He drove his rattly old car south and east and downhill, descending first into Spokane's suburbs: newer, balconied twenty-first-century apartments and obscene McMansions giving way at the city limits to twentieth-century split-levels, ranchers, and bungalows, to strip malls and shopping centers, and, as they neared downtown, to late-nineteenth-century craftsman and Victorian homes, miners and loggers shacks, and the brick apartment buildings of a once-thriving extraction metropolis. It was there, however, that the time machine ended. Pointedly, Kinnick thought, they would not encounter renovated tepees, dugouts, or lodges.

He tried to recall when he'd last been to the city. Two and a half years? Yes. The aching tooth. A trip to the dentist. A lot of things you could patch together in smaller towns—the grocery runs in Springdale, books in Chewelah vintage stores, the occasional beer at the Loon Lake Tavern—but sometimes you needed a big city, such as when you required a root canal.

Thoreau was only twenty-seven when he went to live in a ten-by-fifteen-foot cabin on Walden Pond for two years and two months of spiritual reflection and dental decay. By the time he was thirty-three, old Henry David had no original teeth left. Not so for Kinnick, who had outlasted Thoreau's exile by five years, and who hit sixty with his own choppers intact, thanks to Spokane's dental wizardry.

Then, after that root canal, he had bid big-city civilization farewell again.

"And now, he's back," Kinnick said.

"What's that?" Leah asked.

"Nothing," Kinnick said.

The chess tournament, according to Mrs. Gaines, was being held at an old abbey in West Central Spokane, the city's oldest working-class neighborhood. The Spokane Chess Club met in this nineteenth-century Episcopal Church, a barn-red steepled building with an abbot's house attached. A sign out front read: WE CULTIVATE JUSTICE, JOY, COMPASSION, AND PEACE.

There were only four cars in the gravel parking lot, a few more on the street. Rhys parked and turned back to consider his grandson. "You ready to go get 'em, Kasparov?"

Asher looked up from his notebook, suddenly seeming panicked. "I have to pee."

"I'm sure there's a bathroom in there."

"I hope so!" He was squirming. Hadn't he gone in Rhys's outhouse? And again at Brian and Joanie's? The boy must have a dime-size bladder.

"Try to relax, Asher," Leah said. She looked at Rhys and raised her eyebrows.

"I just want to say, I'm really glad you two came to my house today," Kinnick said, surprising himself a little. "And I'm sorry I was away for so long. I haven't been a very good grandpa or a very good father to your mom. But I'm hoping to change all that." He patted Asher's leg. "Now let's get you to the bathroom before you Ruy-Lopez your pants."

They got out of the car. Across the parking lot, Rhys noticed two men descending either side of a tall black Ram pickup truck. Something about the men didn't scream chess to Rhys. They were round in the chest and belly, wearing black T-shirts covered by matching nylon bomber jackets. One was probably thirty, with a goatee and short, military-cut hair. The other was older, clean-shaven and bald, his head so shiny as to be metallic. It was this older, bald one who seemed vaguely threatening, and oddly familiar to Kinnick, although he couldn't quite place the man.

There was a Gadsden Flag in the window of the truck, and a sticker on its tailgate that at first Rhys thought was an old email logo, until he read it more closely and saw that AOL actually stood for "Army Of the Lord." He looked back at the two men and noticed, underneath the jacket of the one with the goatee: the black strap of a shoulder holster.

"Asher! Leah!" The tall, bald man strode over. "There you are. Your dad has been worried sick about you!"

"That's Shane's friend, Brother Dean," Leah said to Kinnick. Then, louder, to the approaching men: "This is our Grandpa Rhys. He's an author. He lives off the grid."

"Hello, sir," the bald man said as he finished crossing the parking lot. "We can take it from here. Shane asked us to pick up his kids at his apartment today. Their neighbor said you might be bringing them here."

"I really have to use the bathroom," Asher said. He was shifting his weight from boot to boot again.

"Come on," Brother Dean said. "We'll go see if we can use their bathroom and then we can get out of here and call your dad, tell him you're okay. How's that sound?"

"He's signed up to play in this chess tournament today," Kinnick said.

"Is he?" asked Brother Dean. "Well, shoot, his father doesn't know if that's such a good idea right now. What with his mother running off and all." He looked down at Asher. "Your dad asked me to watch you for a couple of days, until he gets back from his trip. Then you and your father and Pastor Gallen can pray about chess later. How's that sound, bud?"

Rhys considered the two men. There was nothing overtly threatening about them. But where did he know the bald one from? It wasn't a good memory. Still, he wasn't sure what he should do.

"Mrs. Gaines asked me to watch them," Rhys said.

"Yeah, that wasn't appropriate," said Brother Dean. "Shane is none too happy about her doing that without his permission. I told her so myself."

"Please," Asher said, squinting his eyes shut.

"I'm taking him to the bathroom," Kinnick said.

"I'll take him," Brother Dean said.

"We'll all go," Kinnick said.

"No," Brother Dean said. "We won't."

Kinnick could see the pain on Asher's face. "Fine. Take him." He turned to Leah. "You want to go with them?"

Dean took the children into the church. The other man stayed, staring at Kinnick, who had the feeling he was being *guarded*.

When they were gone, the man with the goatee said, "We know all about you." His smile was edged with jutting eyeteeth.

"Yeah? Well, I know about you, too. I used to get my email from AOL. What's the name of your secret lair, MySpace?"

The smile disappeared.

"Naziscape?"

"Shane said I should watch out, that you're a sucker puncher. Are you a sucker puncher, Mr. Father-in-Law?"

"Depends." Kinnick could feel the blood rising.

"Think you're so smart. You don't seem so smart to me. You gonna sucker punch me, smart guy?"

But Brother Dean emerged with Leah and Asher before anyone could punch anyone. Kinnick and the man with the goatee watched them walk across the parking lot.

"Today is the *adult* chess tournament," said Asher when he arrived, clearly disappointed. "We got 'em mixed up. The kids' tournament is next month."

"Well, I'll tell you what, we'll come back," Kinnick said. He turned to Brother Dean. "You're not taking them."

Dean narrowed his eyes. "Yes. I am. You don't have a choice in this. Their *father* asked me to watch them until he gets home."

"Well, then, I'm going with you," Rhys said.

"That's not what Shane wants."

"Bethany left a note asking *me* to watch them." Kinnick took a half step forward. "And that's what I'm going to do."

That's when the man with the goatee casually pulled his jacket back to show Kinnick the pistol in his holster.

Brother Dean closed the distance between them, getting almost nose-to-nose with Kinnick, and cocking his big, bald head. "You skip out for ten years," he said. "And now you want to play Grandpa? Is that it?"

Rhys felt that one in his gut. *Seven years*, he thought, *not ten*. But this time he didn't say it out loud because he knew it wasn't much better.

Then, out of the blue, he remembered how he knew Brother Dean. "Wait a minute. You're Dean Burris! I covered your trial. You're the Dominion Eagle Killer."

Dean Burris took a step back, confused, his face coloring with embarrassment. Or maybe rage. Kinnick had written about Burris's federal poaching trial ten, maybe twelve years ago. Burris had been a long-haul truck driver who, in his spare time, poached eagles across the West. Mostly on Indian reservations. Burris would shoot a deer, then leave it out in the open, scaring off coyotes and other scavengers until a bald eagle or a golden eagle came for the carcass. From a hunting blind, he'd shoot the eagle and part out the valuable birds on the black market: wings, talons, tails, feathers. Sometimes he sold whole stuffed birds for thousands of dollars. He'd also, in his illustrious poaching career, killed and sold bears, bobcats, cougars, and Canadian lynx. He tried pleading *not guilty by way of dominion over animals*, but the judge hadn't accepted that particular legal theory. Burris had also challenged the jurisdiction of the federal court, of gaming agents, of Indian reservations, of pretty much every aspect of the case, but the judge rejected all of his sovereign citizen defenses and sentenced him to five years in federal prison. Amid rising concern over radical right-wing crime, there had been great interest in these stories, and Kinnick had gotten good play in the paper—three days of front-page bylines.

Dean's eyes narrowed and his jaw tightened. "Kids. Come on." He began to turn.

Rhys tensed, his fingers curling into fists. "Wait—"

"Grandpa, it's okay," Leah said. She put a hand on his arm, giving him the strangest look. Widening her eyes, as if warning him about something. Or telling him: *It'll be okay. Don't start trouble.* They were Celia's don't-start-trouble eyes. Bethany's not-now-Dad eyes. Clearly, she had adopted her mother's strategy of dealing with people like Shithead Shane—stay back while the pot boiled over. Rhys felt something rise in his throat. "Everything in circles," he muttered. So strange being out among people again. He just kept speaking aloud the words he thought he was only thinking.

Brother Dean grabbed the kids' backpacks out of Kinnick's car, then shepherded them toward the pickup, while the man with the goatee remained watching Rhys, arms crossed, that grim smile still on his face.

What to do now? Kinnick couldn't just let his grandchildren go. Not with the Dominion Eagle Killer. Not so these AOL loons could marry off his thirteen-year-old granddaughter to some pastor's kid and keep his sweet nonprodigy grandson from losing at chess. "Stop!" he said. "Don't do this. Let's call Shane. I'll talk to him. Apologize—" The kids were almost to the truck, and Kinnick had only taken a first step toward them when Dean Burris half-turned back and gave a nod to the man with the goatee.

There was flash of something black. Kinnick's head snapped.

The sound inside his skull was like someone breaking a stalk of celery behind his ear. What just hit him? He didn't see it coming and he didn't see it land. One second, Kinnick was standing, taking a step forward, and the next, he was on his hands and knees, blood pouring from his nose and mouth, his face throbbing. Was his jaw broken? A wave of pain shot through the left side of his head.

Then the word came to him: blackjack. Sap.

Christ. Had he been hit by a goon out of the 1940s?

Kinnick looked up from his knees to see the man who'd hit him walking away, heels of his cowboy boots making little puffs of dust. The goateed man climbed in the passenger side of the extended cab pickup truck. The door closed and the truck pulled away, gravel crackling in the parking lot, Leah's pretty face staring at him through the extended cab window. She had a hand over her mouth. He couldn't see Asher.

"Wait!" Kinnick tried to stand but he was unsteady. Blood pulsed from his nose. He felt the return of an old feeling: hopelessness. *Well, hello, my old friend.* He sat back down in the gravel and watched as the pickup truck turned out of the parking lot. The brake lights winked, and then the truck rolled away down the street.

A young man was running awkwardly from the abbey toward him. "Are you okay? Did that guy just hit you?" He had thinning blond hair and wore a priest's collar under a casual black sweater. His fingertips were warm, gently touching Kinnick's throbbing left cheek.

"You have a fractured zygomatic arch," the young man said. "Sucker-punch injury." He clicked his tongue, then ran inside to get some towels before Kinnick could ask how it was that a baby Episcopal priest could make such a strangely specific diagnosis.

TWO

What Happened to Lucy

Lucy Park strolled across the newsroom, swallowing her anger and striving for that elusive affect, nonchalance, as she went to check on Allison-the-teenaged-cops-reporter, who was bent over her phone at her desk like a nun over rosary beads.

"Hey there," Lucy said, "I don't suppose you're close to filing your story?"

Allison looked up. She was, of course, neither nun nor teenager, but a twenty-four-year-old recent college graduate, still able to conjure a bit of high school indignation on her face when it suited her. "Um," Allison said, "I'm, like, working on it?" She held her phone up with a flopped wrist. On the screen: a photo of crime scene tape around a light pole. She was, like, posting it! If someone would just, like, leave her alone!

Lucy hated this tone. She also hated that reporters were expected to constantly post on social media, before they'd even gotten a chance to report their stories, before knowing what their stories even meant. "No problem," Lucy said, leaving her trademark profanity unspoken— as encouraged by her boss in her last three performance reviews. (*And maybe*, she thought, *when you're done thumb-fucking your phone, you could work some fucking sources and, I don't know, write a fucking news story that I can put in the fucking newspaper, you spoiled fucking child.*)

Language, Lucy, her ex-husband always used to say. *A hundred-and-ten pounds of verbal rage*—that's what he'd called her during a fight on their honeymoon. *Hundred-and-six, you fucking asshole!* she'd said back.

"Right, then," Lucy said to Allison. "So, how long are we thinking?" Lucy glanced at her watch. It was seven o'clock.

"Hour?" Allison said, meaning two, meaning right on deadline, Lucy thinking: *two fucking hours?* For what? This story was a rerun: cops had shot another indigent Freddy, this one threatening people downtown with what appeared to be a syringe. Police responded, stoned guy ran at them, cop lit him up, CAS redux. Cop-Assisted Suicide. Four so far. Banner year.

"I think they're going for a record," Allison said.

"They should call themselves the Department of Euthanasia." Lucy made a casual check of her watch. "Well, let the desk know when you file. I'll have to give it a read from home." She slinked back to her cubicle to pack up her laptop and her empty Tupperware.

Anytime there was a story about a street person on fentanyl—which was pretty much every day—Lucy got nervous about Kel, who wasn't in school, didn't have a job, and whose number of days sober now sat at a personal record sixty-eight. Or, at least, it had been sixty-eight this morning, when Lucy had left for work. Lucy went home nervous most days, worried her nineteen-year-old son was on his way to becoming a full-time Freddy himself.

She texted him: Headed home soon. What sounds good for dinner?

Instant text bubbles. Oh, thank God! When he didn't answer right away—especially when she was at the office late like this—Lucy got sick with worry, afraid he'd pawned his phone again, and was gone, on the streets, in the wind. WTV, the text came back. Whatever. In Kel-speak: *I love you, Mom.*

One more check on her way out, at the desk of Jackson, the intern she'd asked to inquire about a reported fistfight at a school board meeting the night before.

Lucy could remember when a fight at a school board meeting would be unimaginable (*Fight over what? Lunch lady uniforms? Custodian pay?*) but now, with everyone on edge, still pissed off by school closures during the pandemic, angry about the teaching of sex ed or evolution or drag queens or gay rights, or about some book no one had checked out from the school library in a decade, *Random Yelling* was practically an agenda item. She could also remember when there were *two* ed reporters she could've put on this story, one for K–12 and one for higher ed, back when the staff was twice the size it was now. Oh, the extravagance!

Now, the education job was in its third month unfilled. At full staff, Lucy had just fifteen bodies to cover a city of 225,000, in a metro of 600,000—but, of course, they were never at full staff anyway. She had just a dozen reporters today, six in the office, none to cover the 150 or so schools and dozen or so colleges in the region. So, she scratched an occasional ed story out of an intern, or she convinced the less overworked of the two government reporters to make a few calls.

"I haven't heard back from the district," Jackson said. "And I have to work tonight."

Right, because you certainly aren't working *here, you fu—*

Language, Lucy! But of course, the kid had another job. After the Internet co-opted their content and stole their advertising, the newspaper's salaries were frozen, then cut, leading to a flood of buyouts, layoffs, and RIFs. Now, starting pay for a young reporter was barely above minimum wage. Most of her staff had to moonlight—freelancing, teaching, waiting tables, driving Uber, in the hopes that scraps and tips might cover the exploding rents and mortgages and the massive holes in their shitty health care plan.

"Well, maybe go to the district office tomorrow?" Lucy suggested.

"I have to work tomorrow, too," Jackson said.

"Right. Okay. I'll find someone else." Lucy swallowed the swears and walked past the night copy desk chief, who had been an intern himself just six months ago. "I'm out. I'll read Allison's story from home."

Kid saluted without looking up from his screen.

Lucy took the elevator down to the first floor. For now, the *Spokesman-Review* (which, before consolidation, back in the raucous early twentieth century, had been the *Spokesman*, the *Review*, and the *Chronicle* newspapers) still existed in its classic nineteenth-century brick tower, although the newspaper's footprint had shrunk from a couple hundred people on seven floors and a production facility across the street to a couple dozen people on cubicle islands on two floors. Accountants, real estate companies, wine bars, and a gin distillery had taken over the rest of the family-owned news buildings. (Booze and rapacious land-capitalism nudging aside the fourth estate and the public's right to know? Hard to argue with that kind of progress.) The rumor was that the rest of the grand, old newspaper building would soon become condos and apartments. So where would the "newsroom" be relocated? Like other newspaper offices—to a mini mall somewhere, where the baby skeleton staff would be left to "cover the world without fear or favor" between a fabric store and a pot dispensary?

The elevator dinged and Lucy stepped onto the first floor at the same time her phone buzzed. She hesitated. Trouble already? Turn around and go back up? But, no, it was just Kel, with a dinner suggestion. Tacos?

The warm feeling sweeping through her, what was it? Hope? At least one more day of her son being at home, healthy Kel getting another day of sobriety under his size 27 belt. Lucy smiled and typed back, Sure thing, K. Then, she looked up from her phone and gasped as—

—rising from a chair in the lobby—

—she saw—

—a fucking ghost—

"Lucy," the ghost said. "You look amazing."

"Kinnick? Jesus Christ."

"No. It's me. You had it right the first time."

He'd aged, of course, hair grayer than brown. He seemed work-tanned, too, and while he was clean-shaven, and with a recent haircut, there was something feral about him, like the rough men she saw walking the streets carrying everything they owned in backpacks. Or shopping carts. She searched for the right word (they weren't supposed to use *homeless* in the newspaper anymore, but rather the less personalized *unhoused*), but the word she was thinking was much older: *derelict*. "What happened to your face?" Dried blood in his nose and mouth, cheek swollen, eye bruised. His once pleasingly sharp features were mushed and bloodied.

He touched his swollen, dented cheek. "I got punched."

"Who's the lucky girl?"

"There were two of them. Gun nuts. Ram pickup enthusiasts. Knocked me down and stole my grandkids. They want to marry off my thirteen-year-old granddaughter to some pastor's kid. They broke my—"

Kinnick turned to a young man in a priest's collar perched forward in a chair next to the one he'd just left.

"Oh, uh, zygomatic arch," the young man said. He stood.

Lucy looked from the young man back to Kinnick. "Have you seen a doctor?"

"No, but I saw a priest," Kinnick said, and nodded at the young man again. "Figured I'd skip the middleman."

"I was a Golden Gloves boxer." The young priest shrugged. "It's a very common injury. I tried to take him to the hospital, but he wouldn't go. He'll eventually need maxio-facial surgery, but as long as he manages the pain, he should be fine for the time being."

Lucy looked back at Kinnick's face, which did not look fine.

"And I'm technically not a priest yet," the priest added. "I'm a deacon for another month, but our parish doesn't have a priest, so I'm practicing." He fingered the collar. "I mean . . . I'm not a practicing priest yet, I'm practicing to *be* one. Eventually. But people like the collar, so, you know——" Another shrug.

The flummoxed Lucy turned back to Kinnick. "Did . . . did you at least go to the police?"

He nodded. "My car died at his church, so Reverend Brandon here drove me to the cop shop first. I filed a report. Then I asked him to drop me off here."

The deacon-priest gave a small wave. "Speaking of which, I should get back. Chess club will be over, and I need to close the abbey."

"Sure," Kinnick said. "Thank you."

"I hope your grandson makes it back to play chess." And with that, the deacon-priest-boxer left.

Kinnick turned back to Lucy. "I filled out a complaint with the cops, but I only know one of the nutjobs' names. And it's not even the one who hit me. The only thing I know for sure is that they're idiot friends of my idiot son-in-law."

"Bethany's still with——"

"Shithead Shane. Yeah. Anyway, the police seemed pretty dubious of my position as concerned grandfather."

Lucy nodded. She practically bit her tongue to keep herself from saying the next part: *So what the fuck are you doing HERE, Kinnick?* Language, Lucy!

But he'd never needed her to say things out loud anyway, and Kinnick answered her unspoken question by putting his hands out. "Lucy, I need your help."

- - -

YOU LOOK AMAZING. Was that really the first thing Kinnick could think to say? So many other sentiments he could've led with—maybe, *How are your kids?* or better yet: *Hey! Congratulations on becoming city editor*, for surviving the constant purges, RIFs, and defections, for succeeding in a career that spat out so many good people, for putting out a newspaper with a playpen full of interns and twentysomethings. Instead, what were the first words out of his mouth? *You look amazing.* He cursed his male shallowness, which even seven years locked in a cabin with great works of philosophy, science, and literature apparently hadn't cured.

But! In his defense! She did! Look amazing! Slender and fit, formerly short black hair grown out past her shoulders, pulled away from her apple-shaped face, and those runner's legs, and, sure, there were maybe a few more lines around her mouth and next to her eyes—but oh, those dark, patient eyes; one look into them and a rush of feelings had surged through Kinnick's sore body. The old desire heating up the furnace.

The affair between them had started harmlessly enough, as flirty professional admiration—Lucy the young, eager criminal justice reporter asking questions of the veteran environmental reporter thirteen years her senior, a man with a seemingly endless knowledge of bureaucratic work-arounds and records searches and Freedom of Information Act requests: all the boring paper parts of the job that, for a certain ambitious breed of nerd-reporter, were practically foreplay.

They'd danced around their attraction for a while, going to flirty lunches together, exchanging long glances, finding reasons to have drinks after work. Then, one night at an investigative journalism conference in San Diego, they got drunk and made out after his presentation (*Document Dump: How to Go Beyond the Abstract*). They both wrote that night off as a booze-filled mistake—a mistake they reprised three years later at the company's Christmas party. Then, a year after that, they began making the mistake on the regular, meeting once or twice a week at Rhys's downtown apartment for breathless, rather intoxicating sex.

This severe escalation had happened *post-* his divorce, but *pre-* hers, and so, when Lucy's husband, Paul, a skeezy high school teacher and volleyball coach, found an alien sock in the laundry (it must have gotten tangled in her tights as she'd hurriedly dressed at Rhys's place) the jig, as nobody said anymore, was up.

You broke up that poor girl's marriage! was how Celia had put it, lovely, quick-to-judge-but-not-wrong Celia, who wanted to hear none of Kinnick's evidence of the questionable character of Lucy's ex, Creepy Coach Paul. Celia's profound disapproval, even after their divorce, had remained the most powerful force in Kinnick's universe.

I mean, Rhys had pleaded, *can one person* really *break up a marriage?*

Celia had given him her usual sweet, knife-blade smile. *If that one person has sex with one of the two persons in the marriage, then, yes.*

Of course, what Rhys had meant to ask was more complex than that—*Isn't infidelity more a symptom of a failing marriage than the cause? Or a symptom of something else?* But pressing such a weak, clearly self-serving case with Celia would only deepen the hole he'd dug—or cause her to reflect back on the details of their own breakup, and so he'd clammed up.

Even now, years later, with Celia dead (and the lump returning to Kinnick's sore throat) he feared her judgment from the grave more than almost anything he could imagine.

After the office scandal came the space: Rhys giving Lucy some so that she could go to counseling with her husband; Paul giving Lucy some space by filing for divorce and moving to Costa Rica with a former player on one of his volleyball teams. The newspaper gave Rhys some space by including him in a round of layoffs that left the then-fifty-five-year-old reporter rootless and depressed and living off his small severance. Kinnick gave both good judgment and decency some space by diving whole-liver into a six-month bender that saw him closing downtown cocktail bars at 2 a.m. and following the waitresses and bartenders who'd just overserved him to industry joints that could overserve him for *another* half hour. And not long after that, of course, Rhys gave his family some space by punching his loony son-in-law in his conspiracy-spouting face and surrendering to the idiotic whims of the 46 percent by moving off the grid into a little cinder block house deep in the woods. Lots of space up there.

And now, here was Rhys Kinnick, eight years after the infamous *affaire de bureau* with Lucy Park, having tried to heal his soul alone in the woods, back on a familiar barstool a few blocks from his old newspaper office, bruised left eye swollen almost shut, broken cheekbone throbbing with pain from the beating he'd taken earlier that day, frantic to find his grandchildren and his daughter, and waiting for Lucy, who promised to come meet him here after she dropped off tacos for her son.

But that was almost forty minutes ago. Where was she?

Kinnick slow-sipped his soda water. He needed to be sober to talk to Lucy. Sober to find Leah and Asher. Sober for Bethany. Even for Celia, bless her heart. He'd managed sobriety for most of his time in the woods, before lapsing a few times, most recently with Brian and Joanie. Sober was the way back from the edge, back into the world. And that lump in his throat? Maybe permanent.

"Another, boss?" The bartender had a faint Spanish accent and a tightly trimmed beard. He pointed to Kinnick's glass.

"What do I owe you so far?"

"Four bucks."

"For soda water?"

"Heat and lights, my man."

"Still seems like a lot for soda water."

"If you were the designated driver for your party, you'd get a discount."

"What if I'm *my* designated driver?"

"Doesn't qualify."

"What if I have a friend on the way?"

"You need at least three to be a party."

"Seems random."

"Not at all. Three's a party. Two's a date."

"This will definitely *not* be a date."

"That's what they all say. Right after they swipe right."

"I don't know what that means."

"Means soda water is four bucks."

"And how much is soda water if I qualify for the designated driver discount—"

"Three-fifty."

"You know what? You win." Kinnick threw up his hands. "I'll pay the two quarters." The bartender swept away his glass and returned it full, Kinnick taking this opportunity to look around the bar, an old newspaper haunt. It had taken him years to believe that the world was not a series of rooms like this, crowded with people and their cultural noise, their agendas and desires. To remember that the world was the world, and we merely passed through it: twenty-some thousand sunrises, each one with the power to renew us.

It was surreal, being back here again. Everything felt a little bit different, but not as different as he might've expected, after so long in the wilderness. The flat-screen TVs were maybe a little flatter. There were QR codes on coasters instead of menus. Granted, it had only been a few years, and he'd only been hiding sixty-some miles away, and he *had* been in a few bars in Springdale and other small towns since then, and he *had* seen a little bit of television at Brian and Joanie's house, but the changes he noted had a strange quality to them. Not only did they seem broadly unimpressive, but, in some cases, they seemed like steps backward. Like, not only were there no flying cars, there seemed to be more big pickups and SUVs than ever.

At home right now, the crickets would be singing their first flat notes, that lone creek bullfrog calling him out (*Kinnick! Kinnick!*) as the Milky Way began its smear across the night sky. And here he was, sitting on a barstool out of his past, paying four bucks for soda water.

Finally, after almost an hour, Lucy landed with a sigh and the *thunk* of a giant purse, and a jailer's jangly key ring. "You know, Kinnick, if you had a phone, it'd be a lot easier to text and tell you that I changed my mind about helping you."

"Reason number sixty-eight to not have a phone."

The bartender came over and she ordered a dry gin martini. "You want one?"

He held up his glass for a third soda water, and the guy left to make their drinks. Rhys turned to her. "So, your kids—"

"Anna and Kel."

"Right. How old—"

"Anna's twenty-two, a senior at the University of Washington. Kel's nineteen."

"Unbelievable. And is Kel in school, too?"

She let out a breath as the bartender set their drinks in front of them. When he was gone, Lucy took a sip, set her glass back on the bar, and turned to him. "I can't small talk like this, Rhys."

"Lucy, I didn't mean to—"

She put a hand on his forearm and stopped him. "Look, I don't blame you. For anything. It wasn't even about you, really. Paul was a shitty husband. I was a shitty wife. It's fine. We were headed for divorce with or without your sock." She took a deep breath. "But I've spent the last eight years as 'that cheating wife whose kid ended up on drugs.' Like some kind of morality tale. So, forgive me if I'm not in a place where I can just sit here and catch up. Reminisce about the old days."

"I'm sorry, Lucy," Kinnick said. "I know I fucked everything up."

"And now . . . what?" Lucy turned and faced him. "You think you can just drop in and *unfuck* everything?"

Rhys hummed a little laugh. "Technically, I think once you've fucked everything up, the only way to fix it is to fuck everything *down*."

She thought about this for a moment. Then she smiled a little, held up her glass, and they toasted.

- - -

LUCY PARK BURST into laughter when Kinnick asked her, "Who covers the radical right these days?"

"Uh, the government reporter?"

It took him a moment to understand what she was saying—that no longer was the fringe on the fringe. She explained to him that state legislators, sheriffs, and county commissioners—even members of Congress—openly expressed beliefs that would have gotten them labeled as members of a hate group a few years earlier, or at least as extremists, or unelectable loons. "We've got antivaxers and tax protestors, flat-Earth school board members and at least one *posse comitatus* county commissioner. Oh, there's also a rural sheriff who sits in the public library all day looking for books about gay penguins so he can confiscate them. We're on the border of Bizarroland out here." Kinnick explained that one of the men who had taken his grandchildren was a convicted poacher and "sovereign citizen" whose federal trial he had covered years ago. "Think you could get me any clips you might have on this guy, Dean Burris?"

"Clips?" She laughed and pulled out her cell phone. "You think someone at the newspaper is *clipping* stories right now, Rhys? Maybe the elevator operator in her off-time?" She pulled out her cell phone. "Here." She tapped a few things into the phone and read: "Dean Burris? Dominion Eagle Killer?"

"Yeah," Kinnick said. "I actually named him that."

"You must be so proud." She handed her phone to Kinnick.

He held it away, then closer, then away, until Lucy finally handed over her reading glasses, too. "Thanks," Kinnick said.

It was so strange, trying to read on one of these small screens. How did people do it? He tried to move the page down and somehow made it all disappear and she had to find the stories for him again. Then he lost them a second time, and finally, she got closer to him and used her thumb to effortlessly flip through his three front-page stories about Dean Burris's 2012 trial. Their shoulders touching. She smelled great.

"Yep," Kinnick said, "that's him, all right." There was nothing about Burris after those first stories until 2022, when a headline read: "Dominion Eagle Killer Runs for Stevens County Commissioner." The story explained that after serving two years of a five-year federal sentence, Dean Burris was running for office, offering himself as a proponent of the County Supremacy theory, the belief that county governments didn't need to adhere to federal and state laws.

"Looks like he didn't make it out of the primary," Lucy said.

"Well, that's comforting. Says here he's originally from Addy," Kinnick said. "That's not far from where I've been living."

"Wait, so this whole time you've been just up the road?"

Kinnick handed her phone back. "Well, sixty miles away, but yeah, not far."

"I assumed you were harassing women in European hostels, or that you'd run off and joined the merchant marines or something."

"Nah, I moved onto the last bit of our family land, between Springdale and Hunters," Kinnick said. "My grandfather's old, vacant cinder block house. Seemed like a good place to disappear."

"Disappear," she said, not a question, but a word he couldn't help wondering if she'd considered it herself.

Kinnick quoted Thoreau again: "'A man is rich in proportion to the number of things which he can afford to let alone.'"

"And what did you think you were letting alone, Rhys?"

"All of it," he said. "Thirty years of covering science deniers and mindless politics . . . the triumph of utter stupidity. It had even infected my family." Kinnick told her the story of the Thanksgiving fight with Shane at Bethany's house. "My fight with Shane was the last straw. At some point, you look around, and think, I don't belong here anymore. I don't want to have anything to do with any of this."

"The world made me do it."

Pointed, smart Lucy. "No. It was me. Or a team effort, anyway. But I did my part. I had no job. No future. I genuinely thought no one would miss me. I'd alienated everyone I cared about: friends, family, you."

"Don't throw me in there."

"I do recall you saying that you never wanted to see me again."

"And yet here you are."

Kinnick laughed. "Here I am."

"And the last seven years?" Lucy asked. "You've just been up there pouting?"

He laughed again. "No. I concentrated on living simply. It felt like I was repairing my soul or something. I spent a lot of time fixing up the house. I patched the roof. Rebuilt the pump house. Dug a garage for that old, shitty car of mine. Cut a lot of firewood. Tried to rebuild the barn. Failed at rebuilding the barn. Took the barn down. Got into solar power and converting batteries, tried to make my own compost toilet, which is still a work in progress. Walked in the woods a lot. Filled a lot of journals and notebooks. Quit drinking for a few years. Started drinking again. Went fishing. Made some friends. Lost them. Quit drinking again. Read nine hundred books."

"Nine hundred?"

"Nine hundred and fourteen. So far. Classics. History. Philosophy. Novels. Got them at rummage sales. Libraries. Nothing contemporary. I didn't want to accidentally bump into Brexit or Harvey Weinstein or superfund sites or any of the bullshit I'd left behind."

"Let me say, as part of the bullshit you left behind—"

"I didn't mean it that way—"

"—I'm curious: in seven years of reading, what did you learn?"

He thought about telling Lucy about the book he wanted to write, rethinking philosophy and ethics through a naturalist's lens, a book he thought of as *The Atlas of Wisdom*. But he wasn't sure he could survive the teasing she would administer. Instead, a line from *To the Lighthouse* flashed in his head: "'Little daily miracles, illuminations, matches struck unexpectedly in the dark.'"

"Anything that wasn't written by someone else?"

Kinnick smiled: Oh, this tart, intelligent, beautiful woman. Was it any wonder he'd fallen for her? "Let's see. What did I learn? That raccoons are assholes. That water is the most valuable thing in the world. That the sky at night should look like a river of stars." He sighed deeply. "And then, today—"

The bartender interrupted, asking if they wanted another drink. They both shook their heads at the same time.

"Today—" Lucy said.

"Today, I looked outside, and saw two strange kids on my porch. I didn't even recognize my own grandchildren! Can you imagine?" He shook his head. "And now . . ." Kinnick cleared his throat. "I just want to get them back. And find Bethany. Do what I can to help them."

It was quiet. The bartender set out a bill that Lucy quickly covered with a credit card. When Kinnick glanced over he could see her watching him with a pained look on her face.

"What?" he asked.

"Nothing."

"Come on. The way you just looked at me. What is it?"

Lucy sighed. "When I came to work here, you were like a superhero. The stories you worked. The way you'd just dig and dig and dig. I'd come ask you about some federal judge, and you'd tell me where he went to college, what his wife did for a living, what booze he drank at Charley My Boys. You knew everything, and if you didn't know, you'd find out."

Kinnick wished she would stop there. "And now?"

"Now?" She sighed. "Now you tell me that you're trying to find your grandchildren and your daughter, but you don't have a computer or a phone or any basic awareness of the world. Nothing but a broken-down old car and a busted-up face. A ten-year-old would have a better chance of finding them."

"Are you done cheering me up?"

"And if you do find your grandkids, what are you going to do, Rhys? Seriously? They're Shane's kids. Without your daughter, I don't see that you have any rights here."

Kinnick felt his shoulders slump. She was right, of course. "I don't know, Lucy. I just . . . I have to try. Don't I?"

"Try *what*?" He didn't answer and she repeated, "Try what, Rhys?"

- - -

HE WOKE ON Lucy's couch, sat up and saw her son watching him from the dining room table, where he sat eating a mixing bowl of cereal. Kelvin Park-Davis was, of course, *bigger* than Rhys remembered, but then he'd have been only nine or ten the last time Kinnick saw him. He was tall and thin, with dark eyes, shaggy black hair bleached blond at the tips, and more than a trace of his mother's fine part-Korean features. Half-inked tattoos ran from his short sleeves to his wrists.

"So, you're the guy who broke up my parents' marriage?"

"I guess. Sorry about that."

"It's okay." Kel shrugged. "My mom said it wasn't your fault."

"Generous of her."

"I always pictured you different."

"I *was* different then." Rhys felt his swollen cheek. "We met a few times when you were a kid, you know. Your mom brought you into the office to trick-or-treat. I remember one year you were a bird."

"Angry Bird," Kel said.

"Understandable."

"No. I mean, from the game," Kel said.

"Oh, right." Kinnick looked around the apartment. "And your mom is—"

"Also angry. She's showering now." Kel bent forward, as if looking around a corner. "Does your face hurt?"

"Yeah. A little." Kinnick touched his sore cheek again, which was swollen like he'd been to a vengeful dentist. "A lot," he corrected. The Extra Strength Tylenol and the sleeping pill that Lucy had given him were wearing off. "Some guy put a dent in my cheekbone."

Kel squinted. "Zygomatic arch."

"How is it that everyone knows what that is except me?"

"MMA," Kel said. "It's a common injury for fighters. You want some cereal?"

"What kind?"

"Frosted Flakes."

"Maybe later. Do you have any coffee?"

Kel gestured with his head toward the kitchen. Rhys wobbled as he stood up. He walked past the kid, through the dining room—pictures of Kel and his sister on the walls—and into the kitchen, where a glass pot was full of black coffee. He tried three cabinets before he found a cup. The steam felt nice on his face and he nearly wept, the coffee was so good. When this was done, he vowed to get rid of that old, stained aluminum pot of his.

Lucy came out of her bedroom in a wool dress and tights, her hair in a ponytail. "Oh, good. You found the coffee. And I see you met Mr. Kel." She put her hands on her son's shoulders.

"I did. He steered me to the coffee. It's delicious, thank you."

"Why don't you get cleaned up. I'm going to get you situated, but then I need to go in to work."

"Situated?"

"Yeah." She walked away from the table to get herself a cup of coffee. "I might have found someone who can help you."

"You did? Who?"

She glanced at her son, then said, "A retired cop. Does some detective work for law firms, finds missing witnesses, deadbeat dads, that

kind of thing. I called him and he's up for it. He's even had some deal-
ings with the guys you ran into—"

"The Army of the Lord," Kinnick said, "AOL."

Kel laughed. "Seriously?"

"They're apparently the militia wing for this radical church that has
some kind of training compound in Idaho," Lucy said. "They show up
with their guns to Pride parades and shit like that. My friend called
them 'toy soldiers.'"

"It was no toy I got hit with." Kinnick put his tongue into his broken
cheek. "Do I know this cop? Was he around when I was at the paper?"

"Maybe." Lucy took a sip of coffee. Her eyes shifted to Kel and then
back. "I . . . uh . . . I dated him for a while."

"No!" Kel stood up. "You called Chuck?" He laughed as he carried
his cereal bowl to the sink. "Crazy Ass Chuck! Back in the show!"

Kinnick looked from Kel to Lucy. "I'm getting help from a guy
named Crazy Ass Chuck? You *dated* a guy named Crazy Ass Chuck?"

Lucy gritted her teeth: not what she wanted to talk about. "Chuck
is not *crazy*. He can get a little . . . excitable. And he's got some issues."
She shot a glare at Kel. "But who doesn't? Chuck's a good man. And he
was a good cop until they forced him out."

"Wait. Not Chuck Littlefield?" Kinnick remembered stories from
around the time he left Spokane, the jittery, quotable major crimes detective who got sideways with brass and ended up getting transferred.
"You dated Chuck Littlefield?"

Lucy turned the glare from her kid to Kinnick. "You and I are not
talking about this!" She went into the kitchen, filled her coffee cup,
then stalked through the dining room. "Be ready in fifteen minutes,
Kinnick. And for God's sake, take a *fucking* shower! You smell like the
business end of a hobo."

As her bedroom door slammed, Kel's eyes opened wide. "*Day-amn!*
You got a morning F-bomb. I thought only I got those."

Kinnick sniffed his shoulder. "I had a shower yesterday. Have people always been this intense about hygiene, or is this something new?"

"No, I think it's been around for a while." Kel sniffed the air. "Hey, you want to borrow a shirt, man?"

- - -

FOR A DECADE, Chuck Littlefield was the man about Major Crimes, a muscly, fidgety homicide detective who also happened to be every reporter's best source—the only good quote in an otherwise tight-lipped, tight-assed cop shop. His bosses, however, viewed him—and not without reason—as a double-dealing ball hog, a leaky ship, a selfish, glory-seeking nonteam player. They tired of his constant overtime requests and the way details of his cases mysteriously showed up in news stories. And, for his part, Chuck hated the way his bosses rejected his perfectly reasonable requests for fiber analysis and forensic carbon dot powder, for any new investigative tool, which they always dismissed as needless and expensive.

When the funding was cut for a cold case homicide unit that Chuck had hoped to start (and ride into retirement), an anonymous source was quoted in the newspaper, in a story written by the criminal justice reporter Lucy Park, calling the new police chief "a bureaucrat with a toy badge" who had "all the law enforcement instincts of a fat, old bookkeeper."

Two weeks later, Chuck was relieved of his Major Crimes duties and shipped off to Property Crimes, the unit where burnout detectives were sent to die, and where he was tasked with serving out the last nine months of his twenty-five-and-change parked at a desk, herding paper. The problem with this castaway punishment was that Spokane was a property crime town, in the same way that other cities were homicide towns, or gang towns. Every night, meth and opioid zombies wandered the streets looking for open garages, for backpacks left in cars, for anything that could be lifted, looted, or lightened from its owners' unwitting hands.

But since no one would ever mistake a filched lawn mower for "a high priority crime" (especially in a city with twenty or thirty homicides a year), funding for property crimes had remained stagnant for years. That meant just a handful of officers, two clerks, and one receptionist were assigned to the basement unit, a department so overwhelmed they could do little more than shuffle paper and occasionally answer the constantly ringing telephone, all while supposedly on the lookout for patterns that suggested more sophisticated burglary rings. And while property crimes continued to rise each year, even those numbers couldn't capture the full scope of the problem, because most thefts went unreported—once citizens learned that filing a police report was almost as helpful as tossing a coin into a fountain.

And even if it were possible to penetrate the labyrinthian, automated crime-report telephone system, and talk to a human being (it wasn't), you wouldn't find much help there, either. If you were lucky, you'd get a muttering old detective quietly browsing Arizona condos on his computer while he indulged your sob story. "Uh-huh. And did you register your bike? (*nine-hole executive golf course*) Uh-huh. And do you have the serial number? (*community pool*) Uh-huh. And have you checked the pawn shops? (*Maybe I'll try Sedona.*)"

Chuck spent a few weeks in 2017 in this cord of human deadwood, *uh-huhing* his way through dull reports, until one day: epiphany! The "fat, old bookkeeper" of a police chief with the "toy badge" had, like every boss in the world over the last twenty years, gotten his job by selling himself as a champion of "quantitative, measurable units of policing."

Stats.

So, one day, Chuck looked up the numbers of his new unit. The SPD Property Crimes division maintained an "active solution/recovery rate" of between 2 and 5 percent. That's when Crazy Ass Chuck Littlefield devised his cruel and brilliant revenge.

First, he went off his meds. Then, he printed out every report of every property crime that had come in over the last two weeks, and he drove his pickup truck to each pawn shop in the city, one by one. He examined each bike and television and rototiller in the shops and compared them to the stolen property reports, and anytime he found a serial number that was the same, or a photographic match, he confiscated the stolen item and threw it in the back of his truck. He dared the pawn shops to object, but they could do nothing. They knew the score. They were required by law to have on file a receipt with the seller's (i.e., thief's) name, address, and photo ID. But everyone knew what kind of flaccid, disinterested cops worked property crimes, and since they hadn't been visited by a living badge in a decade, the pawn shop workers had gotten lax about checking the fake names on the receipts for the stolen shit they purchased every day. The last thing they wanted to do was rat out their suppliers (i.e., thieves). So, for two months, in the grips of a growing bipolar hypomania, Chuck terrorized both the pawn shops *and* his fellow Property Crimes detectives, solving a record *9 percent* of the property crime cases that came across his desk.

In that time, he also recovered a euphoric sense of purpose that he hadn't felt since he was a young cop in his first car. Returning stolen property was almost better than sex. Bicyclists pumped his hand and thanked him like he'd just delivered their first babies. Contractors got emotional when Chuck pulled up with tool chests taken off their trucks and their job sites. "I have worked in this city for twenty years," one backhoe operator said, "and I've never so much as gotten a crescent wrench back."

"Just doing my job," Chuck said.

One woman, who had her jewelry box (inlaid with mother-of-pearl) recovered by the handsome detective, with most of the jewels still inside, even tried to seduce him, and while he was tempted, Chuck knew better than to mess with this selfless, transcendent feeling. "You're like . . . some kind of hero," she said as he John-Wayned away from her house toward his pickup.

Even his lieutenant was impressed. "What in the fuck do you think you're doing, Littlefield?"

"Just solving crimes, Lieu," Chuck said. "Isn't that what I'm supposed to do?" *And*, he thought, *I am shoving these impossible stats up your worthless ass.*

"You know we can't maintain this," the LT said. "Once you retire, our numbers will drop off a cliff."

"Oh, I don't know," Chuck said, "you've got some good people here."

At that, he and the LT both turned to look at the two souls who happened to be at their desks that day: a receptionist playing *Candy Crush* on her cell while the office phone rang into oblivion; and red-faced Madman McCallister arguing on the phone with the contractor who was rebuilding the dock at his cabin at Lake Coeur d'Alene and apparently doing a shit job. (*Uh-huh, and how much for a dock that actually fucking floats?*)

Chuck's last month on the job, he worked eighty-hour, seven-day weeks, returning stolen goods like some kind of inverse Robin Hood. The pawn shops had tightened up again, and so Chuck struggled to make his target—double digits—but in his last two weeks he hit an astounding *13 percent* solution rate, a number so impressive and utterly unbreakable that even some of his lazier, more cynical colleagues were impressed, two of them giving him a standing ovation when he packed his things to leave on his final day (the other two people in the office gave him the finger).

"You're like the Joe DiMaggio of assholes," his lieutenant said. "And when our numbers fall back to earth, I'm dead."

"Don't sell yourself short," Chuck said, thinking, *No one deserves it more.*

But then retirement came, and along with it, the severe depression that always followed a good mania. But this felt like more than just a dark mood. The only life that Chuck Littlefield had ever known . . . was over. For a while he thought *he* might be over, too—just forty-seven years old and already put out to pasture. He put on weight. Started drinking heavily. One night, he stood on the Monroe Street Bridge, looking over Spokane Falls as it roared and tumbled into the river canyon, and thought, *Why not?* But he didn't jump, and eventually, he found his way back to his mood stabilizers, and vowed to enjoy retirement, the way other cops seemed to. He bought new skis and hit all six mountains within two hours of Spokane. He played on a softball team, and spent his days at the local tribal casinos, where he lost so much money playing poker that he had to get a job. He got hired as an investigator for a law firm, tracking down philandering husbands and wives, interviewing people who were suing their contractors, suing their employers, suing their doctors, spouses, siblings, parents, anyone. It was like being in Property Crimes again, the endless, dull parade of people who wanted to take someone to court.

One day Chuck was in the grocery store, when he saw, in the greeting card and magazine aisle, behind a Covid-19 mask, the former police reporter Lucy Park, who had written the story that effectively ended his career. Something about that mask highlighted her lovely eyes. He could still visualize what she had in her cart that day: Frosted Flakes, red wine, romaine lettuce, coffee, and a *Vanity Fair* magazine. She asked how he was doing. ("Never better," he lied. "Me, too," she lied back.) She apologized for writing the story in which he criticized the new police chief, but Chuck waved this off. It had been the best thing that had happened to him, he explained, getting exiled to Property Crimes. He'd rediscovered his purpose as a cop. She, too, had been exiled, she said, moved off her old reporter beat into a desk job, eventually becoming assistant metro editor.

"You got exiled . . . up?" he asked.

"Exactly. Like being named first mate on a doomed ship."

"The Gilligan of journalism," he said.

It was *she* who asked *him* out, and he nearly knocked over her cart saying yes. He liked her tight dancer's body ("What are you talking about? I was never a dancer.") and her sexy black eyes. ("They're dark brown, asshole.") And he liked the way she smiled at him when he told his old cop stories, as if he were someone special, a man of courage and decency. ("I was actually thinking, 'What a dick you are.'") Most of all, it was that very stubborn argumentative quality—Lucy was a true contrarian—that won him over. He was an optimist, she was a pessimist; he was a Republican, she was a Democrat; he needed fresh air, she went around closing windows; they agreed on so little and yet, somehow, it worked, every argument like a slow dance, electric and filled with promise. They dated for two years, in the manner of divorced people their age, with neither of them pushing for more, just quietly taking refuge in the feeling of having an attractive adult across the table at the restaurant, someone to take a walk with, to share bad news with, to sleep next to. They fit well together, Lucy coiled into his chest, Chuck curled up over her like a protective shell, whispering sweet gallows humor into her ear. ("Want to go watch a murder show? Want to watch some poor wife get strangled by the new curtains?") They shared the love language of two people raised in a cop shop.

He called her "Gilligan." She called him "Fuckhead."

But Fuckhead could be agitated and moody, up-and-down, especially when he skipped his meds. He sometimes said shitty things about her job, or her family, and he didn't always call or text when he said he would. He bought things on impulse, a motorcycle, a fishing boat, another fishing boat, a third fishing boat, a hundred used lawn chairs that he intended to reweave and sell. Gilligan could be moody, too—down, mostly, endlessly disagreeable, bitching about her job and her dying profession. She sometimes said shitty things, too, and yelled at him for not calling or texting when he said he would. Being an editor seemed to put her in a terrible mood, but whenever Chuck criticized the newspaper or suggested she leave it, she went on this insane defense of journalism that made it sound like she was single-handedly saving blind orphans from being eaten by cannibals every day.

Then there was her kid, hapless Kelvin, who, when he wasn't wasting his time playing *Magic: The Gathering* on-line, was wasting himself, cycling through cheaper and cheaper drugs on his way to becoming a street Freddy. Chuck tired of hearing about this messed-up kid, who took up way too much of their conversation time, and way too much of Lucy's energy. And when Chuck offered his reasonable, tough-love advice ("You should toss him out. Be more like me—such a bad parent your kids don't bother you with their bullshit.") Lucy called him "cold and uncaring," and one day, when Chuck happened to suggest that Kel was "a lost cause," Gilligan decided suddenly—just as it had been her idea for them to date—that she was "over your cruel fucking ass."

Fine by him. After two years, Chuck was tired, too, of Lucy's constant negativity, mostly. He suspected there was probably a platoon of hot, hungry, less-complicated women out there for him. So, for a year, he swiped right, slept around, and slipped in and out of various short-term flings. These offered little enjoyment, though, and he found himself devising escape routes on third, second, even first dates. He even made his way back to the jewelry-box woman and slept with her, wishing immediately afterward (or technically, *during*) that he hadn't, that he could have remained an implacable, selfless hero in her eyes, instead of what he actually was: an old, tired, half-horny, twice-divorced cop with bad knees, three estranged kids, and emotional dysregulation and bipolar issues, a guy who didn't really want to hear about your job as a pharmaceutical rep, or how your daughter's new boyfriend was a loser, or how your ex-husband had poisoned the family against you, or, really, anything that came out of your dull, pretty mouth.

So, after two weeks, he ghosted the jewelry-box pharma rep—*How's that for a hero?*—and realized something rather surprising. What he *wanted* was what he'd *had*: low-key, profane, petty, pretty, perfect-fit

Lucy Park. He even started to wonder if maybe he hadn't been *in love* with her. He stared at old photos of the two of them on his phone (her eyes really were brown). He pulled up her number just to look at it, and a few times, he drove past the crappy duplex where she lived with her messed-up kid. He even found himself parking outside the newspaper office once, on the off chance he might see her and casually ask how she was doing. But Chuck had been given no indication that she missed *him*, and he had worked way too many domestic murder cases to go in for a full-on stalking.

Still, he began having elaborate daydreams that involved bumping into her, offhandedly asking if she wanted to get dinner sometime, or, in his more melodramatic moods, rescuing her from thieves, or from international terrorists.

So, to have her just call out of the blue this way and ask for his help—for a former colleague whose grandchildren had been forcibly taken from him—was almost too good to be true. A sign that things were turning around for him, that maybe there was a future with Lucy after all. The very idea filled him with hope. And adrenaline. Especially after she explained that her friend had run afoul of those *Army of the Lord* douchebags, the fanatics who were always skulking around Pride parades and MLK Day marches in Spokane and Coeur d'Alene, and who, during the pandemic and the Black Lives Matter protests, had shown up for unsolicited security-guard duty at shopping malls and downtown stores, in their Don't-Tread-on-Me-I-got-a-small-dick pickup trucks and their Kevlar vests over their black T-shirts, their semiautomatic rifles BabyBjörned to their fat guts like the shithead soldier/cop-wannabes they were (even though none of them had the stones to go and join the actual military, or the brains to pass a simple law enforcement test).

But he was getting ahead of himself. Messing with these buffoons would be fun, a charge to the old battery, practically like police work again, but the real point was getting to see Lucy once more. Helping this old friend of hers (he wondered: *boyfriend?*) and reminding her that dating a retired cop had its benefits. Being of use again. Maybe even winning back his Gilligan, his sexy *little buddy*, and returning as her ever-loveable *Fuckhead*. Chuck got so excited at the prospect, he could barely sit still—he could barely sit still most days anyway—and when Lucy's car pulled up at the Rocket Bakery downtown, Chuck Littlefield leaped up and met them at the door, bouncing on the balls of the Nike Cross-Trainers he wore under his chinos and sports coat, giving her his warmest noncrazy smile, and saying to her friend with the black eye and the broken cheek, in the Glass Animals concert T-shirt: "Dude! Let's do this!"

- - -

THEY SAT IN stiff wooden chairs at a long table in a cavernous coffee shop, Lucy Park and Chuck Littlefield on one side, Kinnick on the other, as he explained what had happened from the moment Leah and Asher showed up on his porch the day before. The big ex-cop had a small pocket notebook open on the table, though he hardly wrote anything down at first. He spoke quickly, in a clipped way that made Kinnick think of a typewriter.

"Uh-huh," Chuck said. "Right. Then what?" Every few seconds, he'd say this, "Uh-huh, right, then what?" as if Kinnick were unaware of the concept of chronology and might suddenly tell some part of the story from the 1940s, or two weeks in the future.

"Uh-huh, right, then what?"

Kinnick repeated what Asher had said, that "maybe Dad killed Mom."

"Smart kid," Chuck said.

"What? You think so?" Kinnick felt suddenly sick. He hadn't really thought Shane was capable of something like that. He'd been trying to *not* think of that possibility.

"No, I mean, that's probably *not* what happened. He just sounds like a smart kid."

When Kinnick got to the part of the story that took place at the abbey parking lot, the two AOL goons taking his grandkids and one of them hitting him with a blackjack, Chuck reached across the table and took Kinnick's chin between his thumb and forefinger, turning his head to both sides. "They broke your zygomatic arch. I can see the dent, even with the swelling."

This was the third thing Chuck wrote in his little notebook, after "Chess Club" and "Smart Kid." "Blackjack. Zygom. arch. Broken."

Kinnick wondered how he could have managed to spend the last seven years reading almost a thousand books and still somehow be the only person in the world to *not* know the scientific name for a cheekbone. He tried not to be intimidated by the retired cop, who was younger and more muscled, with fast-blinking eyes, salt-and-pepper hair and beard, and, evidently, a deep knowledge of facial bone structure.

"So. Can you help him out?" Lucy asked.

"Sure," said Chuck Littlefield. "Sure. It won't be easy. But there are some steps we can take. First, this guy, Shawn?"

"Shane."

"Shane, right." Finally, he wrote the name Shane in his notebook. "Since this Shane is the boy's biological father, and has adopted the girl, your daughter will be the only one with legal standing to stop these paintball yahoos from marrying off your granddaughter. So, first step, find—what's you daughter's name again?"

"Bethany. She might have gone back to Oregon."

"Right." He wrote in his notebook: *Betheny: Oregon?* "We'll find her, but in the meantime I'll have one of the lawyers I work with draw up some kind of writ—and since these shit-sticks can barely read, the writ can say anything as long as we get a *county* official to stamp it—that's the only authority these guys recognize—then we go in strong, present our paper, grab your grandkids, and go find Brittany—"

"Bethany—"

"Right. Bethany, Bethany, Bethany." He underlined her misspelled name in his notebook. "Yep, and if we're lucky, one of those camo pansies will try his blackjack trick on me so I can politely send him home wearing it as a thong."

Kinnick made eye contact with Lucy, who gave a slight shrug of her left shoulder that Rhys took to mean, *Hey, I was lonely. Don't judge.*

"But listen." Chuck slapped the table in front of Kinnick. "This whole thing . . . it could get intense. Are you up for that, the possibility of seeing these guys again?"

Kinnick could feel Lucy's eyes on him. He cleared his throat, suddenly feeling the need to both compete with, and differentiate himself from, this jittery ex-cop, who was clearly trying to impress his old girlfriend.

"'Who then is invincible?'" Kinnick asked rhetorically, then answered: "'The one who cannot be upset by anything outside their reasoned choice.'"

Lucy and Chuck both stared at him.

"Epictetus?" Kinnick said.

Lucy and Chuck continued to stare.

Kinnick's face flushed. "I mean—yeah, sure. I'll do anything to get them back."

Lucy stood. "I should get to work. I have reporters to babysit." She put a hand on Chuck's arm. "Thank you, Chuck. This means a lot."

He put his hand on her hand. "Of course, Lucy. Anything for you."

Kinnick stood, too. "Uh, can I talk to you for a second, Lucy."

"Sure. Walk me to the door?"

They started to move away from the table, and then Chuck said, "Lucy, can I get a minute when he's done?"

Lucy looked from one mistake to the other. "O-okay."

At the door, Kinnick glanced back at the fidgety cop. "I just wanted to say that I appreciate this."

"I hope he can help you."

"I also wanted to ask . . ." He turned back to Lucy. "Are you sure that he's . . . stable? That he's up for this?"

"He's not the one quoting Epictetus."

Kinnick winced. "Ouch."

"How's your cheek?"

"That wasn't about my cheek."

"Good." She reached in her purse and handed him the bottle of Tylenol from home. Then she looked at him a moment. "Just be careful, okay? Chuck knows this stuff. But he can get carried away. If he wants to do something rash and idiotic, I'm trusting you to say no."

"I will."

"Promise?"

"Of course." He felt coddled, like a child, her saying this. Still, it was nice of her to help. And to worry about him. "Thank you, Lucy. I . . . well . . . just thank you."

She nodded and smiled, patted him on the arm, and Kinnick returned to the table. Chuck passed him on the way to talk to Lucy at the door. Rhys watched them out of the corner of his eye—Chuck doing most of the talking, and then, after a moment, leaning in for a hug. From his vantage Kinnick couldn't see Lucy's face, or how fully she returned the hug.

Chuck Littlefield returned to the table and hitched his pants. "Great, isn't she?"

"The best," Kinnick said.

"Okay then." Chuck clapped his hands. "What do you say, partner? Should we go find your grandkids?"

- - -

KINNICK HAD NEVER seen someone drive the way Chuck Littlefield piloted this extended cab Chevy Silverado pickup: perched forward as if bellied up to a bar, steering with his left forearm, which he draped over the wheel, his head snapping left, then right, then left again, like a driving squirrel, zipping between lanes and speeding between intersections. Any space between cars seemed to offend him. "Drive your fuckin' car!" he'd say as he raced around some cautious motorist.

He glanced over at Kinnick. "So. You and Lucy, huh?"

"What?" Kinnick said. "Oh. Yeah. For a few months. But it was a long time ago."

"Long time ago," Chuck repeated. "Right." He worked the phone in his lap with his right hand as he drove, ringing his lawyer's office. He held up a finger to Kinnick and put a single wireless earbud in his right ear. "Shel. Hey. Littlefield here. Look. I need you to run a couple of names for me, standard checks: address, criminal, civil, whatever you got. You ready? First, a Shane and Bethany Collins, Spokane address, and before that, Grants Pass, Oregon. *C-O-L-L-I-N-S*. Bethany's DOB is—" He looked at Kinnick.

"Oh. Uh, April eleventh, 1987. I don't know Shane's."

"Bethany's DOB: Four-eleven-eighty-seven. No DOB for Shane. Next, Anna Gaines, Spokane resident, neighbor, apartment in Northeast, no DOB, husband's name unknown. And a con by the name of Dean Burris, also no DOB. Truck driver. Federal charges a dozen or so years ago—" He looked at Kinnick, who nodded.

"Federal charges for poaching, did some time, apparently ran for office up in Stevens County." Chuck spelled each name and repeated the information Kinnick had given. Rhys couldn't believe this was the same guy who had called Shane Shawn and Bethany Brittany and had barely jotted anything down in his pocket notebook. He seemed to remember every detail now. "Text me whatever you get. We're on the road today, *goin' mo-bile*, so keep the info coming. Thank you, Shel, I owe you."

Chuck ended the call and glanced at Kinnick again. "So, what happened?"

"What do you mean?"

"Between you and Lucy? I'm guessing you didn't break up with *her*."

"Oh." Kinnick laughed. "No. I didn't." He exhaled. "It was compli-cated."

"She does that to people."

"We worked together, so we wanted to keep it quiet. I was recently divorced and she . . . wasn't yet—"

"Ah—"

"Turns out an office scandal is not the best way to start a relation-ship—"

"And yet people keep trying—"

"Meanwhile, she was having trouble with her son—"

"Christ, that kid—"

Kinnick smiled. Having a conversation with Chuck was like playing ping-pong. Rhys looked out the window, remembering. "But honestly? The real problem . . . was me. I was a wreck. All over the place. About to lose my job, estranged from my family, depressed, pushing away anyone who cared about me, drinking too much—"

"Not hard to find yourself there—"

"—until eventually Lucy asked me to leave her alone."

"And you did?"

"For almost eight years."

"Damn. Willpower."

"Well, I left everyone alone. Daughter, ex-wife, grandkids, family, friends. I moved up to the woods and I just . . . disappeared."

"No shit." Chuck chewed his lip. "I don't think I could do that."

"I convinced myself that no one would miss me—"

"I do understand that—"

"—and in the end, it was almost like *I* wasn't the one choosing exile—"

"Right."

"—but like the world was telling me to go—"

"Right!"

"—I had no job and no purpose anymore—"

"Yes!"

"—and it seemed like I was being sent away, like an animal sent off into the woods to die or something. In fact, it was more than that. It was like my whole species had gone extinct."

"Fuck! Yes!" Chuck slapped the steering wheel. "That's how I felt after I retired! Extinct!"

"At first it was a relief," Kinnick said, "being alone in the woods. I worked. Took walks. Wrote. Read. Concentrated on fixing things around my little house. I'd feel this sense of accomplishment from the smallest things. Putting in a new pump for the well. Rebuilding the front porch. Learning to use generators and batteries. For a few years, it was great. But the last couple of years, I've felt something was missing."

Kinnick took and released a deep breath. "Then, yesterday, my grandkids showed up on my front porch. And for just a minute, I didn't know who they were. I find out my ex-wife is dead, my daughter has disappeared, my shithead son-in-law has gone off the deep end . . . and it was like I could see myself, not from *inside* my own head, where I've been the last seven years, but from the outside, where these cute children were standing on my porch, waiting for their broken-down old grandpa to step up and *do* something."

"Jesus." Chuck shook his head. "Damn." He looked over. "Listen to me, Rhys. We are going to get your grandkids back. Don't you worry. We'll find your daughter and her kids, and we *will* set things right again."

Chuck's cell phone had been buzzing during all of this. "No. Don't you worry." The ex-cop thumbed through information while he drove, eyes darting up to the road, down to the screen, up, then back down. "Good, Shel, yes, good, good, good," he muttered.

Kinnick watched the big cop's cell phone with envy. He really needed to get himself one of those things.

"Here we go," Chuck said, "looks like we got an address for your daughter and Shane. We're in business."

They drove to a stucco apartment complex near the Northtown Mall, where Shane and Bethany had most recently lived. Their first-floor unit had a small patio, with a barbecue and two bicycles chained to the metal railing. The smaller bike still had training wheels. Ah, poor, clumsy Asher. Kinnick felt his chest tighten with guilt. So much time he'd missed.

"Nobody's home," Chuck said, arching his hands to look through the patio window. "Place looks well-kept, though. That's a good sign."

"Of what?" Kinnick asked.

But Chuck had moved on, climbing the stairs two at a time to a second-floor apartment, a place with planters and deck chairs on the balcony. "Let's see what the neighbor has to say."

They rang Anna Gaines's bell. She answered in workout clothes, started to smile, then gasped when she saw Kinnick's face. "Oh, my God. What happened?"

"I took Asher to his chess tournament and a couple of Shane's friends showed up and took the kids away. I got this for my trouble." He pointed to his black eye and swollen cheek.

"Was it the men who came here? Two big guys in a black pickup?"

"That's them."

"I'm so sorry! I'm the one who told them where you were going. They said Shane was looking for his kids or else I never would've said anything."

"It's not your fault," Kinnick said. "I'm just glad they didn't give you too much trouble." He turned and introduced Chuck Littlefield. "Chuck's a former police detective. He's helping me find Bethany and the kids."

Chuck opened his little notebook, suddenly all-business. "When was the last time you saw Shane and Bethany, Mrs. Gaines?"

"Let's see. I saw Bethany five days ago. We chatted out by the mailboxes. And I saw Shane a couple of days ago, walking to his truck. Then Leah came over yesterday morning with that note and said that her mom was gone, and that Shane had gone off to find her."

"Did Bethany give you any indication where she might be going?"

"No. I mean . . . not really. I've known she was unhappy. Obviously, she thinks this new church is a little intense. She talked about moving back to Grants Pass, where they had friends. And I do know she had reconnected with someone in Portland recently? An ex-boyfriend?"

"Not Sluggish Doug," Kinnick said.

"Yeah, Doug! I think that was the name."

For the hundredth time, Kinnick thought: *Christ, Bethany's taste in men.*

Chuck turned to Kinnick. "Do you know this Doug's last name?"

Rhys nodded.

Chuck turned back to Anna. "Did Bethany ever say that she felt physically threatened, that she worried Shane might harm her?"

"No, no." Anna shook her head. "Nothing like that. She always said he was a good father, and a good husband, and, honestly, I think he adores her. He just keeps getting deeper and deeper into this church, into conspiracies. Guns. I think all Bethany wants is to go back to Oregon, get the kids back in school, and try to get Shane to ease up on the crazy. I suspect that's why she wanted Mr. Kinnick to watch them while she got some things in order."

Kinnick's head slumped in defeat. One job and he couldn't even do that.

"Did she have her own car?"

"No," Anna said. "That's one of the issues. They just had the pickup, and Shane has that. Maybe she took the bus somewhere?"

Or someone picked her up, Kinnick thought. Or— He thought again of Asher's terrifying comment.

Chuck asked: "Does she have any other friends we might call?"

"I'm sure she does, but I wouldn't know. They just moved here a few months ago. We'd see each other around the apartment complex, and we just started talking, especially after her mother died. We talked about our marriages, jobs she might find around here, about our moms. She was becoming increasingly unhappy, I think. She talked about these panic attacks she'd been having."

Each detail stung Kinnick. He should've been here for his daughter.

Chuck handed over his little pocket notebook. "I assume you have Bethany's phone number. Can I get you to write that down for me?"

Another sting: Kinnick didn't even know his own daughter's phone number.

"Sure," Anna said. She pulled up the number on her phone. "I've tried calling a bunch of times. Goes straight to voicemail. Like her phone is turned off." She handed the pocket notebook back to Chuck. Kinnick looked over the ex-cop's shoulder, as if seeing his daughter's number now might make up for his absence.

Chuck wrote his own phone number on a piece of paper, passed it over, and said to call if she saw or heard *anything*. Anna reached out and squeezed Rhys's hand. "Good luck, Mr. Kinnick," she said. "Those kids are so smart and sweet. It's like they're from another time, you know?"

Kinnick did know. He swallowed and nodded.

"I hope you get them back."

They walked quietly back to the truck, Chuck tapping Bethany's phone number into his own phone, and handing it to Kinnick. Immediately: "You've reached Bethany Collins . . ." Her voice another lump in his throat.

"Straight to voicemail," Kinnick said, and he handed the phone back to Chuck, who opened his email and read the latest information his office had sent over.

"No shit," he said. "Oh man! I know where this is!"

He looked up from his phone to Kinnick.

"What?" Kinnick asked.

"Your guy Dean Burris is living at this pastor's compound in Idaho. Real *Deliverance* vibes up there. They call it the Rampart."

"My grandkids talked about that."

"House, chapel, bunkhouse for ten guys, broken-down cars and farm equipment. I had to serve some legal papers up there for one of our lawyers once. A land dispute. Up in the woods where these half-assed militia nuts train. I said, 'What are you training for? Is douchebaggery a sport in the Olympics now?' Nah, if this Burris took your grandkids up there, that's fucked-up." Chuck looked over. "You got the letter your daughter sent?"

Kinnick patted his pants pocket. "Yeah."

Chuck made a humming noise. Then he chewed his lip again. "It might take a week to track your daughter down. Find this old boy-friend in Portland, see what he knows. And then we'd still need lawyers to draw up papers. Might take weeks.

"Or . . ." Chuck stuck out his lower lip. "You know what? What if we say 'fuck it.' I know a guy who knows the sheriff up there. What if we just drive there now. Put our cards on the table and see if those assholes fold. You in?" He put his fist out.

There would be no Epictetus quotes this time. Kinnick simply nodded and bumped Chuck's fist. "Let's do it."

– – –

THEY DROVE FOR almost two hours through forested foothills and river val-leys, up the Idaho panhandle to a town nearly on the Canadian border, where a retired Tustin, California, police officer stood up from behind a bare oak desk and introduced himself as "Sheriff Glen Campbell." Kinnick glanced over at Chuck Littlefield, but he had no reaction to the name.

Glen Campbell wore a cowboy hat and an epauletted uniform shirt that strained to contain his broad chest and broader belly. Badge over heart, hand-mic clipped to shoulder, he spoke out of the left side of his mouth, like he had a chaw on the other side. And even though he'd apparently lived in Anaheim for forty years before moving up to the muzzle of Idaho, he had a north-country twang that Kinnick recognized as more cultural than regional. "So," he said to Chuck, "I hear you played softball with that worthless ol' fat-ass Dunham."

"He said you might call him that," said Chuck.

"Well, he is a worthless ol' fat-ass. I can't imagine that tub-a-lard gets down the line too fast."

"No—"

"Don't see him beating out a lot of infield hits."

"He ain't exactly what you'd call a base-stealing threat."

They talked this way for a few minutes, about their mutual cop friend, another retiree from Southern California, who apparently was a "hilarious son of a bitch," "a complete asshat," and "a drunken shit-monkey most days," leaving Kinnick to wonder how they'd talk about someone they *didn't like.*

Finally, Chuck got down to telling Kinnick's story.

"Sounds domestic," Sheriff Glen said when Chuck was finished. "I'm sorry for your trouble," he said to Rhys, "but that appears to be family court business, and not my concern."

"Well, no," Chuck said. "These guys forcibly abducted two kids and assaulted their poor grandfather." Chuck turned to Kinnick. "Show him your face."

Kinnick flinched at *poor grandfather,* but he turned so the sheriff could see the full damage.

"Doesn't look too bad to me. Black eye, swollen cheek. Have you iced it?"

"It's a broken zygomatic arch," Kinnick said.

"I don't know what that is," Sheriff Glen said.

"It's the cheekbone," Kinnick said. "I'll have to have surgery to repair it."

"Well, if you were assaulted in Spokane, you really have to take that up with the Spokane police. It's got nothing to do with me. You can take your story and your broken zygowhatever and go have *them* file assault charges. As for this other thing, with your grandkids, the way I see it, it's still just a custody issue. You can take *that* up in family court. Nothing I can do about it, I'm afraid." Then Sheriff Glen turned to Chuck, his splotchy neck reddening. "Look, I appreciate that you're Dunham's friend. But there's no way he told you this was a good idea, bringing me this half-assed custody bullshit."

Kinnick leaned forward. "With all due respect, Sheriff, this is about more than custody. My grandchildren were taken away from me and hauled off to a militia camp. They might be in danger up there."

"What makes you think they're in danger?"

"Well—" Kinnick pointed to his own black eye. "There's this."

"*You* say they're in danger, and *you* say the kids' mother asked you to watch them, and *you* say these guys hit you out of the blue. What do you think these fellas are gonna tell me when I go up there? They're gonna say the kids' father asked *them* to watch the kids. Maybe they'll even say you got hostile with *them*."

Kinnick reached into his pocket. "I have a note from their mother—"

The sheriff held up his hands. "Good. A note from Mommy. And tell me—what's their father gonna say when I ask him, Mr. Kinnick? Is he going to tell me that you're the dangerous one?"

He looked at Chuck. "What is this?"

Chuck's entire body language had changed. He was leaning back in his chair, eyes narrowed, staring hard at the sheriff. "You *do* know who we're talking about," Chuck said. "Those goose-stepping Army of the Lord nutjobs."

The red went from the sheriff's neck up over his face, even as he offered a wide, calming smile. "Sure, I know them. I know Pastor Gallen. He's a good man. A veteran. I know Dean Burris, too. And yes, I know the Rampart. I know that every time I go up there—

because a neighbor complains about gunfire, or there's a dispute over them training in the woods—what I find is a bunch of God-fearing, law-abiding members of *my* community, who, while they might question the federal government, happen to respect the hell out of the role a sheriff plays in a place like this, a sheriff, I might add, who won his Republican primary by a mere sixteen votes against a man with no law enforcement experience at all, a man who openly called for armed rebellion. So, if you want me to be even clearer about it, I will just say that these 'nutjobs' are a powerful constituency in this county. Which, if I may be blunt, you and Broken Cheekbone here are not."

Chuck continued staring hard at Sheriff Glen Campbell.

"Now. If there's nothing else." The sheriff gestured at his empty desk. "I have a lot of work to do."

As they left the sheriff's office, a smiling receptionist said, "Y'all have a good day, now!"

They were quiet as they walked to the truck, Littlefield stewing. "What a fucking coward," he finally said. "Indulging those paranoid dipshits marching around the woods with their semiautos. Guy thinks he can make pets out of rattlesnakes."

They climbed back in the pickup. "So, now what?" Kinnick asked.

Chuck was chewing his cheek and breathing heavily, as if stumped by a math problem. He looked over. "Can I ask you something, Rhys?"

"Sure," Kinnick said.

Chuck pulled out his key ring, reached across Kinnick's lap, and used a key to unlock the glove box. He pulled out a small black case, spun three numbers on the lock, and then removed a black handgun. "You ever use one of these?"

- - -

HIS FIRST DAY in the woods, January 28, 2017, Kinnick carried two bundles of firewood into the house. He'd bought them at a grocery store on his way out of town, along with what felt like a month's worth of provisions. Inside the house, he balled up newspaper and stuffed it through the wrought iron door of the old woodstove, stacked a few pieces of kindling inside, and lit a match. The temperature, outside and in, was 12 degrees Fahrenheit. Kinnick had been preparing the place—sealing up windows, cleaning and bringing in furniture, lugging in books and pots and pans and clothes from the apartment he was giving up in Spokane. And now, with this first fire, he was officially moving in.

The fire caught, and Kinnick got the flue open, but some enterprising swifts had built a nest in the chimney, and the old sticks and brush started burning. Kinnick watched out the window as sparks rained down on the snowy fields surrounding the house. He was glad the roof was made of tin, or it surely would have caught fire. But soon the smoke was drawing nicely out the chimney, and the abandoned cinder block house began to heat up. Kinnick went outside, walked to the creek, broke through the ice, and filled two milk jugs of creek water to carry back. He poured them into a pan on the woodstove, boiled it, and was pleased to have drinking water. He planted a few perishable groceries in a snowbank outside—tied up in bags—and, when the sun set, he rolled a sleeping bag out on the floor, turned on a battery-powered lantern, and set to reading *Walden: Life in the Woods* for the second time since dreaming up this unlikely escape from the world:

> When I wrote the following pages, or rather the bulk of them, I lived alone, in the woods, a mile from any neighbor, in a house which I had built myself, on the shore of Walden Pond, in Concord, Massachusetts, and earned my living by the labor of my hands only.

That's when Kinnick realized that he had company. He looked up. Claws were skittering somewhere upstairs. He climbed the narrow staircase and shined a flashlight into the open attic bedroom and came face-to-face with a hard gang of dead-eyed raccoons that had apparently bunked down for the night. Shit. Nothing worse than raccoons. He'd cleaned some scat around the house, but he hadn't realized the raccoons thought they lived here. Oh, well. He'd take care of it in the morning. But they scurried around all night, fighting, screwing, snarling, laughing. Then, just before dawn, Kinnick heard a noise outside and he went out to find his new roommates were already up and having breakfast, feasting on lunch meat, frozen potatoes, ground coffee—his groceries having been dug out of the snowbank and torn out of the bags from where he'd stupidly left them.

Kinnick clapped his hands. The masked assholes looked at him with sheer disinterest. *Yeah. You got a problem?* Kinnick ran at them, but they didn't budge. He threw rocks, but they just kept munching. One raccoon with a gnawed ear didn't even look up; he was too busy trying to open a jar of dill pickles. Finally, Kinnick returned with a shovel and swung it at the lead raccoon, who hissed and snarled, but slowly backed away, a package of sliced ham clenched in his greedy little fingers.

Kinnick swung the shovel again, this time connecting with the poor, one-eared raccoon holding the unbreachable pickle jar. The wounded creature left the pickles and slalomed away in a daze, the others quickly retreating with him. This battle with the raccoons had lasted about ten minutes, but when Kinnick surveyed the booty—food half-eaten, packages torn—he realized that his provisions were almost all ruined. They'd even sampled his coffee (though, presumably, they preferred a lighter roast). The pickles, some ketchup, a quart of orange juice—there wasn't much to salvage. Well, at least he had the nonperishable food inside the—

Shit.

Kinnick rushed back in, and found three other raccoons, already in the kitchen, again eating without him, chomping on his bread, his granola, his trail mix, even the box of pink Hostess Snoballs he'd thrown in his grocery cart at the last minute—a guilty pleasure since he was a kid.

He sat down on the floor and watched his thoughtless roommates finish the meal. They kept their beady eyes on his, their almost-human little hands working over the pink sprinkles and cake. Two smaller raccoons hissed and fought over the last Snoball.

"Don't worry," Kinnick said. "I'll buy more."

He thought of his dad, Leonard, who'd proudly lived most of his adult life in Seattle—as a kind of rebuke to this very place. After leaving the navy, Leonard Kinnick had married Rhys's mom and taken a job managing apartment buildings in the city and, later on, a golf course. Leonard had called his own father's old house in the woods of Eastern Washington "the back door to hell." Rhys kind of wished his dad could see his predicament now; Leonard had a riotous, peeling laugh, and his son's ineptitude would no doubt bring a great guffaw. ("Reesy, what were you thinking?") Leonard would have thought it was insane, moving into his old man's cinder block house on the Hunters highway. *His* father, Rhys's grandpa Emrys, had moved the family up here from Oakland after losing his shipyard job after World War II. His wife and his two sons, Leonard and Pete, weren't happy in the remote woods of Eastern Washington, where Emrys set out to build the kind of sheep ranch that had sustained generations of Kinnicks back in Scotland and Wales. Rhys's father was only fifteen at the time, but he considered himself a city kid, unimpressed with backward Stevens County and with his father's idea of being a twentieth-century Highlands shepherd.

Emrys's wife didn't care for it, either, and after two weeks, she left her moody husband and his erstwhile sheep ranch for a department store job in Tacoma, taking their younger son, Rhys's Uncle Pete, with her. When Leonard joined them a month later, Rhys's grandfather was almost relieved to not have to make the rustic old house habitable for his sulking wife and kids. He settled into the most basic existence possible, figuring he'd die on this land, not realizing that it would take another forty years.

Rhys could recall his dad taking him to visit craggy, old Grandpa Emrys, who always walked his little ranch in a sheepskin coat that he'd brought from the old country, even though he never got around to having actual sheep on his sheep ranch. Instead, he cut firewood and bucked hay bales and did odd jobs in town to make the ends barely meet. Rhys knew his dad hated visiting his own reclusive father here. "That place destroyed our family," Leonard told him once. But, for some reason, when the old man died, Leonard couldn't bring himself to sell the land. He rented out the house for a while, and sometimes let tenants live there for free. "It's basically worthless," he said. *So, sell it*, Rhys thought. And yet, when Leonard died, the land became Rhys's. And, as it turned out, Rhys couldn't bring himself to sell it, either.

And now look. He'd pulled a complete Grandpa Emrys—blown up his family, lost his job, and run off to the woods, seeking *the tonic of wildness*. But the tonic of wildness had been greatly diluted in those seventy years. When Emrys moved into the woods, his closest neighbor was more than two miles away. Now, Kinnick had four or five neighbors within a mile of his house, and every year, there seemed to be more construction crews and logging trucks plying the two-lane highway, carving dirt roads and driveways into these remote foothills, digging wells, pouring foundations, endlessly converting forests and fields to family farmhouses. When he was a boy, Rhys could remember these woods being full of black bear and elk, moose, coyote, and Canadian lynx.

And now? Here he was, his first morning in the woods, and Kinnick's wildness tonic consisted of a street gang of unruly raccoons working its way through his groceries in his cold kitchen. Watching them he wondered if this was the sort of profound epiphany that Thoreau's writing had promised:

*Live in each season as it passes; breathe the air, drink the drink,
taste the fruit and resign yourself to the influence of the earth.*

For how could one resign oneself *more* to the influence of the earth
than by watching a pack of belligerent raccoons snarf and *chirble* the
last of your supplies?

As he pondered this question, Kinnick had two related thoughts
about his new home: 1. This was going to be more difficult than he'd
imagined. And 2. Until he figured out how the raccoons were getting
in his house, he probably needed to get a gun.

- - -

KINNICK STARED AT the gun in Chuck Littlefield's hand. "Jesus. No!"

"You've never fired a gun?"

"Well, yes. I mean . . . I have a pellet gun at my place in the woods—"

"A pellet gun?"

"Yeah. A Dragonfly air-action rifle. For scaring raccoons."

"An air gun? For *scaring* raccoons? You didn't shoot 'em?"

In fact, after discovering the pointlessness of air rifle *warning shots*,
Kinnick *had* shot two raccoons, in their waddling striped-tail asses, the
feisty leader who always hissed at him, and the poor guy with the battered ear. He could tell it *really* hurt, too. And, mission accomplished,
after that, the pack had limped and hobbled away (pellets embedded in
their furry asses) and had never returned, Kinnick eventually finding
the loose floorboard where they were getting in and patching it.

"I hate raccoons," Chuck said. "They killed my neighbor's chickens.
I would've shot every one of them right between their little black eyes,
and I would've enjoyed it." Chuck shook his head, as if the raccoons
had taken Kinnick's grandchildren. He turned the gun over in his
hand. "Look, this isn't much different than that. Well, except totally
different."

"Chuck, I really don't think—"

"Relax. The last thing I want is you shooting anyone. But since you're going to be my only backup there today, I need you to know how to handle this thing."

"Backup? What are you—" Kinnick couldn't even finish the question.

"We're going in. You and me. Get your grandkids out of Six Flags Reichstag." He nodded at the flat-roofed sheriff's office. "If Captain Fat Ass back there won't help us, then we'll do it ourselves."

Kinnick couldn't help wondering if Chuck's courage (or was it foolhardiness?) had to do with Lucy. If he wanted Rhys to go back and tell her what a brave hero her old boyfriend had been on this adventure. "Look, of course I want to get the kids, too, but . . ." Kinnick nodded at the gun. "Not like that."

"Rhys. I promise. You're not going to shoot anyone. But these are the same guys who hit you in the face with a leather sap yesterday. I'd be a stupid asshole if I didn't at least show you how to handle this thing and give you some way to protect yourself. And I might be an asshole, but I am not stupid."

He put the gun in Kinnick's hand. "Open palm, index finger off to the right, outside the trigger guard. Good. Now close your other three fingers and thumb around the grip. Excellent."

"This is a terrible idea." The gun was cool, weighted toward the front.

"It's a simple .22 Glock, easy to aim and fire. Easy to secure."

"Chuck, I don't—"

"You want your grandkids back?"

"Of course I do!"

"You want to wait two weeks until we can find your daughter and get a writ?"

"Of course not. But I don't want them to get hurt!"

Chuck made an exasperated, grumbling noise. "This is what I can never seem to explain to you squishy liberals. *This is* why *you learn to use a gun! So. That. Nobody. Gets hurt!* Jesus, you people. You're like

Lucy. I gave her a gun for her birthday once, and she told me to shove it up my ass. I promise, you're not going to need it today, but I'd feel a whole lot better if you at least learned how to hold it. So that we don't go in there holding our dicks."

Kinnick sighed. "Fine."

"Okay. At present, this gun does *not* have a round in the chamber. It isn't loaded and it isn't cocked. Now, there are a few more steps to this than there are shooting raccoons with a pellet gun. First, grab that magazine."

Rhys reached into the box and removed the magazine, which looked like a heavy metal PEZ dispenser. A single bullet was poking out of the top.

"Slide that into the grip of the gun."

Kinnick did.

"Now see that little lever by your thumb? That's the magazine release. Click that and remove the mag."

Kinnick did.

"Now slide it back in."

Kinnick did. He marveled at the balanced weight of the gun when it was loaded like this. It felt so intentional, so well designed. Suddenly, he pictured that goateed thug swinging his blackjack and he imagined pulling this handgun out and pointing at his fat smug fa—

Jesus! The shiver that went through his arm! The power! Just holding it, Kinnick felt a rush that he didn't entirely trust . . . but that he rather liked. That word: the *weight*. That was it. The weight of this gun was the exact weight of his anger and his fear and his sense of displacement. That's what the gun weighed. That's where its incredible balance lay.

"Okay, you've got fifteen rounds in the magazine. Now I'm going to show you how to load one of those rounds, how to cock it, how to turn off the safety, and how to fire it. But we are *not* going to fire it, are we? We are not going to shoot my truck." When Kinnick didn't answer, Chuck said again, "Are we going to shoot my truck, Rhys?"

"No, we're not."

"Good. Now step out of the truck."

They did. Chuck came around to the passenger side. Kinnick stood holding the gun just outside his truck door, pointed at the ground, his finger to the side of the trigger guard. Chuck went through the steps again. "Okay, safety off, now it's ready to fire. If we had time, I'd take you to the range, have you practice, but we don't have time. So, I'm going to tell you a couple of things. And I don't want you to freak out."

"I really don't think—"

"I don't care what you think. Hold the gun in your right hand and point it at the fender of my truck, above the right front tire. Finger still out of the trigger guard."

Kinnick did.

"Now, stand with your feet shoulder width apart, your weaker foot slightly in front of your stronger foot. Good. Now, bend your front knee but keep your back leg straight, more of your weight on your front foot, bending forward, elbows slightly bent. Good. Now put both hands on the gun."

Kinnick did. "This seems like a lot of instruction for something I'm never going to use."

"Now, pay attention to this part. Everyone thinks you aim for the chest—that's fine, normally, biggest target. But these para-twats will likely be wearing Kevlar vests. So—don't worry, and it's not going to come to this, but if it does—where should you aim?"

"I-I don't know. The face?"

"You'd think that, but the face is a lot narrower than the rest of the body, a lot smaller, jerkier. That's why turkey hunting is so tough, you gotta pop that sucker's head so you don't ruin the meat. And secondly, you can't believe how tough it is to look someone in the eye and then shoot them there. Moves around a lot. Your conscience will kick in and you'll shift slightly and miss. It's just damned hard, shooting a man in the face."

"Have you—"

"God no," Chuck said, "I've never had to fire my weapon on duty. But I know what to do if it comes to that. Now, here's what you do if someone is wearing a vest. You aim just below their belly fat, to one side or the other. Shoot him in his front pocket. Left or right, doesn't matter, but you want to hit the torso, the hip."

"If you haven't shot anyone, how do you know this?"

Chuck just kept talking. "Shoot a man below the waist and the target is bigger, less mobile. The head flails and flops, but the torso is the last thing to move. You hit a man in the hip, you'll drop him every time. Got it?"

Kinnick shook his head. "I really don't—"

"Also"—Chuck's voice got lower—"the veins are paper thin in the legs. Bleeding is intense. You hit the femoral artery? It's lights out." Chuck was behind Kinnick, talking low in his ear as Rhys stood like a tripod, pointing the gun at the fender of the truck, his hands sweaty and shaking slightly. "Lights. Out." It was quiet a moment and then Chuck's voice got cheerier. "Any questions?"

The high note seemed so insane that Kinnick could only laugh. *Any questions? How about: What the hell?* White Nationalist goons stealing children from church parking lots? Rural sheriffs telling him to go pound sand? A manic ex-cop showing him how to shoot people in the front pocket? Was this just how people behaved now? Is this what the world had come to? Seven years in the woods only to emerge and find everything had gotten crazier?

"It's gonna be fine," Chuck said. "If it comes to it, just think of them as raccoons."

"Raccoons," Kinnick said, and he pictured those remorseless creatures, their dirty little hands, their unblinking eyes, shoving tiny pieces of pink Hostess Snoballs into their greedy mouths; it was harder, though, imagining them driving away with his grandchildren.

Chuck patted his shoulder. "You got this, John Wick. Now, put the gun back in its case and let's go get your grandkids."

Rhys opened the case and put the magazine in, then settled the black handgun back in its little nook. "Who's John Wick?"

"I wouldn't worry about it," Chuck said.

- - -

THE SIGNS BEGAN to appear the minute they left the highway. NO TRESPASS-ING, PRIVATE PROPERTY, and BEWARE OF DOG were practically native plants up here, but these handwritten signs, leading uphill toward the Rampart, took on a more insistent, ominous, and misspelled tone. TURN BACK NOW! TRESSPASSERS WILL BE DEALT WITH! BOW BEFORE THY VENGEFULL GOD! SOVEREIGN ARMED CITIZENS AHEAD! And one large sign at the open gate of a barbed wire fence, which Chuck had to slow down to read: COMMYS, LIBERALS, FEDS, SORROS FBI, AND ALL WHO REJECT THE LORD AND HIS TEACHINGS—STAY OUT!

"I don't see retired cops or shitty grandparents on that list," Chuck said, "so, I guess we're good." These were the first words either of them had spoken since they'd turned down this unmarked road, which quickly devolved into two tracks in the forest, little pine sprigs scraping on the underside of Chuck's pickup.

He eased the truck through the first open gate, feeling a rising buzz of adrenaline. "Here we go . . ." God, how he missed this feeling—and something else that Chuck rarely felt in civilian life: a sense of purpose. He hadn't always felt it as a cop, of course. Some days the job was like any job, filing paperwork, going to training sessions, spending an hour on the phone with HR trying to figure out what happened to your dental benefits.

But four or five times a year, some part of being a cop inspired him, fired up his adrenaline, and, occasionally, moved him to tears.

His first month in a patrol car, Chuck had broken up a party in a vacant field next to an old rail yard. It was a gathering of the lowest of lowlifes, greasy street people drinking fortified wine and huffing old paint cans at a hobo camp amid the tall grass and railroad ties just east of downtown. When Chuck scattered the skank partiers, he found one person sitting on the ground in front of a smoldering campfire. It was a kid: ratty hair, jagged teeth, brown hooded sweatshirt. Maybe nine or ten.

Chuck asked: "Did one of your parents bring you here?"

The kid just stared.

"How old are you?"

The kid stared.

"You don't know how old you are, or you don't want to say?"

Kid stared.

Chuck drove him to the cop shop and waited for Child Protective Services. He got the kid a Coke, and they sat in the foyer while he tried to talk to the boy. "I'll tell you what. I'll get you some Cheetos, too, if you'll tell me your name. Where you live." Nothing. The kid simply stared and sipped his soda. Chuck bought the Cheetos anyway.

Eventually, a caseworker from CPS showed up, took one look at the kid, and started signing with her hands.

When they stood to leave, the deaf kid gave Chuck Littlefield a hug around the waist and wouldn't let go. He smelled like sweat and shit and all the unfairness in the world.

After they were gone, Chuck went to the bathroom and wept. The job was like that. You could see a family of five torn apart in a car accident—blood and body parts everywhere—and not so much as flinch. Make jokes about it later, even. Then some small, seemingly random thing would shiv you—like a deaf kid left alone at a homeless encampment—and you'd feel it pierce and scrape all the way to your bones.

That's what today felt like for Chuck, seeing Lucy, and hearing her old boyfriend tell his story. He'd started out suspicious of Lucy's ex, and Chuck didn't quite get this whole escape-to-the-woods business. He could see someplace like Cancun, or Vegas, but to go live in a cabin in the middle of nowhere? Why? But then Kinnick used that word *extinct*, and something had clicked for Chuck. When he got sent to Property Crimes, and they pushed him into retirement, Chuck had more than once imagined himself as an old bull, worn down by his battles, kicked out of the herd and sent off to die. In a way, he supposed, Kinnick had done the honorable thing in that situation: going out into the woods alone after you were no longer wanted. But the thought of it filled Chuck with deep sadness. His father had always told him that to be a man was to have responsibilities beyond yourself—to protect those weaker than you, to stand up for what was right. All cop-cynicism aside, for twenty-five years, he'd tried to do that (especially when overtime pay was involved). But then, to be suddenly told your services were simply no longer needed? That your kind wasn't wanted anymore? That shit was heartbreaking.

And just imagine, like Kinnick, finding yourself looking out at your front porch and *not recognizing* your own grandchildren! That was the ghost of Christmas future for Chuck, who was ten years younger than Kinnick, and had no grandkids yet, but whose children had been poisoned by his bitter ex-wife and spoke to him maybe twice a year. No, he could imagine the same thing happening to him.

All of that explained why he had made what was probably a rash decision: driving straight into the Church of the Blessed Fire's Idaho stronghold, where the Army of Losers trained for the upcoming holy war against immigrants or the UN or Michelle Obama or whoever the hell they were afraid of (nothing pissed him off more than paranoia; he could never understand these big tough guys being so scared of their own shadows).

The truck eased out of the woods into a clearing below a small hill. There were stumps everywhere, every tree on the hillside, within a hundred yards of the compound, having been cleared; Chuck assumed this was so invading government agents, or Canadian troops, or space aliens, or whomever couldn't take cover behind trees. The Rampart compound itself sat at the top of this hill, and was surrounded by a tall, palisade fence—vertical wood posts of varying heights and widths lashed and staked into the ground. It was the sort of fence that might've surrounded an old cavalry fort. More signs were nailed to the fence: FEAR THEE THY LORD THY GOD and SEND FOURTH LIGHTNING AND SCATTER THINE ENEMY and BULLSHEVIK-FREE ZONE.

The driveway wound around the palisade fence to a second gate, a swinging eight-foot-high livestock gate, which had also been left open.

"You think they're expecting us?" Chuck asked. He looked over. Kinnick was pale, and Chuck felt another wave of sympathy for Lucy's old boyfriend. "Hey, Rhys, if you're not up for this—"

"No," Kinnick said quickly, and then, after a breath, "No, let's do it." He turned, his face grim determination. "I want to get them out of there."

"Okay." Chuck idled the truck just below the gate. "Listen. Don't worry. I've been dealing with asshats like this for thirty years. These guys are like barking dogs on chains. They always back down when you get in their faces. Just remember, this is just a bunch of cement mixers and dishwashers who come out to the woods to play *Call of Duty*."

"I'm good," Kinnick said. "Let's go."

Inside the gate were four buildings: a main clapboard house, an upside-down American flag flapping from its back porch; a small white chapel; a red barn with An Appeal to Heaven flag; and what Chuck recognized as the planked bunkhouse, where the Army of Losers slept during overnight drills, or when their mothers wouldn't let them back into the basements where they lived.

There were a bunch of broken-down vehicles and farm equipment, and angle-parked next to the bunkhouse, three pickup trucks, a Toyota Tercel, and a motorcycle. Chuck parked between the house and the chapel. He turned the truck off. "Wait here," he told Kinnick.

"And the thing in the glove box?" Rhys said, his voice nervous and high. He couldn't even *say* the word *gun*.

"The box is unlocked," Chuck said. "But don't worry about it. And don't do anything unless I tell you to do something."

"Okay. Is there a signal, or—"

"The signal will be me saying 'Rhys, get the fucking gun out now.'"

Kinnick laughed, a nice release for them both. Chuck opened the driver's-side door and stepped out. Gravel crunched beneath his feet. Clouds strobed the sun's harsh light, in and out, then back in.

Between the house and the church was a five-foot hymn board with a badge-shaped sign nailed to it—the sort of thing a different church might have used to alert believers to the songs being sung during that day's services. On one side, Chuck read this:

Thou shalt not be afraid for the terror by night; nor for the arrow that flieth by day; Nor for the pestilence that walketh in darkness; nor for the destruction that wasteth at noonday. A thousand shall fall at thy side, and ten thousand at thy right hand; but it shall not come nigh thee. Psalm 91: 5–7

"The word of the Lord," Chuck said. He'd been raised by an occasionally devout, often-exhausted Catholic mother, who stopped taking her five kids to mass when Chuck was about ten. But such phrases still popped into his head whenever he encountered religion—or whatever this was. "Peace be with you," he muttered, and he walked around to the other side of the hymn board and read this:

Blessing of the Week: When the communist groomers send in the military to control the people, remember this. The Lord

Thy God has His Soldiers in their midst. Top per capita US military enlistees by state: Georgia, South Carolina, Idaho, Alaska, Texas. Be not afraid, for when the Blue Helmets come across the border to rape and kidnap and kill believers, these brave men touched by the Lord shall fight alongside you.

Chuck let out a deep breath. "Well, okay, then."

"You just missed them!"

He turned around. A young woman had come out of the chapel. She was maybe twenty-five, freckled, in a long prairie dress, brown-rimmed glasses, hair tied back in a bun.

Chuck shielded the sun. "Aw, shoot, they're gone already, huh?"

"Yes, Brother Dean said there might be one more coming. He said to tell you they were training down along the south ridge." She pointed the opposite way they'd come in. "He said you could catch up to them down by the fence line. He has his cell if you want to call him."

"Yeah. I'll do that, thanks," Chuck said. "I'll call and tell him I'm on my way." That's why the gates were open. They were expecting more toy soldiers. "Did they walk or—"

"No, they took the ATVs. But they left one." She pointed at the barn, where a red Honda four-wheeler was sitting off by itself. Then she shielded the sun from her eyes to look at Chuck's pickup truck. "Wait, are there two of you?"

"Oh, yeah," Chuck said. "But he can ride on the back. We'll snuggle."

The woman looked confused. And then, from behind her, a young face peered out of the chapel door.

The passenger door to Chuck's pickup opened, and Kinnick jumped out. "Asher!"

The woman turned, just as the little boy stepped out of the chapel, squinted so that he could see better, and said, "Grandpa Rhys? What are you doing here?" He started moving toward Kinnick. "And where'd you get that shirt?"

The woman looked from the boy to Kinnick and back again. "Did you finish the assignment, Asher?"

"Yes," he said, "it was very easy." He didn't look at his teacher as he spoke. Instead, he walked toward his grandfather, who met him in the dirt between the truck and the chapel, dropped to his knees, and took the boy in his arms. Chuck could see him bury his face in the boy's neck.

Asher pulled back to look at Kinnick. "Is your face okay?"

"It's fine."

"What are Glass Animals?"

At first, Kinnick didn't know what this meant, but then he looked down at the shirt he was wearing. "Oh, right. It's a band, apparently," Kinnick said. "Someone gave me the shirt. Because I didn't smell very good."

"Well, it's cool," Asher said. "I like the pineapple."

A girl came out next. "Grandpa Rhys, your eye!" she said. "Are you okay?" She ran toward him.

"I'm fine," Kinnick said, "I'm good," and he hugged the girl, too.

They held this embrace, the three of them, Kinnick on his knees, the kids surrounding him, Chuck alternating between resolve and regret over his own shitty parenting as he watched this little reunion.

"We're in the middle of Bible lessons," the young woman in the prairie dress said to Chuck. "Leah, Asher, you need to get back inside."

"I have a note from their mother," Kinnick said, and reached in his back pocket. "I'm taking them home with me."

Three other children's faces appeared in the door of the chapel, looking out to see what the commotion was about.

"Can you kids go and get your backpacks?" Kinnick asked.

"I don't think—" The teacher looked around nervously. "That's not—"

But Leah and Asher walked past her, and past the other kids, into the chapel.

That's when, from behind them, the back door to the main house opened. "Can I help you gentlemen?"

Chuck turned. He recognized the pastor he'd met when he'd served papers up here before. At the time he had expected David Gallen to be a stern figure with one of those Old Testament beards, but Gallen was a small, clean-shaven man with round glasses and hard-combed hair that looked like it had been parted with a steak knife. In fact, he looked less like a Christian Nationalist preacher than he did the sort of local insurance agent who wore short sleeves with ties and worked out of a mall.

Kinnick straightened up.

Chuck turned to face Gallen. He took two steps, carefully placing himself between the pastor and Kinnick. "Hello, Pastor," Chuck said. "I'm Chuck Littlefield. You might recall, I was up here serving papers last year on a fence line dispute with your neighbors. Listen, you may not be aware of this, but a couple of your church members knocked my friend around yesterday and took his grandchildren. We're taking them back to Spokane as per their mother's wishes."

"I see." The pastor used his index finger to push up the bridge of his glasses. "I was made to understand, by their father, that Bethany had gone off on another drug binge." He shook his head. "Such a shame."

Chuck looked at Kinnick, whose face was knit with worry. "Well." Chuck turned back to the pastor. "I can assure you, that's not the case. Just some good, old-fashioned marital difficulty. Nothing the family can't handle themselves."

"Good. I'm glad. I like Bethany very much. Poor, troubled soul. I should've reached out to her after her mother passed." The pastor smiled and gestured to the house. "I'll tell you what, why don't you two come inside. I'll put on some tea, and we can talk about this."

"You know what," Chuck said, "I feel like we just talked about it."

The kids came out then, returning to Kinnick's side with their backpacks.

The pastor gave a disarming smile. He craned his neck to look past Chuck. "Leah. Is this your grandfather?"

"Yes, Pastor Gallen."

"And you're comfortable going with him."

"Yes, sir. Our mom wanted us to stay with him."

"How about you, Asher?"

"Yes, sir."

"I see." He smiled. "Well then. Maybe you kids can ask your grandfather if he'd like to come inside and have a cup of tea with me. If some of my church members have been disrespectful, I would like to hear more about it. Then we can call your father. I'm sure we can get this whole thing settled."

Again, Chuck interrupted. "Like I said, Padre, I think it's been settled."

That's when Chuck heard the whine of a distant engine. Over a dip in the fence, he could see, on the other side of a thick stand of pines, a dirt trail running along the hill below the Rampart, dust rising from the trees. One of the ATVs must be returning—probably a mile away but coming fast. The pastor must've called them before he came outside. Chuck walked purposefully to his truck, leaned in the passenger door, and opened the glove box. He took out the gun case.

As he opened it, he turned to Kinnick. "I want you to take the truck." He set the key fob on the driver's seat.

"What—"

"I'll be fine. I'm just gonna talk to these guys. Slow their roll. Buy you a little time." He got the gun out, popped the magazine in, and tucked it into the back waistband of his pants. He walked over to Kinnick. "Take the kids and go."

Kinnick stood there, frozen.

"Rhys." He spoke quietly but firmly. "Take your goddamn grandkids. I'll catch up to you later. I promise. Now would you please go."

Finally, Kinnick nodded and hurried the kids into Chuck's pickup.

He jumped in the driver's seat, started it, and began driving toward the gate.

Chuck watched the taillights on his pickup flash once, like a warning, and then his truck passed through the open gate and turned onto the dirt road leading down the hill.

Strangest thought popped into his head then: two more payments and that truck would be paid off.

Through the same dip in the fence, Chuck could see, below the Rampart, the ATV had cleared the tree line and was coming up the hill on the other side. Chuck turned back to the pastor. "I don't suppose you have herbal tea, Padre. I probably shouldn't have any more caffeine."

- - -

KINNICK DROVE QUICKLY down the dirt road, Chuck's pickup truck jostling in the ruts. He tried to go easy, but his adrenaline was spiking, and he kept thinking the word *escape*. Asher and Leah were silently double-buckled in the front seat next to him. As he descended the Rampart's hillock, Kinnick saw another pickup emerge from the tree line, coming toward them on the narrow road. Rhys slowed and pulled over to the side to let the other truck pass. The young man driving wore a dim smile underneath a baseball cap. He nodded and waved, Kinnick nodding and waving back, then watching the truck go by in the dusty rearview mirror. Rhys continued along slowly until he reached the woods, then stepped on the accelerator.

"Where are we going?" Leah asked.

"Not sure yet," Kinnick said. They quickly descended the forested part of the hill, insistent pines seeming to close in and crowd the road on both sides, scraping the side mirrors, until, finally, they came out into a clearing where the dirt road met the two-lane highway. He let out a deep breath.

"Okay," Kinnick said, "okay," thinking maybe they were safe now.

"Your black eye is turning green," Asher said.

Kinnick looked over at his grandson. "Is it?"

And that's when Kinnick heard what sounded like the *pop* of a distant gunshot, echoing in the forest behind them.

He looked back over his shoulder, at the dirt road disappearing like smoke into the trees. *Shit!* Should he go back? Try to help? He looked over at his grandkids. Closed his eyes: *think!* What was the best course of action in a situation like this? But, of course, he'd never been in a situation like this. Nothing even remotely close.

Then came another *pop*, maybe a minute after the first, then another *pop* right after that, possibly from different guns.

He opened his eyes. Leah was staring at him. "Are those—"

"Gunshots," Asher said authoritatively. It was quiet, all of them listening, and then Asher said, "They do target practice sometimes."

"Right," Kinnick said, "they're probably doing target practice." He and Leah kept their eye contact.

Decision time. He could not go back. Not with the kids. Should he turn north, toward Canada? Go to Sheriff Glen Campbell's office, ten miles away? Or go south, toward Spokane, and escape? Kinnick wished for the fiftieth time in the last two days that he had a cell phone. He could call for help. Or call Chuck and ask if he needed to come back and get him.

And just as he thought this, he noticed, in a cupholder between the seats, Chuck Littlefield's iPhone. Wait. So . . . Chuck had stood alone against those militia nutjobs, with only his glove box handgun and no phone?

Kinnick grabbed the phone. He touched the screen and saw the date and time above a photo of Lucy and Chuck, cuddled in front of a fire. Each of them held a glass of red wine. He wasn't sure he'd ever seen Lucy look that happy before.

He tapped the screen, then tapped it again. He tried to remember how these things worked. He turned it over, like a caveman with a garage door opener.

"Do you know his password?" Leah asked.

Kinnick slammed the phone back in the cupholder. Of course he didn't know the man's password! Chuck's last word to him had been: *Go!*

So . . . he needed to go. Kinnick stepped on the gas, spinning tires in the dirt. He turned the truck to the south, toward Spokane, civilization, escape.

As he drove, Kinnick kept checking the rearview mirror, but the only vehicle behind him was a big logging truck. How long would it be safe to stay on this highway? And if he turned, where would he go? With National Forest land on either side, there weren't any cutoffs until Sandpoint. At least twenty miles away.

On a long straightaway he checked the rearview mirror again. A pickup had emerged behind the logging truck. He wished he could recall the models and colors of the trucks at the Rampart, but he'd been too nervous to take note. This pickup didn't seem to be gaining on the logging truck, though. So, it was probably okay. Or was it?

Great, so now he was going to be afraid—

—of every pickup he saw—

—*in North Idaho!*

"You're driving pretty fast," Asher said.

Kinnick looked down. He was going eighty-four miles per hour.

"I guess I am," Kinnick said. He eased off the gas.

"I wonder," Asher said, "how long are we going to be with you?"

Kinnick looked over at the boy. "What?"

"I was just wondering how long we're going to be with you."

"I don't think we know yet."

"Like a week? Or just a few days? Or a month?"

The calendar usually meant so little to Kinnick that he had to concentrate, to visualize the flow of days. Seasons were what mattered to him now. So, let's see: Bethany had apparently left on Saturday. The kids had shown up at his place yesterday, which was a Monday. It was Tuesday afternoon. *Would* he still have them in six days? Ten? Thirty?

"I don't know, Asher, why do you ask?"

"Because I was just wondering—"

"Asher—" Leah said her brother's name not with irritation, but with fatigue.

He spoke louder. "I was just wondering! If we could go back and tell that minister that I want to sign up for the youth tournament? Make sure I get a spot?"

Kinnick took a deep breath. "We'll do that. Don't worry, Asher. We'll have you playing chess soon. And I'll get a board up at my place. You can practice by beating me."

"Okay, but you can't let me win. Or I won't get better."

"Asher," Leah said again. "Enough."

After that, the kids were quiet. Asher leaned against Kinnick and closed his eyes, while Leah mostly looked out her window. They made it to the outskirts of Sandpoint—motels and stores and turnoffs to the ski resort—without anyone from the Rampart coming up behind them. But still Kinnick's mind was racing. (Should he stop and call someone? Where? Who? How? Did they even have pay phones anymore? Was Chuck okay back there? What were those gunshots? What if Shane had already called the police and reported his children kidnapped by their grandfather?) He could feel the adrenaline coursing—a tingle in his arms, an occasional buzzing sound in his ears.

"You're not going to answer that?" Leah asked.

"What?"

"The phone? Do you want me to get it next time?"

Kinnick reached down to the cupholder, where, over the picture of Chuck and Lucy, the screen read: 4 Phone Notifications. He had forgotten what a buzzing phone sounded like. "Shit!"

Asher stirred.

"Sorry about that," Kinnick said.

"It's okay," Asher said. "The *S*-word isn't taking the Lord's name in vain, so it's not blaspheming. Mom and Dad even say it sometimes, but I'm not supposed to."

"I shouldn't, either," Kinnick said. He pulled the truck into a gas station parking lot and let out a deep breath. They were finally at a junction. Two highways converged here, each leading back to Spokane. They could come in from either the north or from the east, and with countless backroads, whichever route Kinnick took, it would be easier to avoid the Pickups of the Lord from this point on. Kinnick turned to the kids. "I'm not used to the sound of a buzzing phone. Leah, if you hear it again, could you—"

And then, as if demonstrating what he was about to say, the phone began buzzing again. Kinnick picked it up and saw the smile of Lucy Park, her eyes behind a large pair of sunglasses. At first, he thought this was some kind of futuristic video call—he knew those existed—but, no, apparently, this was simply how Lucy was identified when she called Chuck's phone. That was new.

Kinnick held the phone out in his open palm, afraid he'd do something wrong—

Leah reached over and swiped the little green telephone receiver image from right to left. She pointed to her own ear, smiled, and mouthed, *You can talk now.*

"Uh. Hello?" Funny, he hadn't spoken into a phone in seven years.

Lucy sounded frantic. "Kinnick! Where the fuck are you?"

"Oh. We're . . . uh . . . in Sandpoint."

"Why didn't you answer earlier? I was worried sick!"

"I forgot how to use this thing," Kinnick said.

"Christ, you stupid fu—" But she caught herself. "I can't believe you guys went up there! What were you thinking?"

I was thinking about raccoons, Kinnick thought, but he didn't say it.

"Listen," Lucy said, "Chuck's on his way to Spokane in a helicopter. Meet us at Sacred Heart."

"The hospital?" The gunshots— "Jesus, what happened to Chuck?"

THREE

What Happened to Chuck

As he watched Kinnick and the kids disappear through the Rampart gate, it occurred to Chuck Littlefield, listening to his pickup rattle down the hill, that he might have made a mistake. He was prone to rash, dramatic gestures like this, when a more patient strategy was often the wiser course. Ah well. Nothing to be done about it now. Recalling the months he'd spent playing poker at the tribal casinos near the Spokane airport, Chuck thought: *Yep. I'm pot-committed now.*

So, he stood calmly in the dirt yard of the Rampart, at the point of an equilateral triangle, Pastor Gallen to his left, the Bible school teacher to his right, the Glock tucked into his waistband in back, beneath his shirt. The pastor said, "Sister Charlotte, why don't you take the kids back into the chapel and finish their afternoon lessons."

She nodded and, without a word, walked back toward the open door, where three wide-eyed kids were peering out.

"Should probably keep them in there a while, too," Chuck added helpfully. He tried to give a friendly smile to Pastor Gallen, who nodded evenly. For the moment, anyway, they seemed to have the same interest. Keeping everything calm.

Sister Charlotte ushered the kids back inside.

When the door closed, Chuck turned back to Pastor Gallen. "Just so you know, I'm hoping to not shoot anyone today."

"And yet you came here with a gun," the pastor said.

"Well, I didn't want to be the only girl at the party not in a dress."

"I think you have the wrong idea about our church, Mr.—"

"Littlefield. Chuck Littlefield. And no, Pastor, I don't think I do."

A truck was coming back up the drive, and at first Chuck assumed it was his. "No, no," he muttered to himself, "what are you doing, Rhys?" But it was a different pickup, an older Ford, that rolled through the open stock gate. From the other direction, the whine of the ATV was coming closer, too.

"So. How do you suggest we handle this?" Chuck asked.

"I assumed you had something planned," the pastor said, and then he smiled and muttered what sounded like a short prayer.

"Yeah, not so much. How about I promise not to shoot anyone, and you keep your guys coolheaded? Then maybe we can talk this over like normal, rational people, and afterward, you can run me back to town?"

"Run you back to town," Pastor Gallen said unsurely.

"Because, I'd imagine," Chuck continued, "the last thing either of us wants is a gunfight between your goose-stepping dipshits and a former police officer."

"I see." The pastor looked him up and down. "Sometimes these things can get . . ." He didn't finish, though, because the Ford pickup parked in a swirl of dust, and a young, white man in a ball cap hopped out. He wore a handgun holstered to a utility belt, tied low on his leg, like someone who had seen too many westerns. He seemed to sense that something was off, and he looked from Pastor Gallen to Chuck and back.

"Everything okay, Pastor?"

Chuck answered for him: "Everything's fine. We were just talking about having a cup of tea. Do you like tea?"

"I'm more a coffee drinker." The man kept staring at Pastor Gallen. He cocked his head, as if waiting for some signal.

Chuck could hear the ATV getting closer, too. Suddenly, this whole thing seemed unwise. Maybe insane. He patted his pocket for his cell phone and realized he'd left it in the truck. Shit! Okay, that was definitely *not* smart.

The red, four-wheeled ATV pulled through the gate and parked at an angle near the pastor's back door. A heavyset bald man in camouflage—no helmet—turned the key and climbed off the rig. He wore a Kevlar vest and had what looked like a .223 Remington assault-style rifle slung over his left shoulder, resting on his broad back. Hung at his waist were a field belt with pouches for ammunition and a holstered, snapped pistol.

"What's going on here?"

The man with the ball cap said to the bald one, "Wait, were we training in full field-dress today? Nobody told me—"

"Brother Dean," Pastor Gallen interrupted, speaking to the bald man with the rifle. "This is Chuck Littlefield. He's a police officer."

"*Retired* police officer," Chuck said.

"He came with Shane's father in-law to get the children."

Dean's eyes narrowed and his head turned slowly. "Where are they?"

"Rhys just left with his grandkids," Chuck said.

"That guy lied about me in the newspaper," Dean told the pastor. "Ruined my reputation. Cost me the county commissioner seat. I didn't realize that was him yesterday."

"I don't know anything about that," Chuck said. "All I know is that the kids' mother left instructions that she wanted Kinnick to watch her kids while she was gone, and you guys beat him up for it."

Dean muttered something, and started for what was apparently his pickup, a black Dodge Ram with a Gadsden flag in back and an Army of the Lord sticker on the tailgate. It was parked with the other vehicles between the house and the chapel.

"I wouldn't do that," Chuck said, but Dean just kept walking.

"I'm serious," Chuck said, and he pulled the Glock from his waistband, spread his legs, flipped the safety, took aim across the yard, and shot the right rear tire of Dean's truck. The gunshot echoed in the high Rampart fence, the tire deflating with a hiss. Chuck was glad Dean had such big tires on his truck, and that he'd hit one on the first try. It would've been embarrassing to have to take two shots. Or to have to get closer.

Dean stopped dead in his tracks. His hand went to his gun belt and his head spun in anger.

"I'm serious," Chuck said.

"Let's all calm down," Pastor Gallen said. "Dean! Mr. Littlefield!"

"I'll pay for any tires I ruin today," Chuck said. "But no one is going after those kids."

Brother Dean stood stock-still between Chuck and his disabled pickup, breathing deeply, seeming to consider his next move. Chuck kept both hands on his gun, which was pointed down at the ground, but in Dean's general direction.

"Brother Dean—" Pastor Gallen spoke evenly. "Let's not let this get out of hand."

"Dean," the ball cap man said helpfully. "We can take my truck."

Chuck turned and aimed his gun at the front tire of the Ford pickup. "No. We're not taking any trucks, Ball Cap. Like I said, we're all gonna just sit right here while those kids get down the road a bit with their grandfather."

To his right, Chuck saw Dean's hand still on his gun belt. To his left, he saw the ball cap man pull his own pistol from its holster and point it at Chuck. "Don't you fuckin' shoot my tire!" Then Ball Cap glanced over to Pastor Gallen. "Sorry for my language, Pastor."

"Please, both of you . . . everyone . . . please." The pastor had his hands out and took a step toward them. "We're all going to put our guns away now. Matthew?"

"Not till he does!"

"Put your gun away and I'll lower mine," Chuck said.

"Those are brand-new Toyo Open Ranges!" Ball Cap Matthew said. "Don't you fuckin' shoot my new tire!"

"Brother Matthew, please—" The pastor, still talking in his calming voice, walked toward the ball cap man.

"I said I'm sorry for the language, Pastor! But I swear—if he shoots my tire—"

Chuck felt a tug at his side in the same moment he heard the crack of the gunshot.

He was spun by the hip, fell, and cried out, squeezing off a round that raised a puff of dirt between him and the truck. From the ground, Chuck twisted his body to return fire, but Ball Cap had tossed his weapon to the ground and thrown his hands straight into the air. "Oh shit! Oh shit! It just went off!"

Chuck hesitated—he couldn't shoot the kid, much as he wanted to—and then he rolled onto his back, to see if Dean had pulled *his* gun, but the big man was standing in the same place, rifle still strapped to his back, hand still on his gun belt, staring coolly at Chuck on the ground.

The pain hit then: a pulsing knife through flesh and bone, the whole left side of his pelvis on fire. Below the waistband of his pants, he could see the blossoming of scarlet-black blood. Of all the ironies—after his careful instructions to Kinnick about where to shoot someone, Chuck had been shot squarely in his left front pants pocket. And he'd dropped like a stone, just like he'd predicted. If it hit the femoral artery—

The pastor reached him, crouched down, one hand gently on Chuck's wounded left side, another on his right arm. He asked quietly, "Can I take this, Chuck? Let's not have anyone else hurt."

Chuck let go of his tight grip on the handgun. "Okay," he said, grimacing in pain. The pastor took the Glock, expertly set the safety, and removed the clip in two smooth motions. He placed the gun and clip gently on the dirt. Then he turned to Chuck.

"Okay, I'm going to look at your wound now. Don't worry. I was an army medic." He turned to Dean. "Brother Dean. Call 9-1-1. Tell them we have an accidental gunshot wound out here."

Accidental? Chuck opened his mouth to object, but a cry came out instead, and the pastor just kept giving orders, this time to Ball Cap, whose hands were still in the air.

"Matthew, leave your gun right where it is, do not touch it, I repeat, do not touch it, go inside, and in the kitchen, under the sink, you'll find a first aid kit. Also grab some towels and give me your belt."

Both men just stared.

"Go!" The pastor raised his voice for the first time.

Dean pulled out his phone as Matthew ran toward the house.

"Lord God," the pastor said quietly, "be with thy servant as I minister and console mine brother here, and lead him to You, Christ Jesus, even as You guide my hands and sustain us both through this troubling time."

"Amen," Chuck muttered. He was hit with another pulsing wave of pain, made a groaning, weeping sound, leaned back in the dirt, and had to give in to the pain for a moment, closing his eyes tight.

"Bleeding's not too bad. He missed the artery," Pastor Gallen said. "I think you're going to be okay. How's the pain?"

"Waves," Chuck said through gritted teeth. "Not good."

"Try to relax." The pastor took Chuck's hand. "Can I ask, Chuck, have you accepted our Lord Jesus Christ as your personal savior?"

Was this a conversion . . . or last rights? Chuck grimaced. "I was raised Catholic."

"Then I'm afraid you have been deceived by false prophets, and by the worst evil I can imagine—a false salvation."

Matthew came out of the house then with a small white first aid kit and two dish towels. He set these down and began taking his belt off. "I'm really sorry. It just . . . went off. I wasn't trying to shoot you. But you were freaking me out! That's a three-hundred-dollar tire, man!"

"I told you I'd pay for the tires!" Chuck spat the words, unsure why he was bothering to argue this point.

"They wear differently when you replace only one," Matthew said. "One tire would be six months newer, and the treads would wear unevenly."

"That's enough about the tires, Matthew," Pastor Gallen said. He worked silently. He cut away a hole in Chuck's jeans with scissors from the first aid kit, put gauze and a square, adhesive bandage over the wound, then pressed the folded dish towel against Chuck's hip. He spoke quietly. "We need to keep pressure on this. It's going to hurt." He pushed, and indeed, it did hurt. "I'm going to put this belt around the towel. You're going to be fine. Your body will recover. But I worry about your soul. You are worshipping in the wrong house. A false gospel. You're on the wide road to destruction. That's not just me saying it. That's Second Corinthians, 11:4."

"I don't go to church," Chuck said, wincing at the pain.

"Well, perhaps this is God's way of opening your heart," the pastor said.

"Are you fucking nuts? Shoot people? Is that your recruitment strategy?"

Matthew paced above them, gesturing with his hands. "I can't go to jail, man. I'm gonna lose my job." He removed the ball cap and ran his fingers through straw hair. "He was threatening my truck! You guys saw it!"

Chuck squeezed his eyes shut. "Please, tell him to be quiet—" The gunshot wound, Gallen's using this opportunity to evangelize, dark-eyed Dean Burris hovering, Matthew's jittery self-pitying monologue—all of it was making Chuck nauseated. "All of you, be quiet."

Dean walked over then. He looked down on Chuck. Such dark, pitiless eyes. Was that a smile on his face. *Isn't the first time he's seen someone shot*, Chuck thought.

"Sheriff's on the way," Dean said. "And paramedics."

"No. I want a helicopter," Chuck said through gritted teeth, the pain coming in another wave. He let out a groan that turned into a kind of yelp. "Have them send a helicopter." He needed to get out of this insane backwater. Twenty-six years as a cop and he'd never been shot at, never fired his weapon, never been seriously hurt, and here he was, possibly bleeding out in the dirt at this nutjob's compound, listening to one yahoo talk about tire wear while another tried to convert him.

He had the clearest thought he'd ever experienced then: *You cannot die here!* "Have them call Spokane," he rasped, "tell them a cop's been shot, have them send a helicopter." He made his voice as steady as possible. And there was one other person whose voice he desperately needed to hear now. "I need to use your phone."

- - -

KINNICK WAS PLAYING it out in his mind as he drove across the border from Idaho into Washington. According to Lucy, Chuck had gotten in some kind of gunfight with one of the militiamen, and was wounded, although she wasn't entirely sure how it had happened, or how serious it was, or if anyone else was hurt. All she knew was that Chuck had called her as he was being loaded into a helicopter that was, at that very moment, taking him back to Spokane.

Surely, the unhelpful Sheriff Glen Campbell would have arrived at the Rampart by now, too, furious that what he called "this custody bullshit" had erupted into such trouble. Pastor Gallen would have called Shane, and with Bethany still missing, Shane would be the only parent involved. He would maybe file a complaint against his abusive father-in-law (*he punched me one time*), for coming to take the kids with some unstable old cop, bursting into a peaceful rural church and taking the kids from the very people Shane had entrusted to watch them.

Imagining it this way was troubling for Kinnick, who realized that his only defense to Shane's version of events would be the note from his daughter and a series of *Yeah-buts*. Like all people, he supposed, when making cases to himself he was prone to forgetting that other people made cases as well.

As a grandfather—one who had seen his grandkids one time in the last seven years—what rights would Kinnick have in this situation? (Answer: none.) And while he could probably expect fairer treatment from the Spokane police, Kinnick also recalled their disinterest yesterday, when he showed up at the cop shop with his note and a broken cheekbone and the desk sergeant had been less than helpful. He hadn't actually *said* Glen Campbell's words, *Custody bullshit*, but he'd seemed to be thinking it.

No, if he went to the police Kinnick might end up in jail, and Asher and Leah would be right back in that crazy militia nest by morning.

He also couldn't take the kids to the hospital. The police might be waiting for him there. He had to find Bethany first. But where? And where would he take the kids in the meantime? Kinnick chewed his bottom lip as he piloted Chuck's pickup into Spokane from the north. Only one place he could think to go. He got off the highway before the city limits, and turned to the west, crossing the woods below Eloika Lake.

"Broccoli and cheese," Leah muttered.

Kinnick looked over at her.

"The color of those trees," she said.

Kinnick looked out at the green needles and orange trunks of the ponderosa pines. "I could see that."

Leah looked over at him. "Mom said you used to make up bedtime stories for her."

Kinnick glanced over again. Asher was asleep, but Leah was staring intently. "I did, yes."

"What were the stories about?"

He could still picture it: coming home after a long day at the newspaper, walking into Bethany's bedroom. After a difficult pregnancy, Celia had been diagnosed with gestational diabetes, so they'd decided early on that Bethany would be their only child. Every year Celia painted some-thing new across the walls and ceiling of Bethany's bedroom, rainbows, pastoral scenes, sea life. He'd peek into her room and see Bethany wide-awake, waiting for him beneath a pod of dolphins. Picking up her favorite doll—Oolya with the blue yarn hair—and holding it in his lap, he'd settle against the headboard, and she'd lean on his shoulder. Bethany would always start it, as if Kinnick couldn't remember: *Once upon a time*—

Celia insisted they not tell their daughter old classic princess stories, in which a prince came to rescue the heroine. But Kinnick had trouble conjuring fairies or wizards or magical beings, and so, somehow, he had decided that what a six-year-old really needed at bedtime was strict realism.

"I had a failure of imagination," he admitted to Leah. "I'd come home from work and tell her versions of the stories I'd written for the newspaper that day."

Leah smiled. "Really?"

"To my credit, I was at least smart enough to realize that an EPA hearing might be boring for a six-year-old, and that a double homicide might be too scary, so, I used to make up magical, happy endings."

"What's EPA?"

"Environmental Protection Agency."

Leah nodded. "Do you remember any of the stories?"

Kinnick did remember one. He had spent two days covering a train derailment. Toxic chemicals. Pesticides and other contaminants. After the second day, he came home and found Bethany wide-awake, sitting on her bed.

"Once upon a time," he said to his granddaughter—

—there was a train that flew off the tracks and crashed in the forest. Luckily, the people on the train weren't hurt. But there were bad chemicals on the train, and they spilled out and it wasn't safe. Firefighters evacuated houses and put fences around the crash site, but the humans spent days

arguing over how to clean it up. Was it a federal job? A state job? A train company job? While they argued, animals came from miles around to sniff at the broken train, and the puddles of mysterious goo leaking out into the forest. Then, an especially smart, curious little rabbit named Bunathy tasted a bit of the goo and realized: it's not safe! She felt her body changing. She stood up on her back legs like a human creature, or like a bear creature, and she realized something else: she could now speak and understand the languages of every other animal! "Back away!" she called to the porcupines and mule deer and coyotes who gathered to see if there was anything to eat in the spilled train cars. She spoke to each animal—in perfect Porcupine, in fluent Coyote, even in the rare Mule Deer dialect. "It's not safe. Do not eat!" The animals all backed away. Clouds were gathering then, and Bunathy could see it was going to rain, but the train wreck was deep in the forest, beneath the canopy of trees, so she gathered the beavers and spoke to them in passable Beaver: "I need you to clear the trees around the crash, so the rain can get in and soak the spoiled ground." As beavers are famously hardworking, and love chewing trees, they dove right in. And just as the beavers were chomping away and trees were falling, Bunathy gathered the smartest birds, the crows. "I need you to fly to nearby farms and bring me tarps from the haystacks and blankets from the clotheslines." Now, crows are notoriously uncooperative, so she had to make a deal with them. "If you do this, I will show you where there is a bin of corn." So, the crows flew off, and when she looked up in the sky a few minutes later, Bunathy saw blankets and tarps, like magic carpets, flying and fluttering into the woods in the clutched talons of swarms of crows. "Cover the train," Bunathy told the crows, and they did, draping the tarps and blankets over the train cars. There was a curious black bear family and Bunathy asked them to get rocks to put over the tarps and blankets, to keep them from blowing away, and, as black bears are known to be playful, they made a game of it, Mother and Son Bear against Father and Daughter Bear, to see who could gather the most rocks, and when the rainstorm blew in, their perfectly placed rocks kept the blankets and tarps from flying away, and kept more chemicals from leaking out. Meanwhile, the rain soaked the contaminated ground, and the chemicals were diluted until they were no longer dangerous. And because Bunathy really did know where there was a big bin of corn—a farmer had filled his bin, but then he'd won a two-million-dollar Power- ball and left his farm for Las Vegas—she brought all the animals to the secret bin for a big corn party, all except the squirrels, who hadn't helped with the cleanup and were too fidgety anyway for parties. By this time, the humans had stopped arguing over who had to clean up the derailed train, but when they came into the forest, they saw it had been done for them! They stood there, amazed. And just before the chemical potion wore off, Bunathy hopped out of the woods, stood on her little hind legs, and spoke to the firefighters, train people, and government types in the elaborate but boring human language: "You still need to test nearby wells and aquifers for contaminants, and mitigate the existing damage," Bunathy said. She could feel herself changing. "And, please, from now on," she said as the languages seeped out of her body, "be more," she said, falling back onto four legs, and then, just before she hopped back into the forest, Bunathy the heroic bunny finished the last human sentence she would ever utter, "careful."

"That's a good story," Leah said. A wide smile broke on her face. "Did Mom like it?"

She did, Kinnick thought, although, as he remembered it, no matter how happy he tried to make the endings to his magical news stories, she always looked gravely concerned afterward.

"Bunathy died, didn't she? From the chemicals?"

"No! I told you. It was temporary. She went back to being a regular bunny. Only now she had a hundred new friends because of the corn party."

But Bethany had just stared at him, with that same look, as if she were steeling herself for the trouble that lay ahead, as if she already understood something harsh about the real world.

Or perhaps about him.

A shiver went through Kinnick as he remembered this. It was as if, even then, Bethany sensed that he couldn't protect her from all the dangers of the world, from the craziness and the instability. That, in the end, he might not even be there for her at all. (He recalled, again, Asher saying, *Or maybe Dad killed her . . .*)

Kinnick rubbed his face. He could feel the panic rising in his chest. If anything happened to his daughter—

"It's gonna be okay," Leah said.

"What?"

"You shouldn't worry so much about Mom." Leah gave a thin smile. "Asher doesn't know what he's talking about. Shane can be a weirdo, and none of us really like this new church, but he would never do *that*. Mom is fine."

How had she known that was what he was thinking? She was so perceptive, just like her mother. But there was something strange in the way she'd said this. "Wait, how do you know?" Kinnick asked.

"What?"

"How do you know she's okay?"

"I guess . . ." Leah shrugged with one shoulder. "I don't?"

Kinnick recalled what she'd said on his porch yesterday—that Bethany had left the note in Leah's snow boot. But it was almost May. And she'd made fun of her little brother for wearing snow boots. So, why would Leah suddenly go looking in her snow boot?

Unless her mother had *told* her to look there. Unless her mother had *told* her that she was leaving. Kinnick pulled the truck over onto the shoulder, turned and faced his granddaughter. "Leah, do you know where your mom is?"

She was staring up at him with Bethany's eyes. With Celia's eyes. She shrugged with the other shoulder. "I can't say."

"Leah, please."

"Mom and I made a promise to each other."

"Leah. If you know something, you need to tell me."

- - -

ASHER WAS SUPER glad to be back at Joanie and Brian's house. The sun was going down, the pellet stove was warm, the lazy dog was nice, and Asher was happy to be on a stool at Joanie's kitchen counter, about to get some dinner. Best of all, he was out of the Rampart, even though his dad had wanted Leah and him to stay there, and not with Grandpa Rhys. But Asher didn't like being there without his dad. Everyone was so serious. Brother Dean and the AOL guys were kind of scary. And the Rampart School was even more boring than home school. He liked Miss Charlotte fine, but he hated rereading the same old Bible stories, which, in his opinion, weren't even that good of stories! (*The worst one was Abraham almost sacrificing Isaac! What was that even about? Like, God is a bully who does practical jokes?*) Pastor Gallen said that Bible literacy was the cornerstone of any education, but Miss Charlotte taught even less science and math than their mother. What kind of education was that?

Joanie set sandwiches in front of the kids, and, as she poured them glasses of lemonade, Asher followed her eyes out the window, where Brian and Grandpa Rhys were on the porch, talking about something.

Asher turned a half sandwich over in his hand. "What did Brian's people eat?"

"Oh, they ate like kings," Joanie said. "The rivers were so full of fish then they didn't even need bridges. You just walked across the salmon to get to the other side. Deer and elk would run up and demand to be cooked that very minute."

Asher laughed. "Did they live in tepees?"

"Sometimes," Joanie said. "But Brian is interior Salish. Do you know what that is?"

"No."

"You should. We live in their country. Salish people lived from the

Rocky Mountains to the Pacific Ocean, from Oregon to Canada," she said. "Nobody owned the land, they just followed fish and game and dug roots, and they got together for powwows, potlaches, stuff like that. Hundreds of tribes and bands. Sometimes they lived in tepees, but sometimes they lived in lodges, and some nights, when they were out on a hunt, or on war parties, they slept under the stars."

"I've slept outside," Asher said. "In a sleeping bag. I like to look at the stars. I know most of the constellations."

"You know Sagittarius?" Joanie asked. She glanced out the window, to where Brian and Grandpa Rhys talking, pointing, gesturing with their hands. "That's me. Loyal to a fault."

Asher continued: "The funny thing about constellations is that when you're little, you think the stars must be really close together, but did you know they're millions and millions of light-years apart?"

"That so?" Joanie was still staring outside.

"Yes. Did you know a light-year is how far light can travel in a year? It's very far. The light we see left those stars millions and millions of years ago. Those stars might not even be there now. They might have blown up back when there were dinosaurs!"

"Dinosaurs, huh?" Joanie said distractedly, still staring out the window.

"Our new church teaches that God hung the stars in the firmament, and that they move around the Earth, but Mom says it's okay if I don't believe everything the church teaches, because that's just what people *used to think* when they wrote the Bible, before there were telescopes and rockets and good scientists."

"Uh-huh," Joanie said.

"Asher," Leah said. "That's enough."

Asher knew Leah didn't like it when he questioned church teachings out loud. She didn't believe everything the Blessed Fire taught, either, but she got mad when her brother talked like this. She liked to say what Pastor Gallen's son, David Jr., had told her: your faith was personal, and God did *not* need you defending Him. David Jr. had told her (and she told Asher) that his divinity professor said it was pointless to use science to argue against the Bible, because if scientific principles governed the universe, then they were, by nature, designed by God. In other words, if it was true, then God was its author, since God was *truth*. And if He was all-powerful, why couldn't He be the one who hung the stars millions of light-years apart? What would time matter to Him? And why couldn't He be the one to light the spark to the Big Bang? What was thirteen billion years to the Creator of the universe?

Asher had to admit, these were hard points to argue.

Brian came inside then. He avoided eye contact as he marched to a back bedroom and emerged a moment later with a long brown leather bag strapped over his shoulder.

"Whoa, whoa, whoa!" Joanie stepped between him and the door, hands on her hips. "Where are you going with that?"

"Joanie, don't start with me—"

"Me start? You're the one walking through the house with a rifle!"

"These people Rhys has got himself balled up with—"

"Rhys got balled up, not you!"

"I'm just going to follow him into town, so he can return the man's truck and his cell phone. Then we'll come right back here."

"I don't want you involved in this, Brian."

"Well, I'm involved, Joanie."

"No. Not like that."

"He needs my help."

She reached for the soft rifle case. "He doesn't need this."

Brian pulled the case back toward himself. "Joanie, please. Can we not talk about this here? In front of them?" He pulled her by the arm back to the bedroom, the door closing behind them.

Grandpa Rhys came inside then. He lingered at the bar, took a half sandwich from the plate Joanie had prepared, and looked from Leah to Asher. "How are you guys doing?"

"Fine," Leah said. Asher noticed that Leah hadn't had much to say since they'd left the Rampart. She sometimes got into moods like this. Their mom said it was "adolescence," but sometimes he thought Leah was just kind of a b***head.

"You won't tell Mom, right?" Leah said to Grandpa Rhys. "About what I told you?"

"What did you tell him?" Asher asked.

Leah spun on him. "Asher! It's none of your business!"

Yes, Asher concluded. Leah was being a total b***head.

"No, I won't say anything, Leah," Kinnick said. "Don't worry. Right now, Brian and I are going to run into town to check on my friend at the hospital. You two stay here with Joanie. We'll be back in a few hours, and tomorrow, we'll go get your mom."

Leah opened her mouth to say something but stopped.

"Why does Brian have a rifle?" Asher asked.

"For turkeys," said Joanie. She was coming out of the back bedroom, Brian behind her with the rifle case. "It's spring turkey season. You kids like turkey?"

"Not really," Asher said. "I like—"

"Asher—" Leah said again.

"I do like pressed turkey *slices*," Asher said. "In sandwiches." And then, as if he couldn't help himself, "But I like ham better."

"Well, he'll try to shoot a pressed turkey," Joanie said. "Or a ham."

Brian nodded at Joanie, who mouthed some words to him.

"Love you, too," Brian said. Then: "You ready, Rhys?"

Grandpa Rhys nodded. "Yeah. Okay." He looked back at the kids, as if there was more to say. "Okay," he said again, then turned for the door. "Okay."

- - -

KINNICK STEPPED WARILY through the double sliding doors, half-expecting to see Sheriff Glen Campbell, or the dismissive Spokane police sergeant, or maybe a full SWAT team ready to arrest him for kidnapping his grandchildren. Instead, he smelled *hospital* and immediately thought of his poor mother (*embolism postsurgery, only forty-four*), and years later, the claustrophobic and helpless feeling of coming to various emergency rooms as a parent. (*Bethany at six, falling off a slide at school and needing five stitches, at thirteen, coughing up blood for no apparent reason, at seventeen, a broken clavicle from a car accident with friends.*)

Every chair in the Sacred Heart Emergency Room waiting area was filled with some manner of suffering—twitching addicts and bleeding head wounds and people struggling to simply breathe. Just inside the doors, a triage nurse was helping a skinny barefoot girl with a screaming, thrashing toddler, who was trying to squirm out of his footie pajamas, or maybe out of his skin. The child let out a harrowing scream as Kinnick stood there, unsure if he should try to help.

"Come on, Mom," the nurse was saying, "you need to keep moving. Let's get your boy back here and start fixing him up." But the young mother had frozen just inside the door, as if this were suddenly more than she could handle.

"He got burned," she said.

The nurse looked over at Kinnick warily, then cocked her head slightly to look more closely at his bruised face. "Looks like you took quite a shot. Zygomatic arch?"

"So they tell me," Kinnick said.

She nodded to a window. "Head over to intake with your ID."

"Oh, no," Kinnick started to say, "I'm not here for—"

But the nurse had turned back to the young mother. "Come on, Mom. We can do this. I'm with you. Your boy's gonna be okay, but we gotta get him inside."

She guided the young woman and her writhing son deeper into the hospital.

Kinnick walked past the intake window, and farther into the waiting room, but didn't see any sign of Chuck or Lucy. Or the police, for that matter—

"Rhys?" She came in behind him, through the open double doors, a Styrofoam cup in her hand. Lucy wore jeans and a sweatshirt, her hair pulled back in a distracted ponytail, strands coming out on all sides. She looked like maybe she'd been crying.

"Oh, no, he isn't—"

"No, he's fine," she said, and strode over. "Sounds like he got lucky. The bullet didn't fracture his hip, and it didn't hit any arteries or anything. Just sort of settled in. The surgeon is on her way down now to debride the wound and remove the bullet."

"Oh. That's good, I guess."

"Where have you been? I thought you'd be here hours ago."

"I didn't want to bring the kids, so I took them to a friend's house."

Niceties over, Lucy smacked him in the chest with her open hand. "What the fuck were you thinking, Kinnick!"

"I didn't— I wasn't— What?" Kinnick had been so worried about the police, or that small-town sheriff, or the Army of the Lord, that it hadn't occurred to him that the real threat to his safety might be Lucy. "I was just going along with Chuck."

She hit him in the chest again. "You don't go along with Chuck fucking Littlefield! Not when he goes manic like that! What did I tell you? Where's your common sense?"

"You're the one who set me up with him!"

Another shot to his chest. "Yeah, because I assumed you'd know better than to go half-cocked into some militia compound with him!"

Kinnick looked around, worried that people would think this angry woman was the cause of his black eye.

"Do you have any idea what you've done?"

"Today?" Kinnick asked. "Or, like . . . lifetime?"

She smacked him again. "It took me six months to break up with

Chuck! And now, because of you—and me—he almost gets killed. The guy has no one to take care of him, Rhys! His ex hates him. His kids won't talk to him. Who do you think is going to have to take care of Chuck now?"

Of course, he hadn't thought of that. "Lucy, I didn't—"

"I honestly don't know how you do it. One day back in my life and it's a steaming bucket of rotten fucking fish heads."

"I am *so* sorry. I really didn't—" He held up Chuck's phone and key fob. "I just came here to give back his truck and his phone. He's got a lot of messages." In fact, the thing had been buzzing nearly nonstop for the last hour.

She sighed. "Come on. I'll take you back to see him."

Kinnick followed her through the misery of the waiting room, past an aide taking a blood sample from a quietly weeping old man. The aide paused from his work to buzz them back into the treatment area, where another set of doors opened.

"Also, this sheriff's deputy from Idaho was here earlier," Lucy said. "He wants to talk to you."

"Did you give him my number?"

"Funny. You're fucking hilarious, Kinnick. No, I told him I'd pass *his* number on to you."

"Well, I'm not sticking around. And I'm not calling that sheriff."

"Right. Good move. You'll make a good fugitive."

"I've got to find Bethany first, and once I bring her back, we'll get this all straightened out with her kids."

Lucy looked back over her shoulder. "You know where she is?"

"I think so," Kinnick said. "She told Leah where she was going."

"She did?"

He thought about telling Lucy what Leah had begrudgingly told him, but he didn't want to put Lucy in the position of having to withhold anything from law enforcement. "Yes," Kinnick said simply.

Lucy paused outside Chuck's treatment room. She put a hand on the curtain and turned back to Kinnick. "He's pretty jacked up on pain meds right now."

From the other side of the curtain: "Gilligan? Is that you? Where'd you go?"

She pulled the curtain, and there was Chuck, in a hospital bed, cabled to a heart monitor, electrodes all over his bare chest, a blood pressure cup on his arm, IV drip above him, catheter bag below him. He looked so small in that bed, hooked to all that equipment.

"Hey! There he is!" Chuck said. "My new partner. Hey, we pulled it off, didn't we?" He held up a fist for Kinnick to bump.

"How are you feeling, Chuck?"

"Me? Shoooot." His fist fell to his side. "I'm fine. All things, you know, considered." His eyes were glossy with pain meds. "Anyway, it takes more than a bullet to slow me down. How are your grandkids?"

"They're fine. Thank you. I left them with some friends for a while. What the hell happened up there?"

"Ah." Chuck waved the question away. "One of those toy soldiers got nervous and his gun went off! I was trying to keep those idiots from following you, and this kid pulled his piece on me, shot me, and then shit his own drawers."

"I'm so sorry, Chuck."

"Guy was weirdly protective of his tires. I would've buried the poor kid, but he threw his hands in the air and practically started crying like a baby. I felt sorry for him."

"Did they arrest him?"

"Nah, Sheriff Yahoo says he's still investigating it. But I doubt he'll charge the kid. Your eagle-killer was there, too, and he and the pastor are claiming the kid shot me in self-defense. Now, there's a cold fish, that guy Burris." Again, a quick glance to Lucy. "But even Brother Dean knew better than to draw on *me*."

Lucy muttered something.

"I shouldn't have gotten you into this," Kinnick said.

Chuck waved this off again. "Are you kidding? This is my job."

Lucy muttered again, but this time louder. "Not your job."

"I shouldn't have left you alone up there," Kinnick said.

"Bullshit. It was the only way to get those kids out of there." He glanced briefly at Lucy, as if making sure she was hearing this. "I had the whole thing handled. Just didn't count on a nervous kid not knowing how to handle a firearm. That *stupid fuck*!"

Kinnick took a half step back.

Lucy put a hand on Chuck's chest, between all the wires. "You should rest. You're getting worked up again."

"I can't tell you how much I appreciate it, Chuck."

"Yeah, well . . ." Chuck shrugged. "I'm no hero." As if someone had been arguing that he was. "We just did what had to be done, am I right, partner?"

Kinnick nodded.

But the air seemed to have gone out of Chuck. He leaned forward and adjusted the blanket covering his lap and his legs. A catheter tube led to a square bag clipped to the side of his bed. Bloody piss was dribbling into it. Chuck sighed, leaned back, and closed his eyes, as if the enormity of the past day had suddenly hit him, and he realized how close he'd come to not coming off that hill.

Kinnick looked at Lucy, who wouldn't return his stare and was watching Chuck's face. "I brought these back," Rhys said, and he held out the key fob and the cell phone for Chuck to see. "Your truck's in the parking lot. Do you want me to move it somewhere?"

"I'll take care of it," Lucy said. She held out her hand without looking at Kinnick and he gave her the key fob.

"You got messages and calls on your phone, too," Kinnick said. "It's been buzzing nonstop. Seems like a lot of people care about you."

Chuck made no effort to reach for the phone. Instead, he looked away and swallowed. Lucy reached over and took the phone, too.

The curtain was pulled open again, and a tall woman in white scrubs entered.

"Mr. Littlefield, I'm Dr. Eltman, your anesthesiologist. I understand we're taking a little souvenir out of your hip today?"

"Okay," Chuck said, his energy totally sapped now.

"I should go," Kinnick said. "But I'll be back to check on you in a couple of days, hopefully with my daughter."

He'd planned to bring Chuck up to speed on the latest development—Leah telling him where he might find Bethany—but the wounded old cop had lost interest, or perhaps the drugs had just kicked in. He leaned back again and closed his eyes.

Kinnick had just started to edge out when Chuck spoke again. "Watch out for those guys, yeah?"

Rhys turned back. "I will." But Chuck's eyes were still closed.

On his way out, Kinnick saw two uniformed police officers, a man and a woman, standing in the hallway. He stiffened, but as he got closer, he could see they weren't waiting for him. They were talking to the young mother who had brought the screaming toddler in.

"How did the baby get burned?" one of them asked her.

The girl shrugged.

"These look like chemical burns, Lisa," the male cop said.

She shrugged again.

"Is someone making meth at your house, Lisa?"

The boy's mother met Kinnick's eyes as he passed, and the regret he saw in that brief look crushed him. How could life be so hard?

As he walked away, Kinnick could still hear the female officer's voice. "I don't want you to lose your baby over this, Lisa. That's all."

That's all. That's all.

Kinnick was crying by the time he stepped out into the dark evening.

Lisa was going to lose her baby. That's all.

Bethany, too. And him, he'd lost his baby a long time ago. Oh, this world.

He was still teary as he walked through the parking lot, to where he'd left Brian, sitting alertly in the driver's seat of his Ford Bronco, scoped .30-06 hunting rifle across his lap.

Kinnick climbed in the passenger seat. "Would you put that thing away." He wiped at his eyes. "What do you think, an elk's gonna walk by?"

"Elk season is not until fall." Brian got the leather rifle case from the backseat. "Spring is protect-your-friend-from-racist-assholes season."

"I just don't want you accidentally shooting *me*."

Brian showed Kinnick a ribbon pinned to the leather case. "You know what that is?" It was small, black in the middle, gray on either end, with two beige stripes.

"Boy Scout badge for stubbornness?"

"Marksmanship ribbon. Lackland Air Force Base, 1982. Second in my training class. Hit sixty-eight of eighty targets. You know what my instructor said . . . Nice shooting, Cochise."

Kinnick winced. He often had the urge to apologize to Brian for things other white people said.

Brian carefully placed the gun back in the case. "Your cop friend gonna be okay?"

"I think so. Surgeon's about to take the bullet out. Lucy's with him."

"How about you? Are *you* okay?"

Kinnick nodded. "I don't like hospitals." He rarely thought about his mother anymore, who went in for emergency gallbladder surgery in Seattle and simply never came out. Kinnick was in college then, and only heard about it afterward; the suddenness still struck him, a feeling like someone had been left behind. His mother was alive one day and then, simply . . . not. And poor Celia. How terrified she must've been. He remembered when they got flu shots, how she needed to stare into his eyes and squeeze his hand; he couldn't imagine her going through chemotherapy alone. Or radiation. Was Cort with her? Was Bethany at Celia's side? Did she die alone? It made him feel nauseated that he didn't know how his ex-wife had passed.

He looked over. Brian was staring at the hospital, too, a familiar, pained look on his face. He knew that Brian had lost both parents, a sister, and a nephew to cancer. Two of them rare sarcomas. It was the reason he and Joanie had begun their protest of the Dawn uranium tailings pond in the first place.

Kinnick turned his body. "Thanks, Brian. You're a good friend."

Brian nodded. "Xest sxĺxalt."

Good day. It was a Salish phrase Kinnick had heard Brian use before, his own personal all-purpose, bone-dry, conversation-ending punch-line, shorthand for everything from *See you later* to *It's a good day to die.* Brian set the rifle case in the back of the Bronco.

Kinnick looked back once more at the hospital, where Chuck was about to go into surgery. As nuts as that guy was, Kinnick couldn't help wishing he still had Chuck's help. What was it he'd said this morning in the coffee shop?

"What do you say, partner?" Kinnick turned to Brian. "Should we go find my daughter?"

FOUR

What Happened to Bethany

She got too high.

This was in the spring of 2002. High school. Sophomore year. Monica's weed. Or, rather, Monica's *boyfriend's* weed, well, actually, Monica's boyfriend's *stepbrother's* weed—hot pocket Connor Brand, brooding senior who claimed to know the B.C. growers personally, from his junior hockey days, before he tore his ACL and had to give up sports for simply looking *hot* (and dealing weed), and who cruised the halls of their high school as if still on skates, and who had never even *looked* at Bethany before today, but who now stood dreamily in her kitchen, watching her try to make a sandwich with hands that suddenly felt like walrus flippers.

"This lettuce feels weird." Bethany held it out for Monica and Connor to see. "Look. It won't do what I want it to do."

"I warned you," Monica said.

"I'm serious. It won't go on the sandwich."

"I don't like lettuce on tuna fish anyway," Connor said, and he grabbed the slices of bread, pressed them together, and took a bite. "Thanks."

Bethany was left holding the unruly lettuce.

"You got too high," Monica said with some level of told-you-so irritation.

This appeared to be true. Also, as Monica had warned her, this appeared to be better pot than the ditch-grown compost they usually smoked. It felt to Bethany like a life preserver of happiness had been gently placed over her shoulders and chest. And a helmet of interestingness. No, that wasn't right. That was stupid. It didn't feel anything like that. It felt like her skin was alive, pores open, nerves firing, like she was too perceptive and too sleepy all at once, too anxious and too peaceful, too chill and too rushed and too buzzed, like . . . like she wasn't sure if this was the greatest high she'd ever had . . . or the worst.

"Paranoia," Connor said.

"We should get back," Monica said.

"My mouth keeps falling open," Bethany said.

Connor took another bite of his sandwich, looking from one girl to the other as they talked.

"Look at my mouth," Bethany said.

"You're not saying words," Monica said.

"I *am* saying words. I'm saying that my mouth keeps falling open."

"Are you taking second-year French?"

"I'm not speaking French!"

"I didn't say you were!"

Bethany felt a creeping panic. "Are you messing with me?"

"It's cute," Connor said through the tuna fish and mayo. "Your mouth."

"We have to go," Monica said. "Now."

"I can't go back like this." Bethany pointed to her open mouth with the hand holding the unruly lettuce. Wait, did Connor Brand just say her mouth was cute?

"We'll miss English."

"I am speaking English!"

"I said we'll *miss* English!" Monica was totally exasperated now. "Jesus, Beth!"

"Shit." Bethany did *not* want to miss English. It was her favorite class. But no way could she go back to school with wild lettuce, walrus flippers, and an open mouth.

They had bailed on computer science, which was an easy skip, being both patently uninteresting and, like, incredibly boring. The teacher, Mr. Dunn (Dunn-Heap, Bethany called him), made the class worse by treating them like mascots, two of only three girls taking the course, like, *ooh, isn't it adorable*, girls taking computer science when everyone knows programmers are boys—as if this were auto shop in 1958 and they'd only taken the class to meet future husbands.

Computer science was also fifth hour, right after second lunch, which made it a prime skip target, since their high school had an open campus and they could go eat at nearby restaurants and come back late, or just ditch food altogether, like today, when they found themselves sitting in Connor's car under the freeway, getting stoned with him and Ian, Monica's boyfriend. Ian had gone back to class, because he had soccer practice that day, but Connor said he was hungry and that's when Bethany offered to make him a tuna sandwich at her empty house four blocks away (her parents both worked during the day); and then she looked at Monica with her *please-come-with-us* eyes, and Monica looked at her with the *I-don't-want-to-miss-class* eyes and Bethany came back with the *it's-just-computer-science* eyes and Monica gave her back the *fine-but-I-don't-like-this-one-bit-and-we'd-better-be-back-for-English* eyes, and boom, here they were, smoke-show Connor Brand standing in *her kitchen*! Eating *her tuna fish sandwich*! While she held a defiant piece of lettuce in her walrus flipper.

But Monica was right. Sixth hour was English, with Ms. Candless, who they agreed probably had sex with both men and women (no reason, except she'd lived in Spain for two years, and she just seemed cool that way) and who let them read all kinds of racy feminist books from her official reading list. No, they *had* to get back for sixth hour.

"I'll drive you back after I finish this sandwich," Connor said.

"I'm going now," Monica said suddenly, and she left the kitchen and was out the back door before Bethany could even throw away the lettuce.

"That was sudden," Connor said.

Bethany opened the cabinet beneath the sink and finally threw the lettuce away. Okay, at least that was done. She was getting her shit together. That weird lettuce was gone. But clearly, her best friend was mad at her now. Maybe they could pick her up on the way back to school and Bethany could apologize. But for what? Getting too high?

"I guess there's no reason to rush back now," Connor said. "Maybe you want to show me your bedroom?"

Wait. Did Bethany want to show Connor Brand her bedroom? This was not a question she had been prepared to answer. Did she want to go to a dance with delicious Connor Brand? Yes. Did she want people at school to see her holding hands with brooding Connor Brand? Definitely. Did she want, perhaps, to make out with juicy Connor Brand in his black Volkswagen Jetta? Sure. But he had just spoken his first words to her less than one hour ago—"You ready for a hit, Monica's friend?"—and so a tour of her bedroom seemed a bit premature, perhaps even creepy, and maybe smooth Connor Brand realized the same thing, because he proceeded to try making up some of the intermediate steps between sandwich and sex, crossing the kitchen, taking her in his arms and kissing her, and at first she thought it was weird that one of the best-looking seniors in school had tuna breath, but then she recalled making him a tuna sandwich, and it made sense and was even kind of endearing, so she opened her mouth and kissed him back, but she wasn't sure what to do with her hands while handsy Connor Brand ran *his* all over her back and butt and sides, so she put one walrus flipper on the back of his neck and the other on his chest, and that felt amazing, maybe she *should* show him her bedroom, but, wait, she had a *City Guys* poster above her bed, what a weird thing *that* would be—like, what, she was ten?—and wait, was she going to lose her virginity? Now? Like this? Stoned and skipping school with a senior she barely knew? And wait again, was his hand going up her shirt—and that's when she heard the familiar sound of footsteps on her front porch and—

"Shit! My parents," she whispered, and pulled away from tuna-breath Connor Brand and pushed him toward the back door, opened it, and shoved him out, following him just as she heard her father's voice in the living room:

"—a bargain when we bought it—"

She gently closed the back door behind her, pushed Connor down the back steps, along the lattice that her distracted dad had put up for the herbs and clematis her earth mother mom planted, toward the side of the house, right through her mother's favorite rosebush. "Stay down!" she whispered, and they snuck low past the big dining room window, and into the driveway. Thankfully, she'd had Connor park up the street, so that no neighbors would tell her parents that a car had been in the driveway or out front, and they crept past her dad's Audi and broke into a run until they arrived at Connor's car, and she opened the door and fell into the passenger seat, heart pounding in her ears. "That was so close!"

"Yeah," Connor said, with slightly less enthusiasm.

She wondered for a moment if they would continue making out in his car, and she thought more about the ramifications of getting in-volved with someone like Connor Brand, who would no doubt go off to college next fall, so she'd be looking at a potential boyfriend window of, what, four months?

But, by then, she could tell something had shifted with wearisome Connor Brand.

"Better get you back to school," he said, like her parents had asked him to drop her off at kindergarten.

"Yeah, cool," Bethany said. And even though she hadn't really wanted to show her bedroom to step-skipping Connor Brand, she still felt like she'd messed things up somehow, and she was feeling sad about that, when Connor drove them right past the front of her house— before she could tell him not to—and she looked up and happened to see her father on the front porch as he started down the steps— apparently, he'd just popped in to grab something—his eyes making contact with hers and following her as she passed, giving Bethany the *is-that-who-I-think-it-is* eyes.

"Shit!" Connor Brand said. "Did your parents see you?"

"I don't know," she said—but no, her *parents* had not seen her, maybe just her dad, because A. she wasn't sure he'd registered that it was her, and B. whoever that petite Asian woman was on the porch with him, it was *not* Bethany's mother.

"I . . . I don't know," she said again, feeling kind of sick.

And, no, she decided, as Connor Brand pulled up to her high school and dropped her off for sixth hour English, this was *not* the best high she'd ever had.

- - -

BETHANY FINISHED THE story of Connor Brand's sandwich and her father's mysterious female friend, leaned back in her kitchen chair, and bit her lip to keep from crying. This was April 2020. Month two of the coronavirus pandemic. Shane was at work, the kids were playing in the backyard, and Bethany was having an online meeting with her therapist, Peggy, who had asked her a simple question: When did the trouble between Bethany and her father "begin"? They'd established that it was *before* the Thanksgiving Day blowup of 2016, Bethany telling her therapist how her "Daddy" had been her favorite when she was little, but that, somehow, during her teen years, they had begun to drift apart.

Peggy had said that an adolescent breach was common for girls and fathers, and asked if she recalled any specific incidents. And that's when Bethany flashed on the day she made Connor Brand a sandwich, almost had sex with him, and almost got caught skipping school by her possibly cheating father.

"How did that make you feel?" Peggy asked for roughly the one billionth time in the fourteen months Bethany had been her client. "Seeing your dad like that."

"Um. Nervous. Confused. Angry."

That afternoon, as Bethany told her therapist, she was also suffering the severe paranoia that came with a weed upgrade of that magnitude, along with Monica's cold shoulder in English class. The last hour of school seemed to take nine hours, then she raced home to find the tuna fish, pickles, mayo, mustard, and bread still out on the kitchen island, and she hurriedly put these things away, dreading the moment her dad came home from work and yelled at her for ditching school. Her mom arrived first, from the urgent care clinic where she worked, and immediately sat down and started reading a book. Wispy Celia always hummed while she read—and always off-key—which drove Bethany crazy, but especially that day, with the smell of tuna fish lingering in the house, and Connor's walrus-weed still making her feel like her stereo knobs had been cranked up.

Then . . . her dad came home. Braced for trouble, she had workshopped a few stories in her mind, finally settling on doppelgänger: *There's a girl who looks just like me at our school, maybe it was her?*

But . . . nothing. He didn't say a word about it. No funny looks, nothing. He asked if she had homework. He sat with a beer watching the Mariners game on TV.

"And how did *that* make you feel?"

Peggy made her background out of focus during these online meetings. It was disconcerting, as if she didn't want Bethany seeing what was on the walls of her therapist's home—perhaps a *New Yorker* cartoon about a psychologist and a dimwitted patient, or maybe the shrunken heads of past clients. Oh well, a fuzzy Zoom call was still better than crying and blowing snot bubbles through a mask.

"Let's see." Bethany blew out air. "Nervous? Confused? Angry?"

"Maybe he didn't see you after all," Peggy said.

"Oh, I was pretty sure he saw me," she said. "But, yeah, maybe my face didn't register. Or he thought, *Nah, Bethany's in school.* At one point, during dinner, I did catch him giving me a look, and I wondered—"

"Wondered—"

"If he wasn't saying anything because of—" A lump in her throat.

"The other woman."

"I mean, it could have been nothing. A friend, someone from work, a source he was interviewing. But the fact that he didn't mention it—"

"That had to be hard. Like you were being asked to keep your dad's secret."

Was it hard? Bethany wondered. Maybe? Honestly, she hadn't thought about that day in years, but here it was, almost twenty years later, and just telling the story nearly brought her to tears. "I guess . . . if anything, on that day, I began to choose a side."

"Choose a side?"

Bethany wondered if she shouldn't get a discount for all the times Peggy simply repeated her words back to her. "Yeah. My loyalties shifted, I guess. I'd always been a daddy's girl. At fourteen, I would have said that I was more like him. That I *suffered* my mother, this embarrassing, dull woman with all the stupid rules. I couldn't wait for my dad—the smart, hilarious, *fun* guy—to come home from his cool job and get the party started.

"But after that, I started seeing him in a different light. Selfish and detached. Kind of arrogant. Spending the weekends working on his 'book.' Of course, I was changing, too. I was so confused and anxious over the way boys were looking at me, the way they treated me. They like you; they don't like you; they only want one thing; they get that thing and they call you a slut. Looking back, it was like this daily battle—their eyes and their hands and me holding them off while desperately wanting them to like me. It was like this game where they had been given the rules and I hadn't.

"And that day, when I saw him on the porch with the woman, it was like I began to realize, *Oh, he's one of* them?"

"You never mentioned what you saw to your mom?"

"I mean, how could I? I was skipping school, getting high, thinking of screwing an eighteen-year-old drug-dealing hockey burnout. And what did I really see? Dad dropping by the house briefly with a woman? Could have been a photographer from the newspaper. They went out on assignments together all the time."

"But because you were fairly sure he'd seen you, and still he didn't say anything, you assumed the worst."

"Maybe that was unfair, treating my mom like some kind of victim. I mean, they were having trouble anyway. They divorced two years later, when I went off to college. They were essentially separated during my last two years of high school. Apparently, they only stayed together because of me. And I guess it was mutual. In fact, Mom had already met Cortland. But by then, I had chosen my side. If Dad was home, I went to my room, put on my headphones, cranked the music. I rolled my eyes when he started lecturing me. I started going out with friends, getting wasted. Sometimes I didn't even come home. He'd become furious and I'd just think, 'Okay, what are you gonna do about it?' I couldn't wait to get out of that house."

Peggy gave her most satisfied therapist smile. "Do you recall what we talked about at the beginning of this session? Is it possible this urge to escape relationships is something that began with your father?"

Bethany cocked her head. This is indeed how they had started the session, how they started most sessions, talking about Bethany's recurring desire—almost a panicked compulsion—to run away when things got hard. She'd broken it off suddenly with every boy she'd ever dated in high school and college, and she'd left Leah's hapless father, Doug, without so much as a goodbye, taking the baby in the middle of the night and escaping to her mother's house the moment she realized (eleven months too late) that the itinerant bass player for Days and Contusion might not be up to supporting a child.

Over the years, she grew more aware of this urge to bolt, and for almost a decade with Shane, she was able to keep the feeling at bay (partly through therapy) and yet, here she was, again, in the early months of the quarantine, hearing that voice in her head again—*Run!*—this time about her increasingly devout husband. She'd met Shane in Narcotics Anonymous, not long after she left Doug. She was shaking off Doug's drug of choice, coke; Shane had quit meth and was just beginning his deeply Christian period. She appreciated Shane's earnest embrace of religion. In fact, they connected over the spiritual idea of "giving in to a *higher power*." They read the Bible together, joined a young couples' prayer group, and found a cool big-box church in Grants Pass—which they jokingly called Godsco—with guitar music and a ready community of nice, young believers.

But Shane was a seeker, and not the kind of person to be satisfied with a nonevangelical, low-key, do-unto-others church. He needed things to progress, to go higher, to go deeper, to learn more; he lived to find answers and make connections. What he read and heard began to make sense of a senseless world. He listened to AM radio at his carpet-laying job, and later, driving a truck and delivering wholesale produce, and this caused him to want to trade up in churches, to find a pastor willing to address "the real world"—how secularism and socialism were ruining America. He was seeking a church, he told her, that was "more scripture-based," and "ready to engage in the final battle with evil," and "fighting to return America to its Godly foundation."

For the last few years, Bethany told her therapist, Shane had gotten into conspiracy theories. And, the deeper he went, the more Bethany felt that old urge to leave. It never rose to the level of a plan, though. More like a daydream. Sometimes, in this dream, she took the kids with her, throwing them into the car and simply driving off. ("Where to?" Peggy asked. "I don't know," she said. "We never arrive.") Other times, it was more like a fantasy, a handsome stranger pulls up on a motorcycle and she runs out and jumps on back, no helmet, leaving Asher and Leah behind with Shane, who, despite his radical religious bent, was a caring, thoughtful father, a reliable builder of tree forts and thrower of snowballs; shoot, he was even a decent cook, at least of things that could be grilled. He would do just fine (her fantasy-self justified) raising the kids alone.

"It's not like I'm really going to do it," she said to Peggy. "It's more like a reaction to this feeling I get, this claustrophobia."

But she'd never connected it to her father before.

"So, you're suggesting this all has something to do with . . . my dad?"

Oh, that patient smile on Peggy's face as she stared with unblinking eyes through those big fishbowl glasses. This was the other frustration of therapy, alongside the repetition, and the *how-did-it-make-you-feel*, Bethany sensing that Peggy was always trying to inch her toward some obvious realization. It reminded her of an old geology teacher in high school, who would slowly try to get students to say the word he was thinking of. ("Pre-? Come on folks. The age of early life? Describes most of Earth's history? Precam- Surely someone did the readings. Precambri-? Anyone?")

Bethany looked at the clock in the kitchen. Four minutes to four. "Can you just tell me, Peggy? We only have a few minutes left, the kids are going to come inside at any minute, and this seems important. I don't have time to guess."

Peggy laughed, one of her shoulders briefly disappearing into the blurred Zoom background. "Yes. Sorry. I just think it's interesting: you describe years of this same feeling, of wanting to escape, to run away, to disappear. And it seems like this might be connected to you pulling back from your father when you saw him in your house with a woman before your parents divorced. This father who you say is more like you than anyone. You saw something that day that wounded you, and for years, you kept it secret. You kept *his* secret. Meanwhile, when life gets difficult for your dad, what does he do? Disappears. Escapes. Like he did from you and your mother. Like he's done now, going to live off the grid in a farmhouse in the woods. Like you've always wanted to do. Maybe this behavior was modeled for you. Maybe the urge to run comes when these men remind you of your father. And maybe you and he have been running away from each other for twenty years."

Here was the final frustration of therapy. That when the answer came, it was so stupidly apparent. So easy to see. Right in front of her. She suspected that being a therapist was ultimately kind of boring—a bunch of transparent people showing up every day, like walking aquariums, sloshing around, complaining that they couldn't quite figure it out, but it felt like something was swimming around inside them.

And how does that make you feel?

It made Bethany feel like a small bomb had gone off in her head. She'd always assumed the fissure with her father had opened on Thanksgiving 2016, with the punch heard round the dinner table. But what if it had started years before that, the day she almost lost her virginity and saw her father with another woman.

Bethany had the craziest urge—to pack up the kids, nine-year-old Leah and five-year-old Asher, and drive ten hours north, in the middle of a global pandemic, to go see her father in the woods. To ask him if he saw her drive by with her drug-dealing wannabe boyfriend that day when she was fifteen. To ask who that woman was on the porch with him. To ask why he was so disappointed in her all the time. To ask how it felt to disappear from the lives of everyone who cared about you. Suddenly, she found herself wondering if her elusive, vexing, stubborn old man might be the key to her own restless heart.

On the screen of her laptop, the therapist Peggy leaned forward. "Can I ask what you're thinking right now, Bethany?"

"Oh, I guess I was thinking—" Bethany laughed. "Precambrian."

"Well," said Peggy, glancing down at her watch, "why don't we start there next time."

- - -

IT WAS EERIE, three days later, in that strange spring of 2020, to be driving on the highway with the kids, and see so few cars on the road. For weeks, she and Shane had talked about how odd it was to see no traffic in front of their house, and to have the sky free of airplanes and contrails. But to be totally alone on the highway? This was the strangest experience yet. Long-haul trucks were parked on the shoulders, as if their drivers had been snatched away by aliens. A lone sheriff's deputy stood on an overpass, hands in his pockets, watching her drive underneath. When she did see a car, every five miles or so, it felt almost like they were fellow survivors of some Apocalyptic disaster, Bethany thinking to herself, *Where could you be going?* just as the other driver must be asking themselves, *Where could you be going?*

Asher mostly slept in the back, in his booster seat. In the passenger seat, Leah stared out the window as they hurtled through the stark terrain of Central Oregon and Eastern Washington: dry canyons, craters, buttes, and the sudden sharp ledges of rocky foothills; abandoned gas stations, tumbledown barns and lonesome farms, miles and miles of wheat fields and soybean and onions, giant metallic windmills slowly turning in the breeze. It was all so desolate, so far removed from the lush, windward side of the Cascades. And then, suddenly, they came upon the Columbia, the massive dark river seeming to have pulled every drop of water from the surrounding plateaus, as it carved its way through all of this rock to the sea.

When Bethany had told Shane that she wanted to go to Spokane to see her mom and then drive up to see her dad—without him—he forbade it at first. As she always did when he tried to play his recently acquired *submit-yourself-to-your-husband-as-you-would-to-the-Lord* card, she laughed in his face. Then he gave her the pouty lip that signaled that his endlessly hurt feelings were once again hurt. "Is it because of what I said to your mom about the Wuhan flu?"

"No," she'd answered, but she thought, *Yes*. Celia loved Shane and wasn't put off by his loud opinions on *everything*; she knew that, beneath his born-again bluster, Shane Collins was a good man with a good heart. And a very good father. But, as a retired nurse, Bethany's mom had no patience for the way his weird conspiracy theories had spread to the coronavirus. ("Does he think three million doctors and nurses got together and just . . . made up a worldwide pandemic? For fun? Does he not know thousands and thousands of people are *dying*? That we're all just doing our best?")

She and the kids would be staying in the apartment above Cortland's garage, and only seeing her mom and her stepfather outside, staying six feet apart, and possibly even wearing masks in the yard. And since Shane had mocked the idea of masks and quarantine bubbles, and had continued hanging out with his buddies, making deliveries at work, going to church and to the gun range, she didn't feel comfortable having him around her frail, almost sixty-year-old mother and her seventy-five-year-old stepfather, even outside and six feet apart.

But it wasn't just that.

Bethany was also planning to go see her dad on this trip, and there was no way she was going to let Shane and Rhys near each other again. Especially in front of the kids.

It was windy and cool when they arrived at her mother's place. Instantly, it was harder than she'd thought it would be, staying this far apart. She ached to hug her rail-thin mom. It was almost easier to meet on-line than to have sweet Celia stand right in front of her and not be able to get any closer than this. They stood awkwardly in the backyard, the slate patio table between them, her mother asking the kids the kinds of questions you'd ask strangers' children. "Do you miss school? Do you miss your friends?"

"I wouldn't miss my friends if Mom would let me have a phone," Leah said.

"Not till you're fourteen," Bethany said.

"Right. When I will literally be the last person in my school with a phone."

"What about Saylor and Skye?" Asher asked. His sister spun around and glared at him, Asher's explanation to Grandma Celia wilting under Leah's glare: "They're twins and their parents are even more strict than . . . ours."

Cortland kept inviting them to come inside, and Celia kept putting a hand on his arm and reminding him: "Darling, people can't come in the house right now, remember? There's a new disease."

"Oh, yes. I saw that on the news. Have you heard about this, Bethany?"

"I have, Cort." Bethany made eye contact with her mother. "It's very scary." Poor old Cort. Poor old Celia.

The next day, she made sure the kids used the bathroom, and then they started driving north, toward her dad's place. No GPS, of course, she only had the directions Rhys had mailed her three and a half years earlier. Once they got out of the suburbs, the forest seemed to crowd the highway on both sides, then to back away again, the tree line moving in and out like a giant green and brown bellows. They passed farmhouses, taverns, gas stations, trailer parks. Signs pointed to dirt roads promising lakes named for animals (*Loon* and *Deer*) and who-knew-what (*Jump Off Joe Lake*)? Ten miles on this two-lane highway, twelve on that one, turn on this dirt road, cross that creek and turn left at the second drive, through the birch trees. Like a treasure hunt.

Finally, she eased up his dirt driveway and parked between the cinder block house and the outhouse.

"What if he's not home?" Leah asked.

"He's home," Bethany said. "Where's he gonna go?"

And sure enough, he came walking over from the barn—or what was left of it. He appeared to be taking the structure down, piling boards on that old 1950s flatbed truck. "Bethany?" He set a crowbar down on the truck bed, removed his work gloves, and made his way over.

She wasn't sure what she'd expected, but the man striding toward her looked more like her father than the anxious, strung-out Rhys who'd punched her husband and stormed off three and a half years earlier. The only other time she'd driven up here, the summer after he moved in, he was halfway to recluse—long hair and beard, disheveled, complaining about raccoons. But now he looked lean and muscled. Sharper. His salt-and-pepper hair had been recently cut and his beard was trimmed. But more than that, there was a clarity in his eyes that hadn't been there in the years before he left.

He wore a brown chore coat over work jeans and a faded Portland Trail Blazers T-shirt that she remembered him wearing back in the day. He tilted his head and squinted, almost as if he suspected he might be imagining them.

"What are you . . . Do you . . . do you want to come in? I . . . I don't have any . . ." He rubbed his hair. "I actually don't have much food at all. I have coffee and some pancake mix. Dried fruit. Smoked salmon. Some pasta. You caught me between supply runs."

"We can't come inside, anyway."

"You drive all the way up here and you can't come in?"

"No, Dad. There's a pandemic. We're supposed to be social distancing."

"Oh. Right." He put a hand to his head. "I keep forgetting. The woman who cuts my hair made me wear a mask. She was talking about it just the other day."

"Dad, everyone is talking about it. Everyone's wearing masks."

"Of course they are. Yes. I'm sorry."

How was it, Bethany thought, that the only two people who didn't seem to know that the entire world had been shut down were her father and stepfather? For a moment, she envied them both.

Kinnick started toward her, as if to give her a hug. "Is it . . . Can I . . ."

"We have to stay six feet apart." She pulled a mask from her pocket. "And I should probably wear this."

"Even outside?"

"I mean, no one knows for sure. But I don't want to be the one who gets you sick."

"Of course. Well, don't put that on. I'll keep my distance. But can I at least bring out some water for the kids? Or some . . . uh, dried fruit?"

Both kids looked at their mother. "That's okay," she answered for them. "We ate at Mom's." She nodded toward where he'd been work-ing. "Are you fixing your barn?"

"The barn?" Kinnick scratched his head, as if he'd forgotten what he was doing. "Oh." He turned to look. "No, I'm taking it down."

"Why?"

"Well, I found my grandpa's old landfill up here. Thirty years of garbage. Old car bodies. Metal and wood. He just threw everything in that hole. I dug it all out of the ground, hauled it off, and cleaned it up, planted some trees, and it just felt so good . . . I realized that's what I want to do with this place. Slowly return it to nature. Eventually leave no trace that anyone was ever here."

No trace. Sure. She couldn't say why this rankled her, but it did.

They walked to the little stream beyond his house, small-talking as they went. Leah and Asher tossed rocks into the water, trying to make the biggest splash, even though the creek was only a few inches deep.

Bethany kept glancing over at her dad. Unlike with her mother, it felt rather natural being six feet away from Rhys. When she was little, she attached herself to her father's hip the minute he got home from work. He'd tell stories about his job and ask her about the books she was reading. She loved seeing his byline in the newspaper. *By Rhys Kinnick. Staff Writer.* He'd light up when he read her middle school book reports and her English papers, as if they shared a secret language—which was . . . of course, language. She loved to write, and everyone said she would grow up to be *just like your father.* And then, as she'd explained to Peggy, in high school this chasm had begun opening between them, and eventually, she stopped saying she wanted to be a writer like her dad.

"How's the writing coming?" she asked. The other time she'd been up here, he'd admitted he was trying again. He had started keeping a journal of his progress in the woods, like Thoreau.

"Slowly," he said. "I guess I'm still mostly *preparing* to write? Reading a lot and making notes toward . . . well, toward something."

"Another book?"

He flinched at this. "I mean, I don't—yes? What makes something a book? You know . . . can I just bind two thousand pages together and pronounce it, 'Book!' I mean, there must be some inherent value to a thing outside its form, or its public recognition, right?" She had noticed this, too, the last time she came up here, the way her father seemed to be debating himself whenever he spoke. "Then again," he said, "maybe not."

"Did you say two thousand pages?" she asked.

"What's that?"

"You just said 'You can't bind two thousand pages and call it a book.' Have you written two thousand pages, Dad?"

"Are there fish in here?" Asher turned and asked.

"There were a *lot* of fish when I was a kid," Kinnick answered. "Little brook trout. About the size of your hand. Not anymore, I'm afraid."

"Where did they go?" Asher asked.

"Where indeed," said his grandfather. "People build houses in these hills, and dig new wells, and the groundwater eventually dries up. There isn't enough water for trout anymore. Or much of anything."

Bethany smiled to herself. That was not the way you answered the question of a five-year-old. You said something like, *They went to another stream*, or, *They swam to the ocean and turned into salmon*, or, *They went to fish heaven*.

"What grades are you two in now?" Kinnick asked the kids. This question got under Bethany's skin, too. *Does he really not know?*

"Kindergarten," Asher said.

"Fourth," said Leah.

And they went back to throwing rocks.

"What are your favorite subjects?"

"English," Leah said.

"Rocks," said Asher.

And they went back to throwing rocks.

"Good subjects," Rhys said.

Until that moment, Bethany had been looking for a way to bring up the reason for her visit, the breakthrough she'd had with her therapist, and how the frost between Bethany and Rhys maybe hadn't started four years ago, but almost twenty, when she'd seen him at the house with that woman. And to ask him: Did you see me? And do you know where it comes from, this desire we both seem to have to escape? Is it genetic? Are we running from each other? And how does it feel—to actually *do it*?

But now, she wondered, what would be the point of any of it? This man didn't even know what grades her kids were in. He hoped to leave no trace of himself, including, she supposed, his people. *That* was the answer to her question.

Rhys Kinnick was the personification of selfishness.

"Did you see my solar panels when you drove up?" Kinnick asked.

"No," she said, "I guess I didn't."

They turned back, and he pointed out a single row of heavy, shiny panels mounted on the tin roof of the old house. "Turns out it's not too hard to put them on a tin roof, even with that kind of pitch."

"Is that right?"

"Yeah. The electrical part was tricky, though, as you might guess. There's a guy who lives up in Ford, this friend of mine, Brian, he was an electrical systems specialist in the air force. He's been helping me. It's easy enough to generate electricity, especially in summer. Storing it is the real challenge."

"Is that so?"

"Yes." And he went on for another five minutes like this, about marine batteries and inverters and about how the real trick wasn't adding more power, but finding ways to have the power on demand, to only use it when you needed it. "I mean a refrigerator, that's your biggest usage right there."

As he spoke, Asher came over and took Bethany's hand. "Mom. Can we go now?"

"Pretty soon," she said.

Kinnick looked down at the boy, then at Bethany. "I'm sorry. I'm droning on about usage rates. I'm out of practice talking to people. I haven't even asked, How are *you*? How's work going? Are you at the same school?"

"I am." She had been teaching part-time, English and civics, at a little Christian school in Grants Pass, where the kids went. "Well," she said, "we're not in school now, obviously. A lot of parents are starting to get upset about that."

"Oh, right," Kinnick said. "I keep forgetting. The . . . what's the disease called again?"

"Coronavirus. Covid-19."

"Right. Right. And Shane? How's he doing?"

She could hear Rhys trying to sound neutral in asking about her husband. "He's good," she said. "He's driving a truck that delivers food to stores and restaurants. He's what they call an essential worker. He sends his best."

Kinnick chewed his bottom lip. "I think I told you the last time you were here, but I want to say it again: I regret my part in that. It's one of the things I think I'm trying to overcome. My temper. My reactiveness."

I regret my part in that? It was like a politician's statement. He comes to dinner at her house, calls her husband an idiot, punches him in the face, and then drives away forever—and half-apologizes . . . for his *reactiveness?* What did that even mean? She pictured Peggy again. *And how does that make you feel?* Bethany fumed. She needed to get out of there. To escape her father's escape.

"When?" Asher was back at her side.

Bethany looked down. "What's that, honey?"

"You said 'pretty soon.' I was just wondering when. Ten minutes or . . . twenty minutes or . . ."

"Fourteen," she answered. Asher nodded and went back to throwing rocks.

Bethany smiled. "Asher hates imprecision."

"I see that. They both seem . . . well, they seem like great kids. Smart. And so cute. They're . . . well, it's just . . . I think . . . you've done a great . . . you seem like a great parent, Bethany—I mean, of course you are."

"Thanks, Dad." Even when he stammered something nice, it stung. *She* seemed *like a great parent?* She could see the strain on Kinnick's face, trying to figure out what to say, how to say it. "Have you thought about coming back?" she asked finally.

"Coming back?"

"Yeah. Into civilization?" She smiled. "What's left of it."

He ran his hand through his hair. "I feel like I'm not quite done here. Like I'm close to . . . well, figuring something out . . . some kind of . . . I don't know what to call it. Conclusion?" He shook his head. "No, that's not right. It's like Sartre wrote: 'Appearance doesn't hide essence but reveals it.' Feels like that's what I'm getting close to. The *appearance* of something . . ." It was clear he didn't want to say the next word aloud, but he finally did: "profound."

She thought again about the questions she'd come to ask him. "Can I ask . . . what is it?"

He laughed, knit his brow and narrowed his eyes. "Well, the whole tradition of Western thought and philosophy is steeped in humanism, right? Pythagoras, Aristotle, Marcus Aurelius. Even something like the Upanishads. Watts, Sun Tzu, ethics, art theory, Sontag, nineteenth-century economics—it all proceeds from the human mind, deals first with human experience. But naturalism, environmental philosophy, which put us on a neutral footing with the world around us, these are barely fifty years old. So, what I've been thinking is . . . what if you went back over thousands of years of philosophical history from this new vantage, trading human experience for environmental ethics. Which ideas continue to make sense? And from that, can we make a new kind of metaphysical map of the world. Something we could chart, orient on a globe. What if you could write it like an outdoor field guild or a topographical map. A sort of . . . revised *Atlas of Wisdom*."

For just a moment, she found herself listening to the father she'd loved at twelve, the father she couldn't wait to see walk through the door at night, whose newspaper byline she would run her hand over, desperate to understand what he'd written the day before . . . about dam removal, or wolf populations, or nuclear waste . . . stories that were never quite as interesting as the versions he told her when he got home, the father who didn't talk to her like she was a little girl—the way her mom did, the way her teachers did—but who would talk about forestry policy needing to evolve past Muir, or who might randomly quote Sartre or try putting abstract theories into an *Atlas of Wisdom*.

But then, she became a teenager and began to see this other, reclusive father—moody, selfish, aloof, depressed—right around the time they drifted apart. She blamed him when her parents split, even though they insisted it was a mutual decision, and even though Celia went off and married Cortland, like, an hour later.

It was also when she was a teenager that Bethany began to sense

Rhys Kinnick's profound disappointment in *her*—his face betraying it, as if he hated every single choice she'd ever made. He bad-mouthed the guys she brought home, especially Doug and Shane (both of whom reminded her of her father), and he scoffed and rolled his eyes at the cars she drove and the classes she took and the apartments she lived in, as if she were constantly letting him down with her bad judgment, as if she had failed to live up to her twelve-year-old promise. (*And worst of all, what if he was right to be disappointed?*) Even now, she wondered what he saw when he looked at her. Instead of becoming a writer like him, contemplating "metaphysical world maps," she was *just* a part-time teacher, *just* a frumpy housewife with two kids whose ages Rhys couldn't bother to remember, *just* a nearly middle-aged woman with questionable taste in men (as if all of them had lined up and she'd merely had to point out the ones she'd wanted).

No, this social distancing was nothing new; she and her father had been at least six feet apart for twenty years. And whatever insight Bethany might have gleaned by coming to see the man now, whatever key he held to her own mysterious heart, she had the sense, seeing him like this, that her idea of *disappearance* was an illusion.

Maybe that's what Peggy had wanted her to see, the ultimate hollowness of the man standing before her, and the empty promise of her own vision of escape.

Perhaps this character flaw was exactly what she'd seen in her father back when she was a teen. Rhys Kinnick was like the math concept she'd recently helped Leah with—a negative equation. *If the signs are different*, as she'd told Leah, *the answer is always negative.* The signs between Bethany and Rhys would always be different. The answer was always going to be negative.

"Four minutes," Asher said. He held up the red digital wristwatch he'd proudly bought with his Christmas money last year. "It's been ten minutes so far."

"Okay, Ash," Bethany said. "Thanks for keeping track." And that, ultimately, was why she could never do what self-absorbed Rhys Kinnick had done.

She could never turn her back on her children the way he had turned his back on his child. On her. Bethany said to her father: "Looks like we have only four minutes."

"So soon?" He seemed a little panicky.

"Afraid so," she said.

"But you'll come back?"

"Sure."

"I'd like that," he said sheepishly.

Asher came over with a saltshaker-size hunk of basalt. "Can I have this?"

"Of course you can," Kinnick said. "Leah, do you want a rock?"

She looked at him like he might be insane. "We have them at home."

Her father smiled at Bethany. "That sounded exactly like you."

Bethany felt her face flush as she walked the kids toward the car. Leah got in front and pulled her seat belt across her lap. Asher climbed into his booster seat in the back, and Bethany leaned in and buckled him.

When she straightened back up, Kinnick flinched, as if he were about to come in for a hug, but suddenly remembered the pandemic, and stayed back.

She smiled, said, "Well," and got in the driver's seat.

Before she could close the door, he crouched down, careful to stay six feet away. "Bye, kids."

"Bye."

"Thanks for the rock."

"You bet. Come back for more. I've got plenty."

Bethany reached for the door handle but at the last second, turned to her father. "Can I ask you a question?"

"Of course."

"When I was fifteen, I skipped school one day."

"Well, that's okay," he said.

"No, I know." She laughed. "It's just, as we drove back to school, I saw you standing on the porch, and . . . I wondered if you saw me, too."

He stared at her blankly. "Jeez . . . I don't . . . I don't remember that. When did you say this was?"

"It's okay." She smiled. "Don't worry about it. Bye, Dad."

"Goodbye, Bethany," he said. "I love you."

"Love you, too."

Also true, that. Of course. And that is what stung so much. She closed her door, started the car, and drove away, watching him shrink in the rearview mirror, standing in the middle of his driveway with his hands in the pockets of his brown suede jacket. At the end of his driveway, she turned, and when she looked once more in the mirror, he was gone.

- - -

KINNICK STARED OUT the window, pine trees blurring to green and brown bands, like a dull Rothko painting. Brian drove them deeper into the woods, ever closer, Kinnick hoped, to finding his daughter. They had somehow missed the turnoff the first time and were doubling back on this empty two-lane highway.

They'd woken up that morning—Kinnick on Brian's couch, the kids in sleeping bags on the floor. After breakfast, he and Brian had climbed in his Bronco, stopped at Rhys's house to get his passport, then started out for the border, leaving the kids with Joanie. They crossed into Canada above Metaline Falls, drove north and west, passing through pristine forest alongside a series of rivers and streams, past farms and ranches, quaint little towns. And now, according to the vague directions they'd gotten from a gas station attendant in Montrose, they were getting close to Paititi.

Apparently for the second time, since they'd driven past it once.

"I don't see how you missed it the first time," Brian said.

"How *I* missed it?" Rhys was tired of being a passenger in his own misadventures—first with the boxing priest, then Lucy, then Crazy Ass Chuck, and now with his old friend, Brian. When this was all over, when he'd gotten Bethany back to her kids, Kinnick was going to cash out the rest of his sad, little newspaper pension and make two quick purchases: a cell phone and a reliable car.

They drove slowly down a narrow, tree-lined corridor, passing no houses at all, only solitary roadside mailboxes every mile or so, until—

"There it is!" Kinnick said. A hand-painted sign nailed to a tree read: PAITITI. An arrow pointed down a narrow dirt road.

"That's it?" Brian asked.

"I guess so."

Brian looked briefly at his phone again. "No GPS. How does anyone find this place?"

"I suppose that's the attraction," Kinnick said.

"Who's playing anyway?" Brian asked.

"What?"

"At the Pie-Whatever Music Festival? Anybody I've heard of?"

"Let's see. Steely Dan. Elvis. Mozart."

"Good plan: be a dick to the one person willing to help you."

"First of all," Kinnick said, "how would I know *who* you've heard of, especially when the newest band I've ever heard you play is Styx? Second, this is an electronica festival. Do you listen to a lot of electronica, Brian? And third, I have no idea who is playing other than Sluggish Doug and whatever half-assed band he's in now."

"Well. Forgive me for asking a question."

Kinnick sighed. "Sorry. This whole thing has me feeling stupid. But I'll stop taking it out on you."

"I get it," Brian said. "It's stressful shit. If my daughter ran off to some greasy hippie festival, I'd be in a mood, too."

This is what Leah had told Kinnick: her mother had come to her bedside on the morning she left, and whispered a secret: that Leah's father, Doug, was in a new band, The Boofs, and, according to what Bethany told Leah, The Boofs were playing at an outdoor music festival in Canada this week and—this was the part Bethany was most excited about—The Boofs were performing two songs that she'd written years ago. Bethany was going to "take a little vacation" to go hear her songs played live. Kinnick had forgotten that Bethany once wrote songs with Doug. In fact, it was how they'd met, as he recalled, at an all-night coffee shop in Olympia where Doug was playing guitar and Bethany was writing in a journal. The classic failed poet meets failed musician failed love story.

Bethany had once shown Kinnick a song she'd written, a protest anthem about the Iraq War. To his shame now, Rhys had landed somewhere between confused and dismissive as he read his daughter's lyrics. But his response wasn't so much about the song (all he could remember was a single rhyme: *armed forces* and *remorseless*) as it was her writing songs (wasting her talent!) with this perpetually stoned simpleton with blond dreadlocks and sleeved tattoos who smelled like he slept in a drainage ditch. And now, apparently, Sluggish Doug was playing in an acid electronica outfit called . . . The Boofs.

"You do know what that is, right?" the gas station attendant who gave the directions had asked Kinnick. "Boofing?"

"No," Kinnick said, warily. "What is it?"

"Yeah, I'm not gonna say."

"It's a drug thing, isn't it?" Kinnick had asked the gas station kid.

"Oh, yeah," the kid said.

He explained that the Paititi Festival was as much about the drugs as it was the music, that it was held in a clearing abutting provincial forest land, and that if Brian and Rhys just drove twenty-five or thirty miles back up the road they came in on—indicating with the dipped bill of his ball cap—they would pass a little finger lake, then, maybe a mile

later, they'd see a sign pointing into the woods, and if they turned up
that road "you practically can't miss it." He leaned forward to confide.
"It's a cold, muddy, stinky mess up there this time of year, though,
yeah? Way too early for this kind of thing . . . they say it's something
about planting versus harvesting, I don't know, it's beyond me."

Sure enough, past the PAITITI sign, two dirt tracks curled into the
forest, and it wasn't long before Kinnick and Brian began seeing vehicles parked alongside this makeshift road: vans and microbuses in
turnouts and switchbacks, all manner of dented car and old motorcycle, anywhere you could wedge a vehicle, there *was* one, until, finally,
they came to a clearing with more orderly rows of vehicles and a huge
banner hung between two trees that read: PAITITI! And another sign:
VIBES AHEAD.

The clearing beyond the parking lot was surrounded by a high fence
and filled with tents and makeshift structures, banners and flags.
Everywhere, there were young people, some dirty and feral-looking,
like survivors of a natural disaster, others in elaborate makeshift
costumes—furry onesies, tall hats and feather boas, rainbows, headdresses.
Lots of lank, greasy hair.

"God, I hate hippies," Brian said.

"I know you do." Kinnick patted his friend's arm. Growing up on
the reservation, Brian had put up with all manner of pale, communal,
new age, moccasin-wearing Geronimo-come-lately weirdos moving
into the woods, asking for strong medicine and advice on building
sweat lodges and digging camas roots, seeking corny tribal brother-
hood from people who actually belonged to tribes. But worse than
that, Kinnick knew, Brian's second wife had been a hippie who had left
him for her Vinyasa yoga instructor.

"This isn't going to be easy for you," Kinnick said. "I can find her by
myself, you know. You can just wait in the car."

"No," Brian said, "I've come this far. I need to face the patchouli."
He parked the Bronco at the edge of the fence surrounding the festival,

alongside an old army tent with a hand-painted rainbow sign that read: RUSHROOM RIDES AND OTHER AWESOME GUIDED TRIPS. He and Kinnick climbed out.

A bearded white guy, probably thirty, came out of the tent holding a long-stemmed pipe. "I'm afraid you can't park here." He wore a homburg hat whose brim was trimmed with ball fringe, an open yellow shirt with at least ten necklaces and beads layered on his chest, jodhpurs tucked into high boots, fingerless gloves, and an intricately beaded fanny pack that announced him as JEFE.

"What are you the chief of?" Brian asked. "Police?"

"Sorry. Didn't catch that reference, I'm afraid." He spoke with a slight affectation, as if he'd spent a week at a British boarding school.

"Your fanny pack. It says you're the *JEFE*."

He looked down and the affectation disappeared briefly. "Oh. No, I'm Jeff." He brushed some stems off the fanny pack and sure enough, the JEFE became simply JEFF. "But truly, you can't park here." He pointed down the road, the way they'd come. "Parking is limited to the full lot you see before you"—he nodded with his head, the fringe balls on his hat shaking—"and back yonder, along incoming road."

"We won't be here long," Kinnick said. "I just need to find my daughter. It's kind of an emergency. It's her kids."

He felt bad making it sound like Bethany's children were hurt, or in immediate danger. They were safe and sound with Joanie in the trailer back in Ford, filling up on maple cookies and hot chocolate, Asher no doubt grilling Joanie about Native Americans while the increasingly quiet Leah kept her own adolescent counsel, seeming more and more like the teenaged Bethany of his memory.

Jefe Jeff was still staring at Brian's Bronco, parked in front of his RUSHROOM RIDES sign. "I'm really not trying to be difficult, but you absolutely need tribal approval to park here."

"And what tribe is that?" Brian asked. He was already getting agitated.

"Right," Jeff said, "the Paititi Tribal Council." He pointed. "Thataway."

"I have a cousin on the Spokane Tribal Council," said Brian. "Does that count?"

Looking to keep Brian from getting too worked up, Kinnick cleared his throat. "Do you happen to know where the bands might be staying?"

"There is another campground, near the stages, up the hill." Jeff pointed through the festival grounds. "Some of the musicians stay up there."

"What are 'rushrooms,' anyway?" Brian asked.

Jeff leaned in and confided, his faint accent disappearing again. "Oh, it's just regular psilocybin, man," he said. "I got the name from *Legend of Zelda*. I thought it sounded cool. I'm a guide. You know? For trips? Acid. Shrooms. Whatever you want."

"Do you happen to know where I might find The Boofs?" Kinnick asked.

Jeff scrunched up one eye. "Yeah, I would not do that if I were you. Not at your age."

"Do what?"

"Boof. But if you do, there are a couple of things you really need to remember." He looked from Kinnick to Brian and back. "First, do *not* share straws. And second, whatever you do, do not reverse the straw. That thing only goes in one way."

"No," Kinnick said. "The Boofs is the name of the band I'm looking for. It's my daughter's old boyfriend's band."

"Oh, oh! I see," Jeff said. "Clever."

Kinnick didn't want to ask the next question, but he knew he had to. "But you might as well tell me, so I stop making an ass of myself—what is it?"

"Boofing? Ah, yes." Jeff laughed. "Ass of yourself, indeed. Well, it's having someone blow drugs, usually ketamine or molly water, straight up your butthole."

"Of course it is." Brian had to turn away, every preconception confirmed.

"The kids are quite into it," Jeff said, as if he and Kinnick and Brian were suddenly a group of wizened old peers. "Supposedly it gives you a faster, more direct high." Again, with the confiding, nonaffected voice. "But between you and me . . . the day I resort to blowing drugs up my shitter to get off? Well—" He put his hands out, as if—enough said. "But as I am unfamiliar with the particular band of which you speak, perhaps you could go ask the Inkarri. I'm sure he can tell you where to find these Boofs of yours."

"The—" Kinnick wasn't sure what he'd just heard.

"Inkarri? He's like the unofficial mayor of the festival. He's named for the last leader of the Incas. The real Inkarri's body was cut up by the Spaniards and spread out for miles, but legend has it that his body will reform itself one day and lead the people to a new paradise."

"Which is . . ." Kinnick screwed up his face. "An electronica festival?"

Jeff laughed. "I guess. Here at Paititi, we choose an honorary Inkarri on the first day, and he's in charge of the *Pachamama*, the grounds, and he runs the *Runakuna*, the tribal council, in *Cusco*. *Paititi* being the last paradise of the Incas."

"You *do* know you're in Canada, right?" Brian said. "Not Peru."

"Hey." Jeff held his hands up. "I'm just a humble shroom salesman at the beginning of festival season. I don't make up the bullshit, I just ride it."

Brian seemed to be warming to Jefe Jeff. He nodded at Jeff's Rushroom tent. "Don't suppose you sell beer in there, too?"

"Regrettably, this is an alcohol-free festival."

"Wait. So, you can blow hard drugs up your ass, but you can't buy a Bud Light?"

This may have been the funniest thing Jefe Jeff had ever heard. "Ha! Right? I never thought of it that way." He held out a fist, Brian shrugging to Kinnick before bumping it.

"Hold on a minute," Jeff said. He went inside his tent and returned wearing reading glasses, staring at a concert bill and carrying two lanyards. "You don't mean The Buffs, do you?" He pointed to one of the smaller names on the bill.

"Maybe?"

"I haven't heard them play, but"—Jeff glanced at his tent—"the guide business is a little slow right now, and since The Buffs are playing on the Tonatiuh Stage in about"—he checked an expensive-looking silver watch—"forty minutes, come on, I'll take you up there."

- - -

BETHANY SAT UP in her sleeping bag, breathless and cold. The awful prickly feeling was back, along with the shakes, the tightness in her chest, the twitching, and the sensation that she might, at any moment, rattle right out of her skin. What had she been thinking? Leaving the kids and running off to a music festival in the woods with her ex-boyfriend? Did she really think *this* would solve anything? Make her feel less anxious? Less depressed? It was like treating a burn by setting fire to it. She'd been having these panic attacks on and off since her mother died, more than a month ago. She'd lost her therapist when she'd quit her teaching job and her insurance went away, and now she wasn't sure what to do. When the attacks came on, the anxiety was like this wall she couldn't see around. And, as it turned out, panic attacks were not something you could just run away from by going off into the woods.

She put her head between her knees and tried to breathe. In deeply—hold. Out slowly. Hold. (Breathe in a square, Peggy used to say.) But then another wave of panic ran through her chest and arms. *My God!* She covered her mouth to keep from crying out.

"Hey, B." Doug's round face slid into the tent opening. "You get some sleep?"

Bethany looked up from between her knees, glad to have him here. "It's happening again." Her voice sounded weak and raspy to her own ears.

"Oh, B, I'm sorry." He came a little farther into the tent, and reached out a hand, but didn't get any closer. She still wasn't used to seeing Doug like this; her once 125-pound, dreadlocked wispy blond boyfriend was a middle-aged 200-pound bald man now. Still those same kind eyes. "Maybe we should get you to a hospital."

"No. I'll be fine." She checked her watch. "Aren't you supposed to be onstage?"

"Pretty soon, yeah," Doug said. "We just set up. I wanted to make sure you were okay before we went on."

Amid all of this—her mom's death, Shane's new church, the trouble at home, the rattly feelings, the waves of panic, her lack of sleep and resulting questionable decision-making, this insane music festival— Bethany really appreciated how caring Doug had been with her. And how respectful.

Four days ago, sleepless and jacked up on coffee and adrenaline, she'd crouched next to Leah's bed, waking her daughter at six thirty in the morning. Shane had left at dawn to go train for the coming holy war with his yahoo friends up at the Rampart, and Bethany whispered to Leah that she was going away for a few days, to Canada, to hear some songs she'd written played by her father's band, and to not tell anyone. ("It's not a lie if no one asks.") There was a week's worth of lunches in the refrigerator, and reading assignments in their desks, oh, and should Shane go after her, there was a note for Anna in Leah's snow boot about where to take the kids. Then she kissed her daughter, told her to go back to sleep, left a short note for Shane ("I need some space. Please don't come look for me."), grabbed her passport and her packed duffel bag, and ran out the door, to where Doug was parked across the street, waiting in his father's old 1972 Firebird, which he'd lovingly and half-assedly restored. She climbed in, and off they flew, toward the Canadian border. The ride was beautiful—warm spring day, windows half down, air rushing in, old cassette tapes playing Traffic and Violent Femmes on Doug's car stereo. She felt an unburdening. They high-fived when they crossed the Canadian border, and high-fived again when they lost their phone signals for good. During the last part of the trip, she had put her hand out the car window, and let the rushing air move it like an airplane, the way she had when she was a kid.

That first night, they'd set up their tent near the other early settlers, in the area reserved for bands and their crews, and she'd continued to feel that open-car-window sense of freedom, pure elation. She smoked pot for the first time in a decade, out of a pipe shaped like a little Volkswagen Beetle—just a quick toke, to remind herself of the feel in her throat, and to send the signal that she wasn't trapped by Shane's reactionary rules anymore. She let the woman in the tent next door, a big gust of hippie life who called herself Mama Killa ("Goddess of the moon, my love," Mama said), paint crescent moons on both of her cheeks, and she reveled in the other weirdos that gathered around the campfire Doug had built for them (although Bethany insisted on the "straight" marshmallows for her s'mores, not the far more popular marsh*mellows* that had been soaked in liquified marijuana). It was a magical night, guitarists taking turns playing while the stars blazed insistently above them, and a cool mountain breeze sent them under-blanket, and she managed to keep her guilt at bay, cuddled with Doug on one side and fleshy Mama Killa on the other, all of them giggling as they watched the fire. That night, with their sleeping bags next to each other, she'd even let Doug kiss her a little bit—

And that's when the first panic attack had set in.

What was she doing up here? This was not who she was anymore. How would she feel if Leah did something like this? She started weeping, gasping for breath.

Doug sat up. "Are you okay, B?"

She made him promise not to give her any more drugs.

"I did *not* give you drugs," Doug protested. "You smoked on your own!"

"No, I know! I just . . . I can't do that again. And this . . ." She gestured to their sleeping bags. "I don't think I want to do this. I don't . . . I don't know." She started crying. "I'm sorry, Doug, but— I just— I—" She didn't finish.

He put his hand on her forehead. "B, you have nothing to be sorry for. And I would never pressure you into anything. I hope you know that." She *did* know that and she calmed down and eventually fell asleep, humming like a mantra the thing she'd been telling herself since she left: *The kids are okay, the kids are okay.* True to his word, since that first night, Doug had not so much as tried to kiss her. And he'd worked to keep drugs *away* from her, no small feat at a festival where LSD, ketamine, ecstasy, and psilocybin were known as "the four food groups."

Doug handed her a bottle of water now.

"Thanks," she said. "You should go. I'll be right behind you."

"When you're ready, walk up to that side-stage area again. Remember it from yesterday?"

"Yes."

"You got your backstage pass?"

She held it up for him to see.

"Cool. Hey, we're playing 'Don't Be Misled' right before our encore."

"Are you really?"

He did his deep DJ voice: "The boys say it's a banger, B."

She laughed. "Go ahead, Doug. I'll be right there."

He left the tent. She climbed out of her bag in her yoga pants and a sweatshirt and switched off the little battery-powered space heater, which sat beneath a metal table between their two sleeping bags. The Paititi Festival, as she'd learned, was held from the end of April to the beginning of May to mark the first Incan harvesting festival, *Aymoray qu.*

But British Columbia in the spring was damp and cold, a fair description of how she'd felt the last few days. Sometimes she couldn't tell when she was shivering from the wet air and when she was shaking from anxiety and lack of sleep. Of course, it was ridiculous, holding a six-hundred-year-old South American harvest festival in the woods of Canada. But the utter strangeness had caused her to reflect on her own life; was it any more random than her family being in the thralls of a repurposed, overly literal, two-thousand-year-old offshoot of an ancient Middle Eastern religion? Before Shane's frog-in-hot-water conversion, faith had been personal to her—a voice in her head that seemed to come from somewhere outside her being, offering her a sense of purpose, a chance to experience something *more*, something communal and quiet, a peaceful path out of the self, out of drugs and alcohol, away from the loneliness and insecurity of her younger years. When she had gone to some Narcotics Anonymous meetings—her mother's idea—Bethany found she took comfort in Celia's chill Unitarian beliefs, and even in Shane's wide-eyed Christian enthusiasm.

But this path that Shane was on now—which had eventually led him to the Church of the Blessed Fire and the Army of the Lord— there was nothing quiet about that. And certainly not peaceful. He had become obsessed with the end-times—Pastor Gallen describing his church as "a quivering bride awaiting the return of our King." It changed Shane, this mixture of paranoid masculinity and Apocalyptic Christian absolutism: a dark communion of fear and testosterone. But, if she were being honest, it wasn't *just* Shane's involvement with this church that had her wanting to run away with the circus. And it might not even have been her mother's death (although that was the thing that had unmoored her). It was something older, something deeper.

She put on her coat, hat, and gloves and ventured out of the tent.

Every time she went outside at Paititi, it reminded her of the scene in *The Wizard of Oz* where Dorothy comes out of the black-and-white house into a bizarre world of color. She wondered what Leah would name some of these new hues: *sunburned butt-cheek*; *beach-ball-in-mud-puddle*. There were bright, angular tents and small geodesic domes, rainbow flags and tie-dyed banners and Indian blankets, signs advertising vegan tacos, fresh fruit, and energy drinks, body-painted dancers floating by like ghosts. She weaved through, tripping briefly on a tent rope but catching herself. It was nice to be out in the sun, her panic dispersing. (*The kids are okay, the kids are okay.*) She joined a line of people walking the path toward the Day Stage, *Tonatiuh*, named for the Incan god of the sun. (She was glad The Buffs were playing here, although it meant they were a minor band. She couldn't even pronounce the name of the larger, nighttime main stage.) Along the trail, a dozen people were standing in front of a half-naked woman live-painting something abstract on a huge canvas. Bethany had seen more than a few furries at this festival—people dressed in fuzzy animal onesies—perhaps because of the cold weather. But there were just as many people in shorts and open shirts, in tank tops and halter tops and bikini tops. For the life of her, Bethany couldn't understand how these kids could dress this way in the cold, wet woods. It made her wonder at the power of the drugs they had now.

Yes, the drugs. She was fifteen years past her festival-going, chemical-ingesting prime, and she had decided she didn't want to slip back. After her single Beetle-toke the first night, she'd only been tempted once, during an anxiety attack on their second day, when Doug was off meeting with the festival organizers and Mama Killa heard her weeping and gasping for air, came inside her tent, and opened her hand to reveal a round pink pill with a heart in the center.

"What is it?"

"It's comfort, darlin'." Mama Killa was all comfort herself, in a soft, fuzzy sweater over a patterned corduroy dress, purple leggings and red boots, feather earrings dangling from her big lobes.

"Yeah, but . . . what is it?"

"It's peace, my love. And sleep."

Oh, that little heart. It looked like the Valentine's candy she used to give Asher and Leah, before Shane informed her, via a pastor he'd met in Baker City, that Saint Valentine's Day had evolved from a pagan Roman fertility ritual, and that nowhere in the Bible was the celebration of such saints condoned—just one of the reasons Catholics were hell-bound.

"What is it?" Bethany asked the big, comforting Mama Killa again.

"Just a little ketamine. It'll calm you down, child."

Child. She pictured her own then, Asher and Leah (*The kids are okay, the kids are okay*), and she thought, *As long as I don't take this pill, as long as I don't sleep with Doug, as long as I don't fall into this life again, I can still go back, if I choose to.*

"I can't take that," she said to Mama, who smiled, threw the pill into her own mouth, and pulled Bethany into her big, comforting chest. She held her tightly, rocking back and forth. "It's okay, darlin'. It's okay, love." (Bethany, relaxing into the woman's flesh, pictured her own frail mother, and thought, *That is the drug I want.*)

The line of people slowed as they approached the Tonatiuh Stage, where apologetic security guards did a cursory check of badges, tickets, fanny packs, and backpacks and the crowd passed through a gate beneath a massive black *Chakana*, an Incan cross. Bethany showed her backstage pass and was directed down a different path, between crowd-control panels ribbed with steel posts, like lines of bike racks, all the way to a small, fenced-off grassy area at the side of the stage, where other musicians, girlfriends, roadies, and hangers-on sat on blankets and in folding chairs.

Onstage, a bearded man, bare-chested, in leather leggings, with a red Batman mask painted on his face, hands in his back pockets, was imploring the crowd to adhere to posted quiet times, to follow recycling rules, and to report overdoses to the medical tent. "And with that," he said, "my friends, lovers, soon-to-be lovers, fellow worshippers at the altar of joy and togetherness . . . please help me welcome . . . The Boofs."

Doug had explained to her that while the band was *spelled* The Buffs—three of the four members had met at the University of Colorado, home of the Buffaloes—they had gained fans by jokingly pronouncing it "boofs" at one of these outdoor electronica festivals, a winking nod to the stoned-off-their-asses fans who had begun downloading their songs. "Or, stoned *in* their asses," Doug said. And since then, it had stuck. "The name, that is."

At forty, Doug was almost fifteen years older than his bandmates. He'd given bass lessons to one of the Colorado kids soon after The Buffs moved to Portland, and he was invited to join the band after he introduced them to a hobby of his, tweaking an old Roland TB-303 bass synthesizer, queering its accent to make a bassline that was both pleasingly poppy and edgy at the same time, a sound that he said was a throwback to 1980s techno, as well as old acid house, German Trance, and Belgian rave music. Then, in a real stroke of brilliance, he slowed that beat down, achieving what he called "a funky-folky, minimal, Flemish EDM-on-Prozac vibe."

"Ooo-kay," Bethany said, not understanding a word beyond 1980s.

But here was the thing. She *liked* The Buffs! Their music was the only thing that had calmed her these last few days. The other bands all sounded the same to her—one song bleeding into the next, and she grew edgy listening to their monotonous, robotic beats. But The Buffs' rhythms were slower, chiller, funkier, folkier, more hypnotic, and when the singer chimed in, he brought an ethereal quality that slowed her pulse. Maybe, in that hesitant, faux-futuristic bassline that Doug was setting, she could hear the shadow of his old music, too, the sweet, hopeful, acoustic songs he'd played her during their five years together. The rest of the band was equally tight, and the airy, wispy singer brought it all together, though Bethany feared he might just get blown off the stage by a gust of wind, like a tumbleweed. Still, she was proud of Doug, who had somehow gone from *eternal child* to *band grown-up*, donating his van to schlep their instruments, managing their "finances," and continuously warning the youngsters away from harder drugs. (Doug had suffered a respiratory illness that a doctor flagged as a precursor to more serious health problems, and was mostly just a weed guy now, with an occasional cup of ayahuasca tea.)

The band sauntered out, picked up their instruments, made eye contact, nodded heads, and started playing, the three young kids front and center, Doug off by himself on his little rhythm island, with his bass and his synth equipment. The music immediately washed over Bethany, and she started to feel better. One thing she liked about The Buffs was that they broke between songs; so many of the other bands turned their whole set into a kind of time-dilated techno-medley. Bethany sat on a folding chair in this side-stage area, closing her eyes, bouncing her head, tapping her foot. Just over the fence line that separated her from the crowd, people danced in every imaginable way, so long as one's imagination tended toward the Grateful Dead: whirling dervishes and people reaching for invisible ropes, women spinning sundresses over leggings and men bopping their bearded heads like chickens eating scratch. A row of people spun Hula-Hoops around bare waists. Few of them seemed to have found the actual beat, but their awkwardness was charming. As strange as it was to find herself here, Bethany appreciated how the festival felt mostly judgment-free. You come as the rhythm-challenged reincarnation of a Mesoamerican shaman; I will dress as a dancing racoon. You paint your body head to toe; I will leave my children for a few days to go hide out in a tent and cry myself to sleep.

And still, Bethany felt separated from it all. Older, soberer, she felt like exactly what she was: a runaway housewife who'd left her kids with her severely religious husband, or—if Shane tried to find her, as she doubted he would do—had sent her kids to stay with her cranky, old, reclusive father in the woods. She smiled imagining that unlikely scenario, her distracted dad, who hadn't even known the ages of his grandkids the last time he saw them, stuck with the nonstop-interrogating Asher and the ever-moody Leah.

But this thought stopped her cold. *Wait, what day is it?* If Anna *did* bring the kids to her dad's place, would Leah have remembered to bring pads with her? If there was one thing her dad would not have on his crappy little ranch, it would be menstrual products. So far, Leah's early periods had been as irregular as Bethany's had been when she was thirteen. Suddenly, Bethany was filled with guilt again (*The kids are okay, the kids are*—) just as another Buffs' song rose into misty crescendo, and the refrain playing inside her head became: *What in the world have I done?*

The last half year had been so trying, for so many reasons—the move to Spokane, Celia's illness and death, Bethany's inability to find a job in Spokane beyond substitute teaching, Shane's attempts to immerse the whole family into the Church of the Blessed Fire (only Leah seeming even mildly interested, mainly because of her crush on the pastor's son, David Jr.). No, this year had completely undone her. Had she lost her mind, coming up here? Was this some final break from reality?

Bethany closed her eyes and tried to let the music calm her again. She gave in to the vanilla smell of the ponderosa pines and the sounds of the crowd and The Buffs' angelic singer intoning those long vowels— she swayed a little, time passing along with their smooth set list, until she heard the singer say, "Thank you. We're The Buffs. Or The Boofs. You do you." He nodded toward her side of the stage. "This one's by our friend, Bethany Kinnick." Her maiden name—*oh, the freedom of that*. Applause, cheers, and a familiar rhythm rose up as they began playing *her* song, the sneakily creepy "Don't Be Misled." She'd written it about the power of obsessive love after following Doug on a much earlier concert tour, in 2008, with his most successful band to that point—*successful* meaning they could sometimes afford to sleep in hotels while on tour.

Don't be misled, she'd written in the chorus, *I am not your friend / I'm here to own you / to clone you / put your heart / in my pocket / pull your arms / out of socket / so I can keep them / around me forever.*

The Buffs' singer—working in his high, feathery register—made her lyrics sound even more haunted, like the young man was predicting his own demise. She glanced over at the dancers, who had mostly stopped spinning and reaching for ropes and were just watching the band, as if at the theater. The pride she felt! *That's my song!* And Doug's smart arrangement—a precisely picked guitar, harmonized chorus, a cymbal wash that sounded like gently breaking glass—made her proud of them both.

The music faded into applause and cheers, and the singer gave a soft "Thanks y'all." The singer pointed with an open hand to the small side-stage pen where the girlfriends sat on blankets and in folding chairs; Bethany smiled shyly, then waved to the back of the stage where Doug put his hand on his heart and extended it to the side pen, toward her.

Someone in the crowd apparently appreciated the song, too, because a voice called out "Bethany!" She was confused at first, and glanced to her right, scanning the stoned and painted faces on the other side of the fence. Again: "Bethany!" A familiar voice, but out of context.

An altercation at the right edge of the dancing throng caught her eye, someone pushing through the crowd—and what she saw next refused to constitute itself in her mind: her father was trying to climb the six-foot chain-link fence separating the girlfriend pen from the dancers and Hula-Hoopers. And two security guards were rushing to stop him. An older Native American man in a trucker's cap and an open-shirted bearded man in a homburg hat were pulling at the security guards as Rhys, perched on the fence, yelled again, "Bethany!"

He freed himself from the guards' grip and flopped over the chain-link, falling six feet onto his back. "Bethany! That song!" He got up. "It was great!" He ran to the shorter steel crowd-control railing, his leg catching as he crawled over it.

She rose out of her folding chair and began moving toward him, the quavering voice that came out of her not her adult voice, but a scared ten-year-old's: "Dad?" He looked terrible. He was wearing a Glass Animals T-shirt. His cheek was swollen, and he had a black eye that was beginning to turn yellow and green. "What are you doing here?"

They were only fifteen feet apart now. Her dad opened his mouth to answer, but he was knocked to the ground again, a burly security guard hitting him with his shoulder and falling on him, slamming his already battered face into the trampled grass.

"Okay, Gramps," the man said. "That's enough."

- - -

ON THE WAY out, Kinnick paused to look back over his shoulder. With the sun setting behind them, The Buffs were playing an encore, and they were surprisingly . . . *not terrible.* Like an edgier, synthesized Seals and Crofts (a reference that he suspected the band would either not know or certainly not love). One of the security guards yanked on his arm again and Rhys continued being escorted out by these angry toughs. Bethany, Brian, and Jeff walked behind him, as they were all herded through the side-stage pen, against the flow of the swaying dancers, through the back of the crowd, past people sitting on the hillside, and finally, to the entrance gate of the Tonatiuh Stage. Bethany kept staring at her dad between the big security guards, as if still not convinced that it was him. Kinnick had tried to explain to the *couldn't-care-less* guards that he'd been looking for his daughter in the crowd and had gotten excited when the band pointed her out, but the tackling one had interrupted him: "Buddy," he reiterated. "Could not. Care less."

The other security guard said, "Maybe just try *calling* your daughter next time." Rhys thought about pointing out that they didn't have phone service up here, but instead, he promised that he would do just that.

It was only once they were outside the gate—"Peace!" Jeff said to the security guards—that Bethany turned to Rhys. "What are you doing here, Dad? Where are the kids? And what happened to your face?"

"The kids are fine," Kinnick said. And then he explained the whole ordeal, Anna showing up on his porch two days ago with the children, Rhys driving them into Spokane for Asher's chess tournament—

"You took him to his tournament? How did he do?" Bethany gave a slight smile. "He's not very good, you know."

"Well, it turned out we had the day wrong. The junior tournament is next month." Then Kinnick told her the rest—how Shane had apparently called his AOL goons to go get the kids, and how two of them showed up at the chess club and, pointing to his cheek and eye, "They gave me this"—

"Oh, Dad!" Bethany's hand covered her mouth.

—and how the militia nuts drove away with the kids, and how Kinnick got help from a retired cop, a "friend of a friend," who helped track them down, and how they drove up to the Rampart to get the kids back—

"Wait, you went up there?"

—and how Chuck the ex-cop sent him and the kids away in his truck while he stayed back to hold off anyone who tried to go after him, and how Chuck shot out Dean Burris's tire and then got shot in the hip by another man—

"Oh, my God, Dad! Is he okay?"

—and yes, Chuck was going to be fine, but a county sheriff named Glen Campbell and maybe even the Spokane police were looking for Rhys now, and how he had been informed that he didn't have any rights as a grandparent ("I suppose I haven't been a very good one anyway."), and how he needed Bethany to come back so she could explain that he had *not* kidnapped his own grandchildren—

"This is a fucking awesome story," Jeff said to Brian.

"I brought a rifle," Brian said.

"As one would!" said Jeff.

Kinnick couldn't place the look that Bethany gave him—somewhere between *I'm sorry I got you into this* and *I can't believe how badly you screwed this up.*

By this time, they had arrived back at her tent. She put her hand to her head, trying to keep everything straight. "And . . . where are the kids now?"

"They're at my house," Brian said.

She turned. "And you are—"

"Oh, right," Kinnick said. "This is my friend, Brian. He lives near me, in Ford. The kids are with his wife, Joanie."

"Girlfriend," Brian corrected, Jefe Jeff putting out his fist for another bump.

"It's more of a common-law thing," Kinnick explained.

"Right." Then Bethany turned to Jeff. "And you—"

Jeff removed his hat and bowed. "The great and powerful Jeff, purveyor of quality hallucinogens, and guide to the furthest reaches of one's consciousness."

"Sure," Bethany said. She nodded, and stuck out her bottom lip, and said, "Okay then," as if she'd processed everything and now was ready to act, Kinnick impressed by her calm. She looked back at the tent. "I'll pack up my stuff. You can tell me the rest of it on the drive."

"I'm sorry to make you leave early," Kinnick said.

"It's okay," Bethany said. "I was ready to go."

"Also, Beth"—Kinnick put his hand out—"I wanted to say, I'm so sorry to hear about your mom." He started to move toward her, to give her a hug.

But she gave a hurried nod, and said, "I'll be right out," and dipped inside the tent to start packing up.

Sorry to hear about your mom? Why did Kinnick have such trouble speaking around his daughter? Everything that came out of his mouth sounded so distant, so cool to his own ear. He looked over at Brian, who shrugged, as if to say, *Children, daughters, women—who knows.*

"You guys look alike," Jeff said.

"She looks more like her mother," Kinnick said.

And that's when Doug came running back up the trail, sweating and breathless, dodging various freaks and furries. "Oh good," he said. "I was afraid she was gone already."

Kinnick couldn't believe this doughy bald man was the same long-haired waste-case who'd swept his daughter off her sandals in 2006, and who Rhys blamed for spinning her into a five-year drug-fueled postcollege eddy, Bethany following Doug's band around aimlessly before snapping out of it one morning and showing up at Celia's house with a two-month-old and a minor coke habit. Rhys had been relieved to hear Bethany had left Doug, but within a year, she was declaring her love for another loser, Shane. ("Out of the frying pan," as Kinnick used to put it, "and into a stupider frying pan.")

Indeed, Shithead Shane had caused Kinnick to soften his opinion a bit on Sluggish Doug over the years, but he could still hear the edge in his own voice when he greeted him. "Hello, *Doug*."

Bethany must've heard it, too, because she emerged from the tent with a backpack, a duffel bag, and a rolled-up sleeping bag. She pushed the duffel into her father's hands, and, as if reading his mind, said, through gritted teeth: "This was *not* Doug's fault, Dad. It was my decision to come up here."

Kinnick accepted the duffel, and Bethany's tone. "I'm sorry." He craned to look around Bethany. "I liked your band, Doug."

"You guys are great," Brian agreed.

"Awesome set," said Jeff.

"Thanks," Doug said. "How have you been, Rhys?"

Kinnick glanced sideways at Bethany. "Trying," he said. "How about you, Doug?"

"Same, I guess." Doug smiled and turned to Bethany. "You're leaving?"

"I am. But thank you, Doug."

"I'm sorry it wasn't all you'd hoped."

"It was just fine. Thank you. And I loved hearing my song. That made it all worthwhile."

"Tell Leah I'll try to see her this summer." Kinnick knew that Doug had had almost no role in his daughter's life—a combination of his own deep slacker instincts and Bethany's desire to start a new life twelve years ago with Shane and her infant daughter.

"I will," Bethany said. They exchanged a long hug, and when it was over, Kinnick shook Doug's hand, gave him a short nod, and turned to follow Jeff the trip guide once more through the festival campsite.

They reached the Rushrooms tent and Brian pulled a slip of paper from under the windshield wiper of his Bronco. He held it up for Jeff to see. On top was another Incan cross. Below that were two stamps: a snake and a flower.

"Parking violation," Jeff said. "Amaru, the serpent god. Luckily, they gave you a *Cantua buxifolia*, too, the sacred flower. Just a warning. If that second symbol had been a lightning bolt, your car would be in a boot. Or they'd be towing it."

"I gotta get out of here," Brian said.

They thanked Jeff, who urged them to come back for the much larger Shambala festival in the summer. "Or," he said, "come up in three weeks for the spring barter faire. I have a booth where I sell homemade soap and leather products." He removed a brown, leather key chain from his pocket and held it out for them to see. It had the dark impression of bird wings stamped on it.

"That's nice," Brian said. "Reminds me of my old air force wings."

"Take it." Jeff took his keys off the chain. "It's yours."

Brian tried to object, but Jeff insisted, so Brian handed him a twenty-dollar bill.

Then, the three of them left, piling in the Bronco.

In the backseat, Bethany held up the rifle case. "Is this necessary?"

"Oh, you can just set that in back," Brian said. He drove them through the parking lot and started back down the narrow two-track dirt road. Kinnick felt exhausted by the last few days, but relieved to have Bethany back. He kept turning and looking at her in the backseat, as if she might disappear again. "Are you okay, Beth?"

She nodded but kept staring out her side window. She had her mother's wide features, and thick eyebrows, and her long, black hair was tied back the way Celia used to wear it, parted almost in the middle, the first loose grays winging out from her scalp. Celia had gone totally gray in her forties, seeming to age faster than Kinnick in that difficult time. He shifted his body, so that he was facing Bethany in the backseat. "I feel like there are some things I need to say to you—"

She didn't look up at him. "I might need a minute, Dad."

"Sure. Of course."

And so, they stayed quiet driving out of the woods, darkness already settling around them. Brian turned off the dirt road and onto the two-lane highway, driving them in silence another fifteen miles, when, without warning, an incessant buzzing began. One, then another, and another. They were coming back into cell phone range. Bethany pulled her vibrating cell phone from her backpack and began looking at the voicemails and texts. "Oh boy," she said. "Here we go. Anna. Shane. Anna. Shane. Pastor Gallen. Shane, Shane, Shane."

In the driver's seat, Brian took out his cell phone, too. Once again, Kinnick felt left out. "Uh-oh," Brian said. He handed over his phone.

On the screen was a text message from Joanie, Kinnick reading it with a renewed sense of dread. Brian! Where are you? Leah is gone! I can't find her—

FIVE

What Happened to Leah

Grandpa Rhys had been gone only a few hours and Leah was ready to strangle Asher, her little brother rising to unheard-of levels of obnoxiousness.

After lunch, Asher sat at the counter, chomping carrot sticks as he grilled Joanie about Brian's Native American heritage. ("Did Brian's tribe ever fight the US cavalry?" *Yes.* "When?" *In the 1850s. With some other tribes at the battle of Four Lakes.* "Did they win?" *For a while they did, riding just out of range of the soldiers' guns.* "Then what happened?" *Well, the soldiers got tired of chasing them around the plateau, so they left the battlefield, went down along the river and burned the Indian villages and shot all their horses.* "Did Brian have a horse?" *That battle happened way before Brian's time, but I do think his family had an old swayback nag when he was growing up.* "What's a swayback nag?" *It's an old horse.* "But it didn't get shot, though?" *No, no, this was many years later.*) At one point, Joanie happened to mention that Brian was learning Spokane Salish, the dialect that had been lost to his family after his grandparents were punished for speaking it at boarding school, and Asher (after asking what a boarding school was) asked what the language sounded like. "Well," Joanie said, "in Salish, you would be, let's see, x̣x̣nut years old"—her voice seeming to come from inside her throat.

"I'm six-nut!" Asher said excitedly to Leah. Then, turning back to Joanie: "How old will I be on my next birthday?"

"Let's see, you'll be *ʔupń*."

"Next year, I'll be open! And how old was I last year?"

"Eight? Let's see. That's *heʔénm*"

"Hey-enim! Cool! How old is Leah?"

"Afraid I can count only to ten," Joanie said. "You'll have to ask Brian when he gets home. He can go a lot higher."

"And how would you say my name?"

"Your name . . . is your name. So . . . Asher."

He held up a carrot. "What about carrot stick?"

In Joanie's answer, Leah heard a small measure of her own fatigue: "Asher, I really have no idea. Like I said, I can only speak a few words."

"Do you think there was a Salish word for chess? Or *Tyrannosaurus rex*?"

"Asher!" Leah smiled at Joanie. "I'm sorry. He gets wound up."

As often happened, Asher seemed to misunderstand what the problem was with his question. "I'm not saying Native Americans lived when there were dinosaurs. I know they didn't. I just wonder if they *knew* about dinosaurs back then, like we do now, from fossils and stuff?"

"Yeah, I don't know that, either, I'm afraid."

"Some people at our church don't believe in fossils, but I do—"

"Asher," Leah interrupted. "You really need to give Joanie a break. Why don't you go play with Billy."

Asher looked over at the sleeping German shepherd, whose coat was a swirl of colors that Leah had decided could be called pulling taffy.

"He's asleep," Asher said.

Joanie took a dog biscuit from a tin, a sound that caused Billy's ears to perk up. "Give him this."

Asher reached for the dog biscuit. "How do you say—"

Joanie cut him off. "I really have no idea."

Asher marched over in his boots and crouched his little legs in front of the dog, who lifted his head with an exasperated groan—his animal instincts no doubt drawing a bead on how irritating this small human was about to be. He accepted the dog biscuit without enthusiasm, crunched it, and licked up the pieces that fell onto his dog bed.

"Take him outside if you want to," Joanie said, "he probably needs to drain the old doggy vein anyways."

"Drain what?"

"He probably needs to pee's what I'm saying. And if you want to play with him, there's a rope with a knot out there. You can throw it to him, or maybe he'll play tug-of-war with you."

"Oh. Cool."

Leah rolled her eyes. Asher was still trying out that word, *cool*, which, coming from him, sounded like the least cool word in the English language. He opened the door and went out with Billy. "Come on, boy!"

Leah noticed that when the door closed, the wall of the trailer shook a little.

Joanie exhaled heavily. "Boy's got a few questions, don't he?"

"It's okay to tell him to be quiet. We do it all the time."

"And does that work?"

"No. Not really." Leah had noticed an old Dell laptop (color: *cave entrance*) that was cantilevered on an alphabetized bookshelf where authors and subjects were blended together (a style of shelving that she'd never seen before). The computer was shoved into the *M*'s, pushing back a line of western paperbacks by authors named McMurtry and Portis, and between them, several books about macramé. (One was called *The Macramé Bible*, Leah recalling a sermon by Pastor Gallen that, among other violations of scripture, chastised people who called various things "the Bible" of this or that.)

"Joanie? Can I use your computer? I need to check my school homework."

"Oh. Sure." Joanie grabbed the laptop, flipped it open, and handed it to Leah at the counter.

"Can you—"

"Oh, of course," Joanie said, and she tapped a few keys, put in the password, and opened an Internet browser. She handed the laptop back, just as outside, there was a scuffling sound.

Leah and Joanie looked up at the same time, to see Asher, still holding the knotted rope, being dragged down the stairs by the dog.

"Uh-oh," Joanie said, and she went outside to check on him.

When the door closed, Leah worked quickly, signing in to her top secret Gmail account. There were two emails right on top from Davy.J.Gallen. She started with the first one, from yesterday, which was about his biblical studies class at his Christian college in Tacoma.

Hey Leah. Today in BS we went over Letter to the Ephesians, 4:1–16, where Paul tells Christians to stop fighting and get along. To "live a life worthy of the calling you have received." (Uh, hello, *Dad*!) The whole time I was thinking about your novel, and that maybe you could name the settlements that the young couple visit after the epistolary books of the Bible. Ephesia, Corinth, Galatia, etc. . . . Then, in the end, your heroes could come back to their own town and kick butt and take names. Like in *Fury Road*, but with less violence. Oh, and remember that hilarious guy I was telling you about, Marsh? The prof asked him what he got out of Ephesians, and Marsh was like, "Uh, that Christians need to stop beefing?" That guy is so funny. The prof was all, "You mean that we must remain united in our faith in Christ, virgin-born and God incarnate, whose redemption through the substitutionary shedding of his blood promises us our own bodily resurrection?" And Marsh is like, "Yup." Classic!

Hey, I'm not sure if you'll be at Bible Study on Saturday afternoon, or at church Sunday, but I have no classes the rest of the week and my parents are bugging me to come home for some reason so if you're around—

Joanie came back in then and Leah turned the screen slightly, so that she wouldn't see the open email.

"You get it all figured out, hon?"

"Yes," Leah said. "Just reading over this assignment. It's . . . confusing."

Joanie opened a drawer and took out a tin of Band-Aids. "You must go through a lot of these at your house."

"Oh yeah," Leah said. "Tons."

Joanie went back out as Leah opened the second email, sent only two hours earlier.

Leah,

Are you OK? My mom says there was some trouble at the Rampart? And that your mother is missing and you and your brother got taken away by your grandfather? And something about a crazy cop getting shot? What's going on there?!?! I hate those militia dudes my dad has hanging around all the time. He's freaking out (more than usual!) and thinks the FBI is going to raid the Rampart. Both of my parents are acting so weird these days. Where are you? I haven't heard from you in days. I'm driving home now. Please write and tell me what's going on!

Davy

She typed quickly.

Davy,

I am fine except my family is seriously imploding. Mom ran off and Shane went to find her. I'm stuck in a trailer in a little town called Ford. My Grandpa Rhys went to get Mom, who's in Canada with my real dad. It's so crazy. Shane thinks she's in Oregon and so he's down there trying to find her and Asher is being a total pain and I can't believe I don't even have a phone! I would call you, but you know my mom's stupid rules. I hope I can see you when you're—

She heard footsteps on the porch and looked up. Joanie and Asher were coming back inside. Leah hit send, even though she hadn't finished the email, as Joanie ushered Asher in the door. He had a bandage on his forehead, just above his left eyebrow, where he always seemed to need a bandage. Leah closed her Gmail.

"That dog is strong!" Asher told Leah. He turned to Joanie. "Are all German shepherds that strong, do you think?"

"Hard to say," Joanie answered. She turned to Leah. "Are you getting your homework all squared away, hon?"

"What home—" Asher started to say, but Leah pointed at him and shot him eye-daggers. *Don't. You. Dare.*

"Yes, thanks, Joanie," Leah said. "Getting all caught up." She narrowed her eyes again and mouthed to her brother: *Be quiet.*

"We're gonna walk to the creek and see if we can see any frogs," Joanie said. "It's just up the road a piece. You want to come?"

"No, that's okay," Leah said. "I think I'll finish this up."

"Sure," Joanie said. She walked into the back bedroom.

"What homework?" Asher whispered. "Mom left us reading assignments is all."

"Asher. Don't say a word about it. It's none of your business."

He looked suspicious, but when Joanie came out of the bedroom with a leash, Asher turned his attention back to the dog. "Ooh, can I hold the leash?"

Joanie glanced over at Leah, who shook her head slightly.

"Why don't I hold the leash for now? Maybe you can on the way back, when Billy's more tuckered out."

"What's tuckered out mean?"

"Tired."

"Is that a Salish word?"

"No, it's American."

"What's doe?"

"What?"

"Doe? Your sign says, Doe lies. And Midnight mine and Dawn something."

"Oh, not doe. DOE. Department of Energy. You know what, I'll tell you about it on our walk."

It seemed to take an hour for them to leave: Asher used the bathroom, Joanie switched her sweater for a jacket, then changed her shoes, then went back to the sweater. Asher used the bathroom again, and finally, the trailer door opened, but before they could leave, Joanie went back in for the jacket again.

Leah simply moved the cursor back and forth until they were finally gone, then she opened her Gmail again, to write Davy back and apologize for sending a half-finished email, and to say she would love to see him this weekend, though it might be hard—when, right there, at the top of her Gmail account, was *another* email from Davy, sent this time, it said, from his iPhone, just a few minutes ago.

Leah—

I was driving back and saw your email. You're in Ford now? I'm on I-90, at a rest stop, less than two hours from there. I just talked to my mom again, too. My parents are losing it. You won't believe why they want me to come home. Can I drive up and see you? Write me back and I'll cut off on Highway 231 and find you.

Davy

Leah typed back frantically.

Yes! There's a little church in the town of Ford. I saw it when we drove up. I will be waiting behind it! I can't wait to see you!

Leah

She hit send and looked at the clock. Had she answered in time? She waited for a moment to see if he wrote back. How far back up the highway was that church? How long would it take to walk there? And what if Davy didn't see her message? She knew it didn't matter. She needed to see him. Should she leave a note? She pulled a pen and notebook from her backpack and wrote:

Joanie,

I went to get some air. I'll be back in a few hours. Don't worry.

Leah

She checked her email once more, but Davy hadn't responded. She didn't want to wait, in case Asher tripped and fell on his dumb head again, or needed to pee for the hundredth time, and came back with Joanie. So, she left the note on the counter, closed the laptop, put it back on the bookshelf, and started out. In the post-Apocalyptic series of books that she wanted to write (a trilogy for sure, maybe more!) the young couple would travel across a decimated country in the end-times (after a plague and civil war), facing all kinds of adventures and hardships as they brought the *true* gospel to these far-ranging places, and taught them to let go of their fear. Some of these communities would be lawless, and would have no faith, while others would be like fortresses, operating under the dark, violent cloud of false prophecies and misguided sanctuaries like the Rampart. The young couple would preach a peaceful and simple Christianity, built around sacrifice and helping the poor refugees from the civil war. She'd had the idea even *before* she met David Jr., who, beneath his thick glasses, had the love-liest celery-green eyes. After she'd told him about her book idea last summer at Bible Camp—and he'd told her that he was beginning to disagree with the way his father ran his church—she could only ever imagine the rebellious boy in her book as Davy, and the courageous girl as herself. She grabbed her backpack, stepped out the door, and started out on what she couldn't help thinking of as their first adven-ture together.

- - -

IT TOOK BRIAN, Bethany, and Kinnick nearly four hours to cross back over the border and pick their way south, through the forests of Eastern Washington, all the way to Brian's place in Ford. It was well after dark by then, and Joanie was frantic. She and Asher had gone on a walk to the creek before dinner, and when they came back, Leah was gone. Joanie and Asher looked around, but they couldn't find her anywhere.

Kinnick read Leah's note and then handed it to Bethany, who was strangely calm—just as she had been with Shane when she'd called him from Brian's car, on the drive back from the Paititi Festival.

That conversation had kept cutting in and out, in the middle of one furious Shane rant or another, first through southern British Columbia ("—you have to be the worst mother in the—"), and then after they crossed the border ("—any idea how humiliating this is for me—"), and again as they skirted the Colville National Forest toward Ford ("—and if you think I'll ever trust you again—").

Even with the spotty reception and Bethany holding the phone to her ear, Kinnick had heard the gist of Shane's blistering take on recent events: Bethany was a harlot, a lying, probably cheating Jezebel who had brought nothing but shame upon their family! And that everyone in the church felt sorry for him, being married to such a woman! And that Shane had been so worried he'd driven all the way to Grants Pass to look for her! And that he'd also looked in Portland, because he "knew you were still in touch with that druggie creep!" And that he couldn't believe she would run off with her ex to a pagan music festival, and how DARE she have the neighbor take the kids to *her father*, of all people "—who you don't even like or respect—" (Kinnick wincing in the front seat). And how dare Rhys come and steal the kids from the very men Shane had chosen to watch them while he was gone— good, protective men, "men of Christ, unlike your sucker-punching father—" and how dare Rhys bring "some kind of crazy, armed cop with him," and if the FBI raided the Rampart, "it will be your fault if good people get hurt," and that, as far as Shane was concerned, she had failed in her role as a mother as surely as she failed in God's eyes, and *he* was the only reliable parent now, so she should bring the kids to him immediately, and it was only near the end, when Shane was softening a little, that he said if Bethany was telling the truth, and she hadn't slept with Doug, and hadn't gotten back on drugs, and if she vowed to bring the kids home to him this very minute, and to repent, to submit to her husband as God commanded her to, that she *might* still have a path to salvation, and if Christ could forgive her, who was he to withhold forgiveness, and anyway, he'd missed her—only then did Bethany say to Shane, "Listen, Shane, I have something else to tell you. Leah may have run away."

The ranting and yelling started all over again.

Throughout this exhausting in-and-out phone call—sometimes

they went twenty minutes of driving without reception—Kinnick had marveled at the way Bethany handled Shane's eruptions, never raising her own voice, saying things like "Yes, I know," and "Of course you'd feel that way," and "Well, to be fair," and "The Bible says a lot of things, Shane," and "Let's talk about that after we find Leah," but he also felt a great deal of sadness, too: that she had grown so adept at keeping the peace, at deflecting Shane's crazy bullshit. It was as if Kinnick barely knew his daughter now, and all she'd been through the last decade, and shame crept back into his chest. He and Brian kept making worried eye contact, and, as he listened to the muffled yelling from the other side of the phone, Kinnick had the urge to punch his son-in-law again—but, of course, that hadn't worked out so well the first time.

"That's got to be exhausting," Kinnick said after Bethany briefly lost phone service near Onion Creek, the phone dropping to her lap. "I hope you know that you don't have to put up with his crazy talk."

Bethany didn't say anything, just looked out her window and waited for the phone to come back into service again. Then, before she took another call, she answered her father, her voice remaining steady and unruffled. "You know what's exhausting?" And, not waiting for an answer: "Your constant disappointment in me."

This landed like a roundhouse to Kinnick's sore face. He opened his mouth to say something, but no words came out. He and Brian made eye contact again, Brian mouthing the word *Wow*.

And when they finally arrived at Brian and Joanie's trailer, Bethany still seemed to be miffed with her father as she calmly processed the day's events. She held Asher against her waist as he filled her in on his version of the last few days ("—and I fell in Grandpa Rhys's creek and we went to my chess tournament but we had the day wrong, and we found out there's another tournament next month, and then Brother Dean took us to the Rampart and we stayed the night there, and I slept in the chapel, but Grandpa Rhys came and got us the next day and brought us here and I slept in a sleeping bag and Billy pulled me down the stairs and in Salish did you know I'm *six-nut* years old—").

Brian volunteered to drive around again, looking for Leah. There were only three directions she could've gone, southeast, toward Long Lake and Spokane, north, toward Springdale, and the least likely direction—west, onto the Spokane Indian Reservation.

"We didn't look that way," Joanie admitted, Brian grabbing his jacket, about to drive to Wellpinit to look for her, when Bethany glanced down at Asher.

"And what do you know about all of this?"

"Well." Asher seemed to think about it for a moment. And then, sheepishly: "I know she didn't really have any homework."

The room was silent for a moment and then Joanie sat up. "The laptop!" She ran to the bookshelf and grabbed it, brought it back to the counter and opened it. "She asked to use my computer to check her homework."

"Look up the history," Brian said, and Joanie ran her fingers along the pad below the keys, Kinnick flushed with the same insecurity he'd had since coming out of the woods two days ago: everyone in the world seemed to have perfect mastery of this most basic and useful tool—except him.

"Gmail?" Joanie looked up. "I don't have a Gmail account."

"Neither does Leah," said Bethany. "Or, at least, she's not supposed to." She explained that Leah had asked recently if she could have a separate email account where she could write David Jr., away from the *collins4:19.family* address, the email that Shane and Bethany had access to, where they checked her schoolwork and monitored her exchanges with friends. "She didn't argue when we said no," Bethany said. "I probably should've known then that she'd just go and do it."

They tried opening Leah's email on Joanie's laptop, but Leah had signed out of the account, and while her username popped up, they didn't have her password. After a dozen guesses (Asher: "What about velociraptor?") they gave up.

Bethany's cheeks filled with air, and she let the breath go out in a deep sigh. For a moment, Kinnick wondered if she was considering going back to Doug's Incan paradise, perhaps taking a guided trip with Jefe Jeff.

Instead, she said, "Well, we may not know *where* she is, but I think I know who she's with."

- - -

BRIAN SAID HE'D keep looking for Leah around Ford that night, even though Bethany told him that wasn't necessary. He and Joanie loaned Kinnick their second car, an old Subaru Outback splattered with road mud and Sierra Club bumper stickers, to take Bethany and Asher back to Spokane. Kinnick drove to their apartment on the city's north side, hopeful that they'd find Leah there. But it was after 11 p.m. when they arrived, and there was no sign of her. No sign of Shane, either. He hadn't answered Bethany's last phone call, when she'd left a message saying that Leah was most likely with Pastor Gallen's son. She'd left a message for the pastor, too, but hadn't heard back from him, either.

They spent a mostly sleepless night at the Spokane apartment, Kinnick curled up on yet another person's couch, startled by the sounds of the city at night, the cars and voices and barking dogs, the bright streetlights making it feel like an endless dusk out there. In the morning, he sipped coffee and looked around the apartment while Bethany showered. Chuck was right when he said the place was tidy. Comfortable. Lived-in. Hard to believe she and Shane had only been here a few months. How could the surfaces remain so neat while Bethany's insides were apparently roiling? Again, he felt this strange sensation: pride alongside confusion, the sense that his daughter was a kind of stranger, unknowable to him. On a bulletin board in the kitchen, home school assignments were carefully pinned up next to Bible verses, Asher's most recent report on Mount St. Helen's (complete with a drawing in mideruption), and Leah's essay on the novels of C. S. Lewis. On the other walls were family photos: of Leah and Asher, of Shane and Bethany and the kids, and one lovely portrait of Celia and Cortland. No pictures of him, of course. There were also a couple of framed political posters, Kinnick reminded of the tamer religious posters and needlepoints (*This is the house the Lord has made*) on the walls of Bethany's former home in Grants Pass.

How different this "art" was—in one, a brutalized Jesus had been crucified against an American flag; in another, a cross of red, white, and blue stood beneath the words: "One Nation Under God," with the next word, "Indivisible," covered by what looked like a red-stamped: "REPENT!"

Bethany came out of the bathroom, dressed in jeans and a sweater, with a towel wrapped around her head. "My hair was so greasy," she said. She checked her charging phone, then set it back on the counter, looking up in time to see Kinnick still standing in front of the framed "REPENT" poster.

"Shane keeps putting that up," she said. "I take it down. He puts it back up."

Kinnick pretended he'd just noticed the poster. "Oh. Really?"

She held up her phone. "Nothing from Leah, or from Shane. Or Pastor Gallen." She bit her lip. "I swear, if anything happens to her—"

"I'm sure she's fine," Kinnick said. But he couldn't help wondering how Bethany would've finished that sentence: —*I'll never forgive myself.* Or—*I'll never forgive* you.

Kinnick said, "I shouldn't have left the kids with Joanie. I should've stayed with them until you came back."

"Not your fault," Bethany said.

"She's most likely with that boy, David Jr., just like you said." Kinnick tapped the edge of his coffee cup. "And I'm sure they're fine. Do you think they're at the Rampart, with Shane?"

Bethany nodded. "I hope so."

"You don't think they'd try to elope or something?"

Bethany shook her head. "No, I don't think so. And I can't imagine any church performing a wedding ceremony with a thirteen-year-old bride. Even in Idaho."

Bethany brought out a hand towel, one of Shane's flannel shirts, and his deodorant. Without a word, she set them on the counter in front of Kinnick.

"I stink again?" he asked, pinching his arms to his sides. "Have people gotten more sensitive about hygiene in the last few years?"

"I don't think that's what's going on," Bethany said. She went to get Asher started in the shower, then walked next door to talk to Anna. Kinnick used the hand towel to freshen up at the kitchen sink, put on Shane's deodorant and his flannel shirt, and walked over to the bookshelves, which were covered mostly with young adult Christian titles. There was a bookmark in one paperback, and he pulled it out and read a few sentences, putting it back when his daughter came inside and said that Anna wasn't home.

Bethany had a thick stack of mail in her hands, and she stood in the kitchen, going through it, piece by piece, unceremoniously dropping the envelopes into two piles on the little round kitchen table. She sighed and looked out the window.

All night, Kinnick had lain awake, trying to figure out what to say to his distant daughter. Spotting her at the concert, running through the crowd and climbing the fence, he'd had the insane idea that he was *rescuing* her, that she needed saving, that all he had to do was reach her, and all would be settled between them. He'd pictured them coming together in a warm, forgiving embrace. But, of course, he'd ended up in a security guard's arms instead. And, since then, it seemed like Bethany hadn't wanted to meet his eyes, or to talk about anything except how to find Leah. Other than the thing she'd said about being tired of his disappointment, and the bit about him stinking, they hadn't really talked at all.

Kinnick recalled her coming to visit four years earlier, during the pandemic, and the icy, six-foot gap she'd insisted they maintain. It felt like that distance was between them still—and maybe would be forever. He had no idea how to breach it.

While thinking about that earlier visit Kinnick wondered if he wasn't maybe going about this all wrong. If it wasn't delusional to think he could simply come back into her life and say he was ready to be her father again, to jump back into their tangled relationship without at least trying to untie the original knots.

"Beth—"

She glanced up, a neutral look on her face.

"Look, I don't know if this is the right time, but please hear me out. I need to say some things." She didn't stop him this time, and Kinnick went on: "I am *not* disappointed in you. I'm sorry I gave you that impression. And I'm sorry that I took out whatever issues I had with your partners on you. That was wrong of me. I have wanted to say that to you many times over the last few years—"

She flinched at *last few years*—as she should, of course, unconscionable he should be out of her life for so long—but Kinnick knew that he had to keep going, to get it all out. "You know, a friend recently asked what I learned living alone in the woods. When people ask me that, the only things I can ever think of are quotes from people who've said it before. Aristotle. Thoreau. But I'm starting to think Thoreau might have been full of shit. If we aren't living for others, maybe we aren't really living."

He took a deep breath. "When you came to visit me last time, you asked if I had seen you skipping school when you were fifteen. Well, I did. I saw you that day. I watched you drive past the house with that boy. And I never said a thing. Because I was with someone I shouldn't have been with, too."

Bethany just stared at him, no reaction on her face.

"But you probably knew that. Bethany . . . I am so full of regret.

And shame. For turning my back on you that way. And not just seven years ago. And not just because of Shane. So . . . what I wanted to say . . . is that I am sorry. For so many things. But maybe we could just start with that?"

The breath seemed to catch in Bethany's throat. She inhaled deeply.

"I've been trying to figure something else out," Kinnick said. "When you were going through such a hard time these last weeks, after your mother died, why you sent the kids to be with *me*? And I could only think of two possible answers. Either you wanted to send me a message. Or you really needed me. And I just want to say, whichever it is, I'm here for it."

Still, that noncommittal look on her face. Then, finally, a small nod.

Kinnick took a step toward her. "I know I've got a lot of years to make up. And I know I can't do it in a day. But I'd like to start now, if that's okay."

Kinnick took a few more steps, reached out, and tentatively took his daughter in his arms. She stiffened at first, then shuddered and began crying, and finally collapsed against his chest.

Kinnick whispered, "I'm sorry," and "It's going to be okay," and "I'm sorry," again.

She managed to say only, "Dad," and he squeezed her tighter.

And then he felt smaller arms around his waist, Kinnick looking down to see Asher, out of the shower, hair wet, barefoot, dressed in sweatpants and no shirt, his arms around them both. "What are we hugging about?"

- - -

IN THE CAR afterward, Bethany felt drained by her brief, cathartic cry. Ever since the panic attacks at Paititi, or maybe since her mother's death, or shoot, maybe most of her life, she'd concentrated on breathing shallowly, thinking clearly, focusing on each small step—trying to get

through the days without her mother, get through the festival, get back
to her kids, talk Shane down from his anger—to keep her thoughts
always near the surface, and therefore, keep her emotions at bay, for
now, at least until they got Leah back.

But her dad's apology had caught her off guard, and she'd allowed
herself to go deeper, into the past, melting into his arms the way she did
when she was nine or ten, even as she'd puzzled over his last question:
Why *had* she sent the kids to be with him? He'd shown almost no interest in them, or her, for so much of her life. *Was* she sending him a
message? Or was she just so desperate for help that she'd had nowhere
else to turn? She wished again she hadn't lost her health insurance, so
that she could see her therapist, Peggy, and ask those questions (and
have Peggy repeat them back to her). But then, immediately after crying in Rhys's arms, predictably, Bethany had thought of a hundred
things her father's apology had *not* covered, a thousand things to still
be angry at him about, a million things he'd missed over the last seven
years, over the last *eighteen* years. But something he'd said—*I'd like to
start now*—had given her pause. When she thought about all that her
father had missed in the last seven years, since his retreat to the woods,
she reflected on how hard those years had been—losing her job, losing
her mother, the pandemic, the kids having to leave their school, and,
in the center of it all, like a tornado, Shane's deepening drift into this
end-times theology. My God, she was tired. She had needed . . . something . . . and it clearly wasn't running off to a music festival in Canada.

So, maybe it was letting her dad "start"? And her, too, maybe she
could allow herself to begin forgiving Rhys, allow him to try to help—
without entirely relying on him, of course, after all, he'd only had one
job: watch her kids for a few days, while she went to see Doug's band
play. And look how that had turned out.

She glanced over at her father now, in the driver's seat of his friend's
Subaru. What exactly did she expect he could do? The man didn't
even have a running car. As a kid, she'd always seen him as so reliable

and knowledgeable, a series of squares: square jawline, square shoulders, square hair, a man of perfect right angles, a paragon of rational thought, like he was a book himself—but the edges had long ago worn off. She used to dread his harsh judgments, the way his lips would set, and his eyes would narrow, the way he'd say, "You did *what*, now?" But here was a softer, more introspective old man, seemingly humbled by life. An old, battered book, its pages faint and yellowed.

"Anything?" He looked over at her.

Right. Her phone. Bethany looked down at the screen (as if she wouldn't have felt the vibration or heard the ringtone). "Nothing." She had tried calling Shane again before they left the apartment, but it had gone directly to voicemail. And Pastor Gallen hadn't answered his phone, either.

And so, she and Rhys and the freshly showered Asher had piled in Brian and Joanie's Subaru and started back through the streets of Spokane, headed east, toward Idaho, and eventually, to the Rampart. To Shane. To the end of days. Or maybe the end of her marriage. So many borders they'd end up crossing this week.

"I'm not exactly excited to go back to that place," her father said.

"Yeah. Me neither." Best case: Cross looks from Shane and Pastor Gallen. A stern lecture that she submit to her man. Daughter married at sixteen. Worst case: the Blessed Fire congregation stoning Shane's wayward wife to death.

Kinnick asked if they could make a quick stop. "I need to check on a friend. It will only take a minute. And it's on the way."

He parked in front of a blue duplex and ran up to the unit on the right. Bethany watched him ring the doorbell and bounce nervously on the balls of his feet. He looked back once and held up a finger: just a minute. Finally, a short, pretty Asian American woman came out onto the porch in a robe, a cup of coffee in her hand. She came all the way outside, easing the front door closed behind her. She and Rhys launched into what looked like a spirited discussion, Bethany wondering if this was the same woman she'd seen on her parents' porch when she was fifteen. So long ago—it was impossible to tell. Maybe her dad had a type. She opened her car door slightly and caught her father midsentence: "—can't believe he's here."

"Oh, he's here," the woman answered. "The doctors said he could go home anytime—if he had someone to look after him. He practically sprinted out of that hospital and into my fucking car."

"Oh, Lucy," her dad said, "I'm sorry."

"You're sorry? Right. And I'm a fucking nursemaid thanks to you—"

"I'll come back and help," he said, "I promise."

"Whose house is this?" asked Asher from the backseat.

Bethany eased her door closed. "Grandpa's shack-job," she muttered.

"What?"

"Grandpa's friend."

"Oh."

The woman went back inside and Kinnick walked back to the car, head down, looking chastened. He climbed into the driver's seat and blew out air, like a tire going flat. "Sorry about that." He had just reached down to start the car when the door to the blue duplex opened again.

Out onto the porch stepped a well-built middle-aged man, a few years younger than her father, with lightly graying hair and a well-trimmed beard. He was wearing a sweatshirt, baggy basketball shorts, and what looked like hospital slippers.

But it was what he carried in his left hand that caught Bethany's eye: a half-gallon catheter bag—like the one she recalled Cortland having to use after his prostate surgery. A tube ran from the bag into his shorts and up his leg. A small amount of bloody urine sloshed in the bag as he shuffled quickly down the sidewalk in his hospital slippers toward them. "Kinnick!" the man yelled. "Wait!"

The woman came back out onto the porch to watch, followed by a skinny young man with tattooed arms, who stood behind her, both of them wearing half-smiles on their bemused faces as they watched the catheterized man hobble down the sidewalk.

"Oh, Jesus," her dad said.

"It's the man from the Rampart," Asher said from the backseat.

Rhys lowered his window. "Hey, Chuck. How are you feeling?"

He arrived at Kinnick's window, smiling. "Great! Much better! Hey, Lucy says your granddaughter has gone missing now?"

"Yeah," Kinnick said. "We're going to look for her."

"You think she's back up there? At the Rampart?"

"We're not sure, but that's where we're going to start."

Chuck glanced back at the house briefly. "Give me a minute. I'll go with you."

"I really don't think—"

"You can't go up there by yourself. Face that douchebag army alone?"

Kinnick couldn't help himself and his eyes briefly darted down. "Chuck, you can't possibly—"

Chuck gestured to the big plastic bag of urine in his hand. "Don't worry. I have a smaller day bag. I'll just strap it to my leg, and we'll go up there together."

"You just had surgery!"

"It was like pulling out a splinter! Took them less than an hour. No infection, no internal damage, piece of cake. A few stitches, a round of antibiotics, doctor says I'm good as new."

"Chuck! You got shot two days ago!"

"Yeah, I was there, remember?"

"Look at you. You're in no condition to—"

"What, this?" Chuck interrupted, holding up the catheter bag again. "This is nothing! I'll be out of this in no time." He flicked the tube. "Get yanked around by my dickhole for a few days until my body remembers how to piss on its own again."

"Dickhole?" Asher asked from behind them.

"Asher—" Bethany said.

"Hey, kid, good to see you again." Chuck nodded at Asher in the backseat. "Hard to believe it, huh, that your body could forget something as simple as how to take a leak?"

"Leak?" Asher repeated.

Lucy stepped off the porch. "Chuck! Why don't you come back inside?"

But Chuck leaned both arms onto the door of the car. "That yokel sheriff wants to charge the idiot who shot me with unlawful discharge of a firearm. You believe that? A misdemeanor! I said 'Why not just charge him with speeding?' Says I could face misdemeanor endangerment charges, too! For what? Second-degree tire assault? Oh, and he still wants to talk to you, by the way. Asshole kept my Glock as evidence, but I've got my service piece at home. You and I could go get it—" He suddenly looked across at Bethany. "Hey, is this your daughter? You found her? Nice work!"

"Oh. Yeah. Bethany, this is Chuck. Chuck . . . this is my daughter, Bethany."

"Thank you for"—Bethany hesitated—"your service?"

"Just doing my job," Chuck said.

"Not your fucking job," the woman said as she arrived at Chuck's side.

"We have to go," Kinnick said. "But I appreciate your help, Chuck. More than you know. And I'll be back soon. We'll get this squared away and I'll come see you."

But Chuck still looked concerned. "You don't want to at least borrow my other piece?"

"No," Kinnick said. "No more guns."

Lucy put her arm around the big ex-cop. "Come on," she said gently. "Let's get you back inside. You're supposed to be resting."

"Okay." Chuck reached through the open window and patted Kinnick once more on the arm. "You go easy up there, partner. Stay out of trouble." Then he backed away, leaned on Lucy, and allowed himself to

be guided away, her hand firmly on his back. As they walked toward
the house, though, Lucy glanced back at Kinnick and used the hand
on Chuck's back to flip him off.

"Sorry, Lucy!" Kinnick said, in a tone that seemed to indicate that
much of their relationship involved his apologizing. He turned back to
Bethany. "So. Those are my friends, Lucy and Chuck—"

In her lap, Bethany's phone vibrated. She looked down at the screen,
then held it up for her father to read the name. Pastor Gallen.

- - -

BETHANY CLEARED HER throat and answered the call. "Hello."

"Sister Bethany? It's David Gallen. How are you?"

She recoiled a bit, hearing his voice, recalling his dark and doom-
filled sermons. She knew that Shane had complained to him about her,
questioning her commitment to the Blessed Fire. She always sensed
judgment coming from the church leader—and that was before she
ran off to a psychedelic electronica festival. "Hello, Pastor. Thanks for
calling me back."

He stumbled through his words at first, as if he'd had a prepared
script for ministering to her and was rushing through it. "I-I've wanted
to talk to you for some time now. I should have called right after your
mother's death and before this business between you and Shane reached
a crisis point. I'm sorry I didn't. You were new to our congregation and
have seemed a little wary of us at times. But I should have told you
how, in our deepest struggles, in times of sorrow and grief, God still
has a plan for us. He calls on a grieving wife to first care for her husband and for her children, even in times of great pain, as He cares for
us even as we disappoint Him. He shows us that we can only begin to
heal through His love—" But then he suddenly shifted to Leah and
David Jr., "—but, obviously, we have another situation on our hands
right now—"

"Are they with you?" Bethany asked.

"No," the pastor said. "I had hoped they were with you."

"No," Bethany said, "but you think they're together?"

"Yes. We're sure of it. David Jr. was supposed to drive home from Tacoma yesterday. But then he called Darlene on his way and said he was making a detour to pick up Leah because her family—your family—was imploding."

"I wouldn't say imploding." Bethany looked over at Kinnick.

Pastor Gallen went on: "His last text said that something came up and he wasn't coming home after all. Darlene wrote back, but Davy didn't even open the text. She can follow his phone's location. I don't entirely understand the technology like Darlene does, but she says his signal cut out last night somewhere up there. Maybe his battery died, or he turned off his phone, or drove out of range—"

"In Spokane?"

"Well, no," he said, "she lost the signal northwest of there. Near a town called—"

In the background, the voice of a woman, his wife, Darlene, saying, "Springdale."

"Springdale," the pastor repeated.

Bethany looked over at her father. She covered her phone and spoke in a whisper, "Do you think they would've gone to your place?"

Kinnick shrugged. "I don't know why they would."

"Sister Bethany?" the pastor was saying. "Are you there?"

She put the phone back to her ear. "Yes. I'm here."

"Can I ask—how is your father's friend? The one who was shot up here."

"He's going to be fine," she said. "We just saw him."

"Oh, good. I'm relieved. We don't need that kind of trouble. The young man who accidentally shot him feels terrible about it."

Yeah, probably not as terrible as Chuck feels, Bethany thought.

Then the pastor cleared his throat. "And, well . . . there's something else that I—that we—well— Um . . ." He seemed hesitant about what he was going to say next, and Bethany heard the woman's voice in the background again.

"Go on, David, tell her."

"I *am* telling her, Darlene," Pastor Gallen said, the first indication of weariness in his voice. "I wanted to apologize to you personally, Bethany. My son is going through a difficult time, as a lot of young people are these days, bombarded with conflicting information, with a culture that worships permissiveness and debauchery, images that confuse and titillate, that go against God's will, and make a mockery of His plans for us, as revealed not only in Genesis and Leviticus and Romans and elsewhere, but also, Jeremiah, 28:11, and I just wanted to say—"

There was a rustling, and she could hear Darlene trying to grab the phone from him. "Darlene, would you—"

"If you're not going to tell her—"

"I *am* telling her!"

"Give me the phone, David. Please." Then it was Darlene's voice in her ear: "Sister Bethany, what my husband is trying to say is that David Jr. is gay."

"We don't *know* that!" Pastor Gallen said in the background.

"Of course we do!" she said to him. "We've known it since he was six!" And back into the phone: "He's never had any interest in girls. And lately, he's been talking about this young man at school, who, we recently found out, is gay, and we overheard Davy say he has feelings for this boy—"

"Darlene!" the pastor said again.

"David. Please." Her voice softened and now she was talking to her husband. "You know it's true. Remember the images we found on his computer? And why else does an almost twenty-year-old boy, when pressured by his father to find a girlfriend, choose a thirteen-year-old girl that he's only met twice, someone he can't even date for two years."

"Oh," Bethany said. "I see." She suddenly felt an ache for Leah, who likely would have fallen for a gay boy at *some* point in her life, so many straight girls did. But, usually, this kind of thing happened a few years later, at seventeen, or at twenty, at theater camp, or in college. To have her first love be gay? At thirteen? This was going to sting. Oh, poor Leah.

Darlene seemed exhausted. She said to Bethany: "David asked him to come home this week. Yesterday, I found out why. So, I told Davy why his father had summoned him."

"I didn't *summon* him, Darlene—" the pastor said. "I just wanted—"

"He wants to send Davy to conversion therapy," Darlene said. "He wants to do it quickly and quietly, before anyone in the church finds out."

"Darlene, I want to offer him the opportunity to talk to someone, that's all," Pastor Gallen said in the background.

"So," Darlene said to Bethany, "I guess you can see why Davy didn't come home last night."

The pastor said, "Please, Darlene. This is hard enough."

Bethany thought she should probably let the Gallens work through this by themselves. "Listen, Darlene, I have a pretty good idea where they are. We'll look for them there and I'll call you as soon as I know something."

"Thank you," Darlene said.

Bethany wanted to say something else, to tell them to go easy on their son, or to have an open mind, but the words failed her, and she hung up in the middle of Darlene saying, "God Bless you, Beth—"

- - -

SHE TRIED SHANE once more, got no answer, and left another message— "Shane, we think we know where Leah is. Please call me back."

Then Bethany called Joanie's number. She handed the phone to Kinnick, who had changed directions and was driving them north out of Spokane, the suburban streets giving way to a straight highway that cut through alfalfa and wheat fields, toward the deeply forested foot-hills and mountains looming in the distance.

"H-hello?" It felt so strange to Kinnick, holding a phone to his head again, seven years after he'd thrown his own cell phone out a car window somewhere in Southern Oregon. How ridiculous the whole concept of a "phone" had become over the years—going from the dedicated over-size receiver of his youth, curved and cupped, fitting so nicely in your hand and covering your ear so perfectly, to this hard, unwieldy deck of cards that doubled as movie camera, personal assistant, consumer tracking device, and anxiety crack pipe.

"Hello," Kinnick said again. He thought he could hear a faint voice but there was no answer. "I don't think it's working," he said to Bethany.

"You have it upside down," Asher said from the backseat.

"Oh."

He flipped the phone over, and there was Joanie's voice. "You're talking into the wrong end, Rhys!"

"Yeah, I just realized that."

He could hear Brian's voice in the background, too. "For Christ's sake, he's like a child."

Kinnick explained that they were, at that moment, driving back to his place, and that Leah and David Jr. might have gone there last night.

"Why would they go there?" Joanie asked.

"Go where?" Brian said in the background.

"He thinks they went to *his* place," she told Brian.

"His place? Why would they go to his place?"

"That's what I asked him."

"I have no idea," Kinnick said.

"What did he say?"

"He said he has no idea," Joanie told Brian.

"Does he want us to go?" Brian asked.

"No, he says they're on their way now," Joanie told him.

Brian said, "What I'm saying is, since we're closer, does he want us to drive up there?"

"Do you want us to go since we're closer?" Joanie asked.

"No, that's okay," Kinnick said. This three-way conversation was making him dizzy. "We're almost to Deer Park already. We'll be there soon enough, and if they *are* there, I think Bethany's the one to talk to them."

"He thinks Bethany's the one to talk to them," Joanie told Brian.

"Makes sense," Brian said.

"Brian thinks that makes sense," Joanie said.

Kinnick said, "I just wanted to make sure it's okay with you and Brian if we used your car a little bit longer."

"He wants to know if he can keep the Outback."

"Here, let me talk to him," Brian said.

She handed the phone over.

"I don't want to *keep* your car," Kinnick said. "I just want to use it a little longer. Just until tomorrow."

"No problem," Brian said. "Use it as long as you need."

"I'm planning to get my car towed out of the Episcopal Church parking lot and taken to a shop tomorrow."

"If by shop, you mean junkyard, I think that's a good move. Hey Rhys, listen," Brian said, "are you sure you don't want me to come up there?"

"No, you've done plenty, Brian. I can't tell you how much I appreciate it."

"No, you probably can't. Okay, well, if you change your mind—"

"You'll be my first call," Kinnick said.

It was another thing about phones now; you didn't get the satisfying closure of hanging up. You just stopped talking. Pressed a button. So anticlimactic. He handed the phone back to Bethany. "Probably time for me to get one of these things again. I don't suppose they have one with a rotary dial?"

"We can check."

They turned past Loon Lake and drove west, down a steep hill and, eventually, through the town of Springdale, turning past the lumber mill on Hunters Road and starting the last ten miles of this journey, back to the place where it had all started. It was a drive that Kinnick could make in his sleep, and he glimpsed, through the trees, familiar old landmarks: listing barns and abandoned cabins, scraggly cattle and sheep moving toward salt blocks and watering troughs. But as much as he'd lived in *this place* the last seven years, he'd also spent much of that time in his head, hiding (behind self-pity and stubbornness) from the people who needed him. Kinnick glanced over. Asher was asleep again. Bethany was staring out her window. But when they were a mile from his house, she suddenly turned to her dad. "Weren't you lonely up here?"

"Not at first, no," he said. "I was happy to be away from the bullshit, the politics and gossip. The division. All the noise I mistook for life. But it sneaks up on you. Eventually, the solitude becomes physical, like thirst. I remember, one day, maybe in my second winter, I started getting this panicky feeling. Like I couldn't breathe. I used to drive to Springdale and park outside the tavern. Didn't even go in. I just sat there and waited for someone to come out. It was like I needed to just *see* another human being, to know I wasn't alone in the world."

Bethany had a pained look on her face, and he wondered if everything he said from now on would be taken as an affront. (*If you were so lonely*, Dad, *why didn't you come and see* me?) Should he apologize again? Should every sentence that came out of his mouth begin with *I'm sorry*?

"Then one day," he said, "I started going *inside* the tavern to see people."

This caused Bethany to smile. "I do understand why you moved up here," she said. She glanced in the backseat, perhaps to make sure Asher was still asleep, and lowered her voice: "I get it, too, the urge to run. I can't tell you how many times. To just . . . go. Leave everything behind. But here's the thing—in my daydreams? I never *arrive* anywhere. There's never a landing place. And . . . turns out . . . it *was not* a music festival in Canada."

They laughed together.

"Do you think I just haven't found it yet? Or does it not exist?"

Kinnick sighed. "Boy, I wish I knew." He wanted to keep talking, to tell her that it was okay to leave Shane, if that's what she wanted to do, that he would help her financially and with the kids, whatever she needed, but he wasn't sure how she would take that.

Bethany was staring out her window as they passed a makeshift house in the woods, the kind of place Kinnick jokingly called a Stevens County McMansion, tin-roofed pole building thrown up over a single-wide trailer, all rust and exposed timbers, surrounded by a dozen wrecked old cars.

"Well," Bethany said, "whatever my place is . . . it's not out here. I can tell you that." She glanced over at him. "That woman we saw this morning, Lucy. Was that—"

"Yeah," Kinnick said. "That was her. Not that it matters now, but back then, when you were fifteen, there wasn't anything going on with us. Not yet anyway."

"Then why keep it secret?"

"I don't know. Maybe because I already knew how I felt about her. Because I *hoped* something would happen. It was like you'd see right through me if I said something."

"You loved her."

It wasn't a question, but it was the same thing Leah had asked about Joanie. This time Kinnick didn't hesitate. "I did," he said. "Very much, as it turned out. So much that I convinced myself, in my deep self-loathing, that she'd be better off without me." He looked over at her again. "I thought that about everyone, for what it's worth, that you were all better off."

"And how did we do?" Bethany asked. "Without you?"

He looked over. "You did just fine, Bethany." He turned the car off Hunters Road and started down the dirt road that led to his driveway.

"Well." Bethany straightened up. "I'm trying," she said, the weariness in her voice breaking him a little.

- - -

THEY EASED OVER the culvert, up his driveway, past the creek and the little stand of birch trees, until they could see the house and outbuildings, the old broken-down pickup. It was strange for Kinnick, seeing his sad little kingdom this way, after being gone for the first time in years. And to have these other people here, apparently inside his house, with his books and his thoughts and his half-finished projects—he felt a moment of panic. What had he accomplished up here?

There was a car parked at the end of his driveway, near the back door of his cinder block shack: a fifteen-year-old Ford Focus with a Jesus fish bumper sticker and a Covenant College parking pass on the back windshield.

"They must be in the house," Kinnick said.

"You don't lock your door?"

"There's no one out here but me and some raccoons. And *they* can't reach the doorknob."

They left Asher asleep in the backseat and opened their car doors, stepping out into the dusty driveway. A gust of wind rustled the leafy birch trees, making a sound like distant shorebreak. "This parent stuff—" Bethany laughed uneasily. "My God."

Kinnick wanted to agree but wasn't sure he had the standing.

The front door of the little gray house opened, and Leah came out onto the porch, dressed in the same jeans and peplum top as the day before. "Mom?" Her voice quavered and she covered her mouth.

"Leah! What are you doing here?"

"We didn't know where else to go." Leah descended the steps, ran to her mother, and fell into Bethany's arms.

"I'm sorry," Bethany said into Leah's hair. "I'm sorry I left you, baby."

So, Kinnick thought, that's how you apologized for leaving.

"Did you get to hear my dad's band play your song?" Leah pulled back and looked up in her mother's face.

"I did."

"And—"

"And it was pretty great."

"Oh, Mom," Leah said. "I'm so glad!"

David Gallen Jr. emerged onto the porch then. He was short and slight, in rumpled khakis and a baby-blue button shirt, his white-blond hair already beginning to recede on his long forehead. He stood with his hands in his pockets, shoulders slumped, squinting through round glasses. If not for his thin hair, he might have passed for thirteen or fourteen himself, Kinnick thought.

"What are you guys *doing* up here?" Bethany asked again.

"Do you know what his parents want to *do* to him?" Leah asked.

"Yeah," said Bethany, "we heard."

"What did they tell you?" Davy asked.

"Well—" Bethany looked over at Kinnick, who nodded. Yes, she should tell the poor kid. "Your parents said they think you might be . . . gay?"

"Unbelievable," Davy said. "They told you that? What, are they just going around telling everyone? Is it in the church bulletin? 'Sunday prayer service starts at nine. Also, David Jr. might be gay!'"

"Of course not," Bethany said. "They're just concerned, that's all."

"He's not gay," Leah said confidently.

Bethany paused a moment, then looked down at her daughter.

Kinnick had what he assumed must be the same thought as Bethany just then: *Wait, how does* Leah *know that. And wait, what did they do inside his house last night.* And, just, generally: *Wait.*

"Oh, Leah," Bethany said, "you guys didn't—" She didn't finish the thought.

"What? No!" Leah looked disgusted. "Gross. Why are parents so obsessed with sex all the time? We kissed is all."

"And I *liked* it!" Davy said triumphantly.

Kinnick briefly wondered if there was an even more remote place he could move to next time.

Still on the porch, Davy folded his arms. "What did my parents say *exactly*?"

Bethany looked over at Kinnick again, who could do nothing but shrug. He felt like he'd dropped out of 300-level parenting, and this was some PhD stuff.

"Well, you should talk to *them* about it, but they told me that maybe there were some images on your computer?"

"I was looking into bodybuilding!"

"And they overheard you saying you had feelings for a boy at school. A boy who might be gay?"

"Marsh! I said I loved Marsh! Everyone loves Marsh. Marsh is hilarious!"

"And Marsh is bi," Leah said, "not gay."

"Yeah," Davy said, "Marsh is bi!"

"What's bi?"

They all turned. Asher was climbing out of the backseat of the Outback.

Leah screamed, "Would you shut up, Asher!"

Davy was still interrogating Bethany. "Wait, so you're telling me my mom thought I was gay because of muscle photos on my computer and because I said I loved a friend at school?"

"Well," Bethany said, "she said something about knowing that you were gay since you were six—"

"Seriously? I don't believe this." Davy put his hands on his head. "That happened, like, three times, total! I mean, what six-year-old doesn't wonder what he looks like in a dress?" For some reason, he looked at Asher when he said this.

"Oh, I'm nine," Asher said.

"And even if I were a cross-dresser, which I'm not, that's not even a signifier of sexuality!" Davy was working up quite a case. "It's like they're stuck in the 1980s."

"What's a cross-dresser?" Asher asked.

"Asher!" Leah yelled again.

Bethany shot another glance to her father, looking for more help, perhaps calling on his parental seniority, but Rhys had nothing to offer in this situation except a change of venue. "Look. Why don't we go inside and talk about this?"

"Not with him!" Leah pointed at her little brother.

Asher was stunned. "What did *I* do?"

SIX

What Happened to Asher

It was a hard decision, but Asher knew what he had to do. He resigned his post as the greatest scout the cavalry had ever seen, effective immediately, telling gruff old General Kinnick that from now on he would only fight on the side of the Indi— er, the Native Americans. *You know my soldiers will have to kill you if they see you,* the general stated. *But I have been the best scout you've ever had,* stated Asher. *I know,* the general stated back. *It's true.* Asher saluted and stated, *I'm sorry, sir, but this is my destiny.* The general stated, *Well, then go with God, soldier,* Asher immediately stating back, *Cool.* The tribe had given him a special name, *Six-nut,* because he was the bravest nine-year-old anyone had ever seen. Nobody could believe what a good scout he was. He talked the chief of the tribe, Standing Water, into moving their horses to a safer river up north, one that he had discovered (and leaped over) on an earlier scouting mission to this remote territory. Six-nut knew that, hidden on this secret river, the horses couldn't be shot by the cavalry solders. Standing Water said this was a brilliant strategy, but that it would be dangerous. He would be taking his life in his own hands. *That's what I do every day,* Asher stated. He found a rifle on the ground, but then he found a better stick and tossed the first one away, and that's when—

"Asher?" It was General Kinnick again, coming out of the back door of the house.

"Yeah."

"We're still talking in here. Are you all right outside by yourself?"

"Yes. I'm fine."

Grandpa Rhys looked all around and breathed in deeply. "Nice out here, isn't it?"

"Yes."

"Stay near the house, okay?"

"Can I go play by the creek?"

Grandpa Rhys looked back at the house, as if wondering if he should ask Asher's mom, but then he said, "Sure. Just don't go very far, okay?"

"Can I jump over it again?"

"Well." His grandfather made a face. "I guess."

General Kinnick took another look around, then settled his eyes on the brave young scout, perhaps knowing that he might be seeing him for the last time. "But come inside if you get wet."

"I will."

And with that, the general went back inside the fort.

And so Six-nut moved slowly into the woods, hiking along the raging river. One wrong step and it would be over for them all. Four braves had been put under his command by Standing Water, surely the first time a nine-year-old had ever led a war party. Asher explained to them the difference between cutbanks and point bars, and they were all amazed. He said they needed to find a good point bar on which they could cross the horses to the other side.

Then he saw a rock that looked a little like a chess piece, a bishop, and Asher bent over and picked it up. It wasn't flat on the bottom like a real bishop, and it was kind of uneven, but it could pass. Bishops were his favorite pieces (even though they couldn't really do very much, and he suspected they would ultimately be his downfall, once he rose to the level of grand master, because he would always rather sacrifice his knights than his preferred bishops) and he wondered how you went about flattening the bottoms of rocks anyway, to get them to stand up, and whether he could find a whole chess set among these rocks. Maybe he could build a board from a log and then find enough rocks to teach the men in his war party to play chess.

Doubtful. He'd need to find sixteen light rocks and sixteen dark rocks, half of them in pairs. And the other sixteen would have to be pretty much the same, for pawns. Maybe these little round pebbles. He bent over and picked one up. For some reason, he had the urge to put it in his mouth, which he did. It was cold and dirty and . . . rocky. He spat it out.

He looked back at the house. Smoke was coming out of the chimney. Grandpa Rhys had built a fire. Maybe for coffee. Was Leah drinking coffee now, too? He didn't like that she was getting to be in the grown-up conversations, while he still got sent outside to play. What was the big deal? So, Leah and Davy had kissed and Davy was friends with someone who was a bi, which apparently meant that you thought boys *and* girls were cute, which he didn't see why that was a problem. Wasn't that how *everyone* should be?

He found himself back at the same corner of the creek where he'd tried to jump before. He set his rifle down on the ground. The other side would be a perfect place to bring the tribe's horses. But, first, it needed to be properly scouted. The last time, his boots had messed him up. So, he took them off and set them in the grass high above the cutbank. He stood in the wild grass in his socks, watching the creek water burble around this corner. He eased forward a step, to the edge, crouched, bent his knees, and jumped.

He landed perfectly on the inside corner, on the dirt of the point bar, just like his grandfather had suggested. "Hey!" he said.

But look, now his boots were on the other side. He wondered if Indian scouts ever went barefoot.

That's when a noise in the woods behind Asher startled him. He turned. From behind a tree stepped a big bald man, dressed all in black, black gloves on his hands, a cool utility belt around his waist, a holstered handgun on his right side. He had a little tube in his hand, a small telescope, like the one that usually went on a rifle.

"Brother Dean? What are you doing here?"

Brother Dean put his finger to his lips.

Asher whispered: "What are you doing here?"

Brother Dean whispered back. "Who's inside the house, Asher? Is that cop in there with your grandpa?"

"No, he got shot, remember?" Asher whispered. "He's at this lady's house. We stopped and saw him. It's just my mom and my grandpa and Leah and David Jr."

Dean looked at the house. "You're sure there's no one else in there?"

"Yeah," Asher whispered, "I'm sure."

Brother Dean pulled a small walkie-talkie from his utility belt. He pressed the button and said into it: "All clear. We are a go. Repeat. We are a go."—Asher wishing *he* had a walkie-talkie like that.

- - -

INSIDE THE HOUSE, Bethany patted David Jr. on the arm. "Look, I know this is scary, and hard, but you need to talk to your parents about it, Davy. They want to help."

"Are you kidding? They want to deprogram me!"

"We'll talk to them. Your mom seemed very understanding. And your dad—" She didn't finish the thought. Davy's dad probably *did* want to deprogram him.

Davy stood and walked to the window. "Where do they get off saying I'm gay, anyway?" He turned back. "It's not like I've even done anything! How are they such experts on what I want when *I* don't even know?"

Leah opened her mouth, as if to reassure Davy about the kiss they'd shared last night, but she seemed to think better of it. She'd explained to her mother that they'd talked all night, gotten blankets from Kinnick's room upstairs and spread them on the floor, among all the books. At some point, Leah had offered to let him kiss her, to see if he liked it. Bethany felt so conflicted. Here, her daughter experiences her first kiss, and they're not talking about that, but about conversion therapy and bisexuality and whether wearing women's clothes had anything to do with one's sexuality.

Bethany sighed. "Let's all just . . . stay calm, huh?"

She sipped the terrible coffee her father had made. She had to breathe through her mouth in here because of the smells in the house. Body odor and dirty clothes and old books. Like the crypt of a mummified philosophy professor. Not exactly how she'd been picturing her own "escape." Meanwhile, her father could not sit still, and kept moving stacks of books, picking things up, setting them down elsewhere—like someone tidying a compost pile. He smelled his armpit, then changed shirts, then smelled his armpit again. She wasn't sure she could handle this new *giving-an-effort* Rhys, who, at one point, went to his pantry and brought out a plate of random canned and dried foods from the kitchen. "Soda cracker? Vienna sausage? Dehydrated huckleberry?"— each offering somehow sadder than the last.

Davy sighed. He picked a soda cracker off the plate and sat back down. "Maybe I should just move to Canada or something."

"It's not so great up there, either," Bethany said, her father giving her a warm smile. "Look, Davy, I'll help you talk to your parents. I'll go with you."

"My dad's not going to listen to you," Davy said.

That was undoubtedly true. Especially after what the church believed she'd done, leaving Shane for her old drug-addled, musician boyfriend.

"You know what would piss my dad off the most?" A sly smile crossed Davy's face, and for the first time, Bethany thought this wispy young man might have a chance in life. "Before they found their new church,

Marsh's parents baptized him in a Catholic Church. I should tell him Marsh is Catholic and that we want to get married in his church. Dad's head will explode!"

"I don't think men can marry each other in the Catholic Church," Leah said quietly, almost to herself, as if it was dawning on her where this was all headed.

Oh, how Bethany wished she were just talking to her daughter about this. She dreaded what was coming for Leah, the teenage years, all that heartache and blooming awkwardness, the cacophonous thoughts and unwieldy feelings. She could already sense her daughter beginning to pull away, slipping into adolescent shutdown mode.

She patted Leah on the leg, and they made eye contact, Leah swallowing hard, Bethany mouthing, *It's okay.*

Then Bethany stood. "Listen, Davy, before we do anything else, can we at least let your parents know that you're safe?"

Davy held up his phone. "No coverage."

"We can drive back toward town and send them a text."

There was a sound outside then.

Kinnick looked up. Dust at the far end of the driveway. "Someone's coming."

Bethany went to the front window and looked out, Kinnick stepping up beside her.

A black Dodge Ram pickup was driving toward the house.

"Shit," Rhys said. "I know that truck." He reached up and touched his yellow-bruised eye, the panic rising in his chest.

The pickup parked right behind the Outback, nearly at its bumper, as if signaling that no one was going anywhere for a while. The driver's-side door opened and out stepped the man with the goatee. He was wearing a black Kevlar vest, his handgun holstered under his armpit.

"That's the guy who hit me," Kinnick said.

Shane got out of the passenger seat, his clean-shaven face gaunt, mouth pinched, as if he hadn't smiled in months. He, at least, appeared to be unarmed. He looked toward the house, trying to see inside.

And then, from the tree line behind them, out stepped Dean Burris, also in black and in a Kevlar vest, a handgun holstered at his waist. He had a hand on Asher's shoulder.

Bethany put her hand to her mouth. "Oh, no."

Asher, who was, for some reason, not wearing his boots, ran to the passenger side of the truck, to his father, who bent down and hugged the boy.

Dean Burris stood with his hands on his hips. He walked farther up the driveway and called to the house, "Oh, Mr. Kinnick! You'd best come out now. You've got company!"

- - -

THE FRONT DOOR opened and Kinnick walked out alone. He pulled the door closed behind him. Let out a deep breath. He could do this. A light breeze had picked up, and the air had gotten warmer; a fine sifting of dust blew off the driveway. Kinnick walked past the wringer washing machine and down the wooden steps toward the three men, trying to look calm and unhurried.

"Hello, Mr. Burris," he said. "What can I do for you?"

The three men before him stood in a triangle, Dean out front, Shane behind him to the right, hands on Asher's shoulders, the goateed man to Burris's left and slightly behind him, leaning against the front of the truck.

"Well, if it isn't Rhys Kinnick, staff writer," Dean said. "You know what? When I asked about you, back in that town where little David Jr.'s cell phone cut out last night, folks said, 'Kinnick? Oh, sure, he lives up Hunters highway. About eleven miles.' And look, here you are."

"Here I am," Kinnick said, willing his voice to sound deep and tough.

"Where's your cop friend?" Dean asked. "He's not here to bail you out this time?"

"He's on his way," Kinnick lied. "With some of his buddies."

"I don't think that's true," Dean said. "Asher says he's at some nice lady's house, recovering from the last time he tangled with us."

Kinnick breathed deeply, still trying to keep his voice from cracking. "Asher," he said evenly, "why don't you go in the house with your mom and Leah while Brother Dean and I talk, okay?"

But Shane kept his hands on the boy's shoulders. Asher looked up at his father, who continued to stare coldly at Kinnick. Still, of the three men, Shane was clearly the least threatening, and the most unsure of himself. The other two, armed, wearing Kevlar, had come here expecting some kind of battle. Who knew what they'd told poor, gullible Shane. He'd probably expected to find blue-helmeted UN soldiers camped on his father-in-law's land.

Kinnick gave Shane his most disarming smile and tried again. "Shane, whatever problem you have with me, let's not put the kids in danger, okay? Maybe take Asher inside? What do you say?" He looked pleadingly at his son-in-law. "And you and Bethany can talk in there. You guys have a lot to figure out."

Shane looked over at Brother Dean, who still had that grim smile on his face. "Don't look at me," Dean said to Shane, "unless you want us to go in there and get your whore wife for you."

"Shane," Kinnick said. "Listen to me. These guys are *not* welcome in my house. Or on my land. But if you want to take Asher inside, and talk to Bethany, please, go ahead."

"Don't let that woman off the hook, Brother Shane!" Dean said. "'For if a man knows not how to rule his own house, how shall he take care of the church of God?'"

"Come on, Dad." Asher looked up at Shane. "I'll show you the house. It's full of old books. And scratch paper. You know what that is, scratch paper?" He took his father by the hand, and they started for the front porch. "I jumped over that creek," he said, pointing beyond the house. "I left my boots there."

"Wait, you made it?" Kinnick asked as they passed. He put out a hand and Asher high-fived it. "Nice job." Then Kinnick said quietly to Shane, "Upstairs." He had told Bethany to take Davy and Leah upstairs and to wait there. He also tried to send Shane a mental message: *please, don't let them get hurt*, but he couldn't read the man's eyes. When the front door closed, Kinnick turned back to Dean.

"I'll tell you what," Kinnick said. "I'll take Shane back to town with his family. Nice of you to bring him up here, but you guys can head out now."

"Can we?" Dean Burris laughed. "But I don't think we're done talking, Rhys Kinnick, staff writer." He grinned maliciously. "You know, I had no idea at the chess deal that you were the one who wrote them terrible stories about me back in the day." He turned to the goateed man. "Did I tell you what this creep called me, Bobby?"

Goateed Bobby, who had presumably heard the story several times, nodded.

"Dominion Eagle Killer!" Dean Burris said. "Man puts it in a headline and everything! Then I go run for county commissioner a few years later, it's all 'Dominion Eagle Killer' in the newspaper and I lose. All because this lousy son of a bitch thought he was being so clever."

Kinnick recalled that old reporter dodge: *I don't write the headlines.* Instead, he said, "I wasn't the wildlife agent who arrested you. Or the judge who sentenced you."

"Well, they ain't here, so I guess you'll have to do." Dean took two more steps toward Kinnick, his boots kicking up dust. They were maybe four feet apart, now, Kinnick trying not to back down.

"Look," Kinnick said, "I'm sorry if—"

But Burris interrupted. "Did you know that I have a copy of them stories you wrote? My mom clipped 'em out. You believe that? And not out of pride, either. How do you think that would make a mother feel, reading those lies about her son, like he's some kind of criminal?"

In some ways, this was more comfortable territory, defending a story he'd written in the newspaper in *don't-shoot-the-messenger* style; it made Kinnick think maybe he could get out of this after all. "Look, Dean, I'm really sorry the story affected you that way," Kinnick said. "It wasn't my intention. All I was doing was reporting what happened in the courtroom."

"I'm just saying I didn't connect your name at first, when Shane told us about his sucker-punching father-in-law. But hell, if I'd known 'Rhys Kinnick, staff writer' was the man at that chess deal, I wouldn't have had Bobby here"—he looked back over his shoulder—"work you over." He turned back. "No, I'd have done it myself."

Adrenaline coursed through Kinnick then. He had the urge to rush Dean, but he knew where that would lead. "Look, I didn't mean to—"

But Dean leaned forward and squinted at Kinnick's face. "*Damn!* Did we bust your cheek, Rhys Kinnick, staff writer?"

"Zygomatic arch," Kinnick said.

"See that, Bobby!" He looked back at the goateed man. "You broke the man's face! What's the matter with you? Where's your manners?"

Bobby chuckled behind Dean.

"Let's all calm down," Kinnick said. He felt almost as if he and Dean had been cast in roles; he knew there had to be a way past that. "Let's not let this situation get out of hand."

"Calm down?" Dean Burris said. "Oh, I'm calm. And the *situation*, as I see it, Rhys Kinnick, staff writer, got out of hand when you brought that lunatic up to the Rampart and he shot my truck. The situation, Rhys Kinnick, is that you got my friend's lawful-wedded wife in there, along with the pastor's faggot son, and I don't see that you have any say in the *situation*. In fact, I just have one question for you, Rhys Kinnick, staff writer." He smiled. "Who has dominion now?"

"Listen—" Kinnick put his hands out in a peaceful gesture.

"Did you know I had a wife, too? Back then?"

Kinnick tried to recall; had he seen a woman in court? He shook his head.

"Yeah, not the sort of woman to wait a couple of years while you're in a federal institution. She lives in Billings now." Dean took a deep breath. "I tell you what." He pulled his handgun from its holster and flipped it over, so the handle was facing out, Kinnick wondering briefly, *Is he going to hand me his gun?* "I'm gonna do you a favor," Dean said.

Kinnick felt a charge go through his legs, and his mouth went dry. Jesus, the man wouldn't shoot him, would he?

"I'll even up our work and then we'll go," Burris said. And with that, he swung the butt of the gun at Kinnick's head. Rhys leaned back and got his arm up, blocking some of the blow, but the gun butt connected hard with his jaw, staggering him backward.

The pain, again, was excruciating. But Kinnick felt perversely proud that, this time, he hadn't gone down.

Burris was red-faced. "Oh, no, Rhys Kinnick, staff writer, looks like I accidentally broke your jaw instead of the other cheek." He turned and looked again at the goateed man. "Sorry. I messed up your work, Bobby."

Bobby didn't answer this time.

Kinnick held his hand against his throbbing right jaw. It felt like, if he let go, the whole thing would simply fall off his face and drop to the ground. He ran his tongue along a cracked molar and tried to stop the moan that escaped his mouth.

Burris turned back. "How about this? What if I break your *left* jaw, then your *right* cheek. Then you'll have two breaks on each side. Top and bottom. You'll be evened up. You'll be—what's the word?" He looked confused for a moment, then turned back to Bobby, the goateed man. "What's the word I'm looking for, Bobby? When both sides are the same?"

"Thymetrical," Kinnick managed to say.

And with that, Burris spun back and swung the gun in his fist again, but this time, Kinnick didn't get his hand up and he took the brunt of it to his right cheek and eye socket, and, hearing the cracking sound of celery stalks again, he went down hard in the dirt. He couldn't stop the scream that came from his mouth.

"Ooh, I *heard* that one!" Burris said.

That's when the front door of the house opened behind Kinnick, Shane coming out on the porch, hands out, peacemaker style. "That's enough, Dean!"

Dean laughed. "Is it, Shane? Is it enough? Boy, it didn't take long to turn you back into a pussy-whipped little piece-a-shit, did it?" Dean turned to Bobby again. "Little man can't keep his woman at home, and he wants to tell me what's *enough*?"

"Dean—" Bobby began.

"I'm saying, you made your point," Shane said. "Look, I appreciate your help. But you can go now. I got it from here."

"You got it?" He gestured at Kinnick with the butt of the gun. "Your asshole father-in-law ruined my life, brought a cop to my church, shot up my truck, and you think you got it?"

On the ground, Kinnick was dizzy with pain. He rolled over onto his hands and knees. He didn't see the next blow coming—a kick, Dean's boot snapping his face back, his nose and mouth spattering the dirt driveway with blood as he landed on his back again.

"*Stay away from him!*"

Splayed out on the ground, coughing blood, Kinnick looked back over his shoulder, through bleary eyes, to see his daughter descending the front porch steps with . . . something in her hands. He squinted. Was that . . . his little Dragonfly pellet-shooting air rifle? His raccoon defense system—she must've found it upstairs. Maybe when she moved the kids up there. She held the gun against her shoulder, and was looking down the barrel, as if she'd fired a rifle before, Kinnick wondering when, and how, and with whom. Shane, maybe? More fatherly failure on his part, never teaching his daughter to shoot. Of course, an air-powered pellet rifle wasn't likely to break the skin, let alone stop a lunatic wearing a bulletproof vest. But as terrified as he was, Rhys couldn't help but be proud of Bethany's effort; hell, maybe Dean would be fooled, and think, for a moment, it was a real rifle, a kid's .22 perhaps, pointed at him.

"Bethany—" Shane sounded a warning. "Don't—" He put his hand out, but she walked past it, the gun pointed at Burris's face.

This latest development threatened to send Dean over the edge. "Shane," he said, "control your whore wife, or I'll do it for you!"

Shane took another step toward Bethany. "Beth. Let's calm down now—"

"Wait. Is that an *air* rifle?" Burris cut him off. He was squinting at Bethany. He looked over his shoulder once more at quiet, goateed Bobby. "You seeing this, Bobby? Whore's got a pellet gun. Maybe she's gonna put my eye out with it."

Bobby gave no answer.

"Beth." Kinnick rolled over again and started crawling in the dirt toward his daughter. "*Pleathe.*"

"We're almost finished working on your father's face, Sister Bethany," Burris said, "but if you want, I can take a run at yours next." He took a step toward her. "Or, if you want, I can shove that gun up your—"

"Stop it!" Bethany said, and the tears began streaming down her cheeks. "Just stop it! Get out of here. Now!" She looked over to her husband. "Shane. Please." Her voice quavered. "They're gonna kill him. And they're terrifying the children."

That's when Dean Burris rushed her, yanked the pellet gun from her hands, and threw it aside. It clattered in the dirt. Bethany put her hands up to stop him, but Burris grabbed her by the wrist, twisted, and spun her to the ground.

"Dean—" Shane started toward him.

From the ground, Kinnick, too, began crawling to help.

But Burris took Bethany by the hair and began dragging her backward toward his pickup. "Lying whore needs to be taught a lesson."

"Dean!" Shane yelled. "Let go of her!"

From the ground, Bethany punched backward, over her shoulder, and hit Burris's arm, but he just kept dragging her down the driveway, her feet kicking up dust.

"Dean—" Shane pleaded again.

Bethany swung again and this time Dean reached down and smacked her in the ear with the gun butt, pulling her by the hair with the other hand. "Someone needs to teach . . . this bitch—"

"Dean!" Shane said once more. "That's enough!" And he started running toward them.

SEVEN

What Happened to Shane

Shane used to have this recurring nightmare: it's dawn and he's outside their old house in Grants Pass, wearing flip-flops (always, for some reason, he's in flip-flops), looking up and down the street, when he hears a buzzing sound, and darkness rises on the horizon, becoming waves of monstrous locusts from the Book of Revelation approaching as helicopters (*the noise of their wings . . . like chariots with horses . . . tails like scorpions*) and demonic hordes of faceless soldiers (. . . *with hair like women's hair* . . .) begin moving up the street, pulling people from houses (. . . *slaying a third part of men* . . .), and in the dream, all he can do is stand there, rooted to the ground, watching as they approach, wishing he'd been more prepared, more diligent, that he'd built a bunker, or moved them to the mountains, or put a better dead bolt on the door, anything—knowing that his wife and children are inside and that he is helpless to stop what is coming . . . How long, he wondered, had he been so afraid? Of something terrible happening to his family? To his country? How long had he suspected it was *already happening*?

No, he *knew* fear.

But this—this was something different: immediate, primal, physical. Systems beyond his cognition fired up: fight-or-flight amygdala signaling hypothalamus, pituitary gland releasing hormones into the blood, nervous system firing adrenaline into the mix, cortisol raising heart rate and blood pressure, skin pores tightened, lungs on fire, pupils dilated, mouth dry, tunnel vision—an enraged Shane running toward this man he'd thought was a friend, this man he'd thought could help *protect* his family, thinking, *I might have to kill him*, this man who was dragging the woman he loved by the hair, and that's when—

A quick vision from the past interrupted this rush of pure instinct.

Nothing more than the synaptic spark of an out-of-the-way neuronal sensor—a fraction of a millisecond in mental processing time, a day forever lodged in his brain—and, as Dean Burris dragged his struggling wife by the hair down the dirt driveway—this was the memory that popped unbidden into Shane's mind:

Junior year high school. First mustache. Hot Sharon Bell invites him to Young Life. (You mean Lame Life!) But Sharon Bell has a butt you'd follow anywhere, even to church, and Shane goes to their dumb picnic where he meets a flock of bland, smiling-Christian types, of no interest socially, *so* lame they are somehow lamer than *his* lame friends. (Shane is a gearhead, a motor monkey, always in the parking lot, comparing tires, speakers, horsepower.) Despite Sharon Bell's righteous backside, religion doesn't stick with Shane that day at Young Life—it will be another twelve years, many of them spent wasted, pissed at the world, before Shane truly hears the call of his Lord and Savior, Jesus Christ— but this one image from high school *will* stick with him—

—and it came to him now, in the instant he moved toward Dean Burris—

A slow kid at his school, known as *Bones* (because he's so fat, an early high school attempt at irony), is being teased by a few baseball players in the parking lot on a warm spring day as Bones waits for his mom to pick him up. They push the kid back and forth like a human Hacky Sack. *What did you have for lunch today, Bones? Everything? You like to eat dicks, Bones? Or just balls?* Submental stuff—no one is more hateful than high school baseball players, hat brims low, chaw in their gums, a-hole subset of the most popular kids in school, and years later, when Shane hears people rail about "elites" and their vicious attempts to control and sabotage good Americans, it is these baseball players he will sometimes picture, confident jerks who come from places like Forest Lake and who think they're so much better than you. But on this day, no one at his school is dumb enough to stand up to these bullying princes, to insert themselves in the trouble. And so, while Bones is tortured, they all look away, or wander off, Shane staring at his Sambas. And that's when one of the Smiling Christians he recalls seeing at the Young Life picnic, a small, nerdy senior in a red polo shirt, whose name might actually *be* Christian, steps between Bones and the baseball players. "What's the matter with you," Christian scolds them. "Do you get off bullying people?"

And that's it. Predictably, the baseball players turn from Bones to Christian, making fun of the nerd's clothes, calling him queer, but Shane is impressed that Christian isn't fazed by this—of course nothing changes that day, life goes on, it's just one of a million daily encounters between high school haves and have-nots—

But twelve years later, when Shane Collins, on probation for possession, found himself weeping at a court-ordered NA meeting in a church basement in Salem, Oregon, he *felt the Lord* come into his soul and his chest seemed to crack open and his limbs began to tingle as he remembered brave Christian, or whatever his name was—

No—it was something even weirder! Charlton, yes, Charlton!

Anyway, he remembered thinking: *That is what God can do.* He can make the fear go away. He can fill you up, the way He filled that smiling string bean in the red polo shirt and gave him the strength to stand up to a demonic horde of baseball players, to stand up to the bullies and the elites—

That was the kind of Christian, the kind of Charlton, that Shane had longed to be, the conqueror of fear, not its slave—

And now, as his wife swung her fists over her shoulder helplessly, and Dean Burris dragged her toward his truck, and his battered jerk of a father-in-law crawled away in the dirt—typical—Shane looked quickly over his shoulder, hoping the kids weren't seeing this—*Oh, God, Asher, please don't be watching*—but if he was, Shane knew what he'd want his son to see, his father *standing up* to the bullies and baseball players of the world, standing up to the demonic hordes, and maybe, just maybe, it was never too late to be a better Charlton, and maybe, if you could be born again, you could also be born again . . . *again*, because Shane yelled, "Hey!" as he wound up and threw a haymaker at Dean Burris, missing his intended target, Dean's bulbous chin, but landing with a dull thump on the man's thick neck—*Yes*, Shane thought, *this* felt right, *this* was good, the endless *fear* turned now to fighting for the people he loved—as Shane swung again, brushing Dean's cheek and nose this time, and he said once more, "Let go of my wife!" which worked, because the spit-furious Dean finally let go of his handful of Bethany's hair, dropped her to the ground, swung his handgun up to the right, and shot Shane Collins in the forehead.

- - -

ALL CRUELTY SPRINGS from weakness. Seneca said that, along with: Ignorance is the cause of fear. Kinnick had always believed these adages to be true, but now, bleeding on the ground, watching Dean Burris stand over his dead son-in-law, Rhys wondered if Seneca might have been a little silly to believe in the causal roots of evil. He wondered if cruelty and its bride, fear, didn't just exist spontaneously, forces as elemental and eternal as gravity.

"Jesus, Dean!" Goateed Bobby was the first to speak, the shot still ringing in the air. "What the *fuck*! What did you do?"

And then Bethany's voice, screaming, begging, crying: "Shane? Shane? Shane!" She crawled toward her husband, who had fallen backward, his head turned away, legs crumpled unnaturally beneath him. She reached his left side, weeping, trying to pull his limp body into her arms.

On the ground, Kinnick crawled in the opposite direction.

"Dean!" Bobby said again. "What the fuck! What do we do now?"

What rubbish, Kinnick thought, his *Atlas of Wisdom*. Now, at the end of life, how short, cruel, and pointless it all seemed, *wisdom*, what a waste that houseful of books before him had turned out to be. He looked up at Dean Burris, who stood in the middle of the driveway, panting, handgun hanging at the end of his big right hand, while, just a few feet away, Bethany held the newly dead Shane and wept.

"He attacked me," Dean said flatly. He took in a deep breath, let it out, and turned to look at Bobby. "Well," he said, "I think we gotta clean this up now." The coldness in his voice.

"No." Bobby shook his head. "No fuckin' way, Dean." He put his hands out to the side, as if saying, *I'm not helping you with this—but I'm not stopping you, either.*

Kinnick had crawled all the way to his target, the air rifle, and he rolled over and picked it off the ground. *We gotta clean this up*, Burris said. Rhys remembered Chuck's advice. If the man is wearing Kevlar, aim for his front pocket. From his side, he blinked the tears from his eyes, brought the air rifle to his shoulder, flipped the safety off, and pointed at Burris's left front pocket (Kinnick always kept the Dragon-fly pumped at least ten times, and loaded with pellets), and, as Burris turned away from his goateed friend, Kinnick pulled the trigger, and with a pleasing *pfft*, a single pellet flew twenty-five feet and hit Burris, not in the left pants pocket or right pants pocket, but right between them, right, as Chuck might have said, in the dickhole.

Of course, even pumped ten times, the pellet wouldn't break the skin, or go through Dean's jeans, but the shot must have really hurt, because Burris doubled over, and with an "Oof," he dropped his handgun to the ground, and instinctively covered his groin with both hands.

Probably too far for Kinnick to get the gun, but he scrambled to his feet, and staggered, listing left, before finally moving toward the big man, pumping the air rifle barrel as he went. One, two—

That's when he saw, over Dean's shoulder, a plume of dust. A car turning up his driveway. Three, four pumps—

Kinnick kept moving and pumping the rifle—five, six—maybe he'd get even luckier this time and hit Burris in the eye. He wondered if anyone had ever won a fight as badly outgunned as he was now.

But even outgunned, Kinnick knew he would not stop, not until Burris killed him, and he was filled with grim determination: *I will never give up. I will protect Bethany and my grandchildren, I will beat this man to death with the stock of this pellet gun, I will beat this man with the broken bones of my own battered face*—

He staggered toward Burris—seven pumps, eight—and from fifteen feet, raised and fired again, but he was on the move, and this time the shot went right, pellet hitting dirt as the big man looked up, picked his gun off the ground, and rose to fire—Kinnick realizing that he wasn't going to reach him in time.

So, he threw the air rifle, which caused Burris to duck, and this gave Kinnick a quick view of the car that had come up the drive, and that had stopped some eighty feet away: a Ford Bronco, Brian already leaning out of the open driver's-side door.

Burris rose again, straightened slowly and said, "You fucking son of a bitch!" He raised the gun toward Kinnick, who apologized again in his mind—*I'm sorry, Beth, I really thought*—when a crack echoed from what he instinctively knew was a larger gun, and Dean Burris's right arm seemed to explode—slivers of bone, mists of blood—the handgun dropping from Burris's destroyed right hand to the dirt, the big man following his shattered arm to the ground with a banshee's scream.

Kinnick managed the last steps to Burris's feet; woozy, he bent over and picked the handgun from the dirt where Dean had dropped it. Recalling his brief firearms training (feet apart, left foot forward, barrel pointed slightly down, thank you, Crazy Ass Chuck) Kinnick pointed the gun at Bobby, but the goateed man had not pulled his own weapon. He dropped to the ground and cried out: "No! Please!" and began scurrying under the truck.

Kinnick thought he might pass out. He steadied himself. Eighty feet down the driveway, he saw Brian, leaning out over the open door of his Bronco, still looking through the scope of his .30-06. Exhausted, Kinnick sat down in the dirt, alternating pointing the gun at Bobby, and at the screaming Burris, then at Bobby again, who was completely under the truck, now, only the pale palms of his hands showing. Kinnick let out a deep breath as his daughter sat rocking her dead husband, her helpless cries joining the whelps of the one-armed Dominion Eagle Killer, rising together in the still air.

EIGHT

What Happened to Brian

With the shot still ringing in the air, he swung the scope to the second man, who looked properly, pants-shittingly, terrified, and who immediately fell to the ground and began crawling under the truck. Brian swung the scope back to the bald man, writhing on the ground in front of Kinnick. His friend's face was plump and bloodied, but he held the handgun steadily, pointing it from the scared man under the truck to the one Brian had just shot.

Oh God, Brian realized, *I just shot someone.*

"Brian?" Joanie said from inside the Bronco. "Is he—"

"It's okay, Joan," Brian said. "I got him."

Only then did he realize how badly he was shaking.

- - -

JOANIE TOOK THE Bronco back up the road until she got a phone signal. She made the first frantic call, and within fifteen minutes, sirens could be heard roaring up the highway in the valley below. They came in waves: paramedics and ambulances from Chewelah and Spokane, Stevens County sheriff's deputies from Colville, assisting deputies from Spokane, the town marshal from Springdale, a random volunteer fire truck, a tribal cop from Wellpinit, a forensics team from Spokane, and a wildlife agent who just happened to be in the area; even a couple of FBI agents would eventually drive up the dirt road to Rhys Kinnick's little house in the woods.

Dean Burris had gone into shock, and thankfully passed out; his tortured cries had been almost as unbearable to Kinnick as poor Bethany's weeping. She'd let go of Shane's body, finally, wanting to go check on the kids, but Kinnick had stopped her and pointed to her chest. "Beth, wait—" His broken-mouthed voice sounding raspy and mushy in his own ears.

She looked down at her sweater, covered in Shane's blood, and began weeping again. Thankfully, Joanie was back, with a jacket she'd had in her car, and she put her arms around Bethany, and covered the bloody sweater with her jacket, zipping it up so that Bethany could go inside and check on the kids.

David Jr. had risen to the moment, it turned out, keeping Asher and Leah huddled in Kinnick's bedroom upstairs, and telling them to stay calm and stay put, even after the gunfire started. Davy had been the one to find the pellet gun, though Bethany had taken it from him.

Pale, unconscious Dean Burris was loaded into the back of the first ambulance, a deputy accompanying him for the forty-mile ride to Colville, to Providence Mount Carmel hospital, and eventually, to the Stevens County Jail. They didn't handcuff him, Kinnick noted, either because he was in shock or because there wasn't enough left of that right arm to cuff. They did put bracelets on Bobby, however, who eventually crawled out from under the truck. "I'm sorry," he said to Kinnick, "I didn't—" But he wasn't able to finish his apology before his head was pushed into the backseat of one of the sheriff's cars, which followed Burris's ambulance off the property.

After twice giving his version of events to a sympathetic sheriff's detective, Kinnick was put on a gurney and loaded into the other ambulance, where he was given ice packs for his face and some pills for the pain. Out the back door of the ambulance, he could still see poor Shane, his body on the dirt driveway. "Can I talk to my daughter before we go?" Kinnick asked.

Bethany had come back out of the house, eyes dusted and teary. Joanie's jacket was zipped up to her neck.

She stood at the open back door of the ambulance. "Are you okay?"

"I think so," he said. "You?"

She nodded, tears spilling over her lower eyelids.

"And the kids?"

"They're okay. Scared." She cleared her throat. "I haven't told them yet."

Kinnick said, "It can wait." Then: "I am so sorry, Beth."

She nodded, and looked back over her shoulder, at Shane's body, surrounded now by sheriff's deputies. She covered her mouth and began crying again, in little gasps, Kinnick wanting to reach for her, but unable to move because he was strapped to the gurney.

One of the medics climbed in and said he had to shut the door of Kinnick's ambulance now, Rhys muttering, "I love you," as the door closed on his daughter's tear-streaked face.

At the other end of the driveway, Brian was explaining himself over and over to various law enforcement officials—more out of their curiosity and respect for his shot than out of any suspicion that he'd done something wrong—he pointed, gestured, reenacted, telling them how he'd been worried for his friend ("He's a real hapless son of a bitch") and that's why he and Joanie had driven up here from Ford, but as they approached, they'd heard a gunshot, so he'd had Joanie unzip his hunting rifle from its case and hand it to him. And, as he'd turned up the driveway, he saw Dean Burris bent over, and Kinnick running at him with what looked like a toy rifle, so he'd slammed the car into park, opened the door, stepped out with his rifle, rested it on the car door, and when he saw Burris rise a second time with the handgun, he'd taken aim, and fired.

"Hell of a shot," the deputies said over and over.

"Thanks," Brian said, keeping to himself that he'd been aiming for the man's back, and had somehow hit his shooting arm instead. He felt sick every time he thought about it. The randomness of it all.

They told him they'd likely need to keep the gun for a while, to do forensics tests.

"All yours," Brian said. "Long as I get it back before elk season."

Kinnick's ambulance was easing past them just then, and Brian gestured toward it. "Okay if I—"

"Oh, yeah, sure." The deputy waved to the ambulance driver, who stopped. The deputy double-tapped the hood, then went around back and opened the door.

When he'd first seen his friend, after Brian ran up the driveway to check on poor Shane and make sure everyone else was okay, Kinnick had been too choked up to thank him. The enormity of it all. How close they'd come to dying. Like poor Shane, who had tried, at the end, to protect Bethany.

God, if anything had happened to her or to the kids—

Now, seeing his friend through the open door of the ambulance, the same feelings of *what might have happened* rushed through Kinnick, and his head fell forward, and he cried silently and helplessly, head bobbing back and forth. Brian leaned into the ambulance and squeezed Kinnick's foot, the only part of his friend he could reach.

"X̌est sx̌ix̌ai̓t," Brian said. He wished he knew a better phrase than *Good day*, but he had only begun taking classes at the Salish School, and, for now, it would have to do.

NINE

What Happened After

We all have to live through a dark season now and then. This is what Kinnick told himself, in the coming months, during his long, painful recovery and the difficult time that followed. Still, he found himself wondering, *How do we get back from something like this?*

He moved to Spokane for his medical care and to help support Bethany and his grandkids as they struggled with Shane's death. Kinnick had forgotten the hardest part of parenting: the realization that *you can't keep your family safe*. That no matter how strong you were, or how much money you had, you could never totally shield the people you loved from the sorrows of life. Or shield yourself, for that matter. For weeks after nearly being killed, Rhys felt like they were all still in danger. He slept poorly, was always on edge, and, at times, felt totally bereft. Post-traumatic stress, his doctor said.

Kinnick wasn't sure if the doctor was diagnosing him or the world.

Pestered by Lucy the day he left the hospital, Rhys had allowed himself to be interviewed by a young reporter named Allison. When the story ran, Kinnick was deflated. She'd gotten his quotes right and the details certainly seemed accurate, but reading about the whole thing in the newspaper somehow shrunk Shane's murder, as if it had been nothing more than a seedy domestic squabble between a flaky wife, her religious husband, and his gun-toting militia friends. Rhys even started to wonder if that's all it was. He had to remind himself of the limits of daily journalism, which was better at posing questions than answering them. Still, he wondered: Where was the story about how fear had infected so many people, how it had killed his poor son-in-law? How a sociopath like Dean Burris had burrowed his way into the Church of the Blessed Fire? How these insane things kept happening, these eruptions of senseless violence, of anger and ignorance and greed and mendacity, like ancient fissures bubbling up under the surface, and what—we were just supposed to go on with our lives? Wake up the next day like nothing happened, like we hadn't lost our minds? Just turn the page, to the baseball scores or the horoscopes or celebrity birthdays? (Nothing to see here, just America.)

The best part of Allison's story was the description of Brian: "a former air force marksman and environmental activist."

"Air force marksman?" Kinnick teased him. "You were an electrician!"

"You want to go back and trust your life to an electrician?" Brian asked.

Brian admitted that he, too, was having trouble sleeping, and that he kept replaying that day in his mind, wondering what would've happened if he'd arrived a few seconds later—or a few minutes earlier. If, say, he hadn't stopped to feed Billy on the way out the door. Maybe Shane would still be alive. ("Or Burris would've shot you, too, and we'd *all* be dead," Kinnick countered.) The sheriff's investigator told Brian that his miraculous shot had hit Burris's arm just above the elbow, and had torn through his forearm and wrist just as he raised the gun to fire, but what Brian couldn't stop thinking about was how off-target and lucky that shot had been, and how easily two other things could have happened: one, he'd missed completely, or two, he'd killed the man.

"I wouldn't want to have killed someone," Brian said. "I've made it this far in life without killing anyone. Be a shame to start now." He told Kinnick that he and Joanie had gone up to the spring barter faire in Tonasket, where they bought some of Jefe Jeff's soap, and a couple of nice belts, and that he'd filled Jeff in on everything that had happened, and that Jeff had offered them a free guided acid tour. He said Joanie was game, but that he couldn't be talked into it.

"Maybe you and I can take a trip sometime," Kinnick said.

"I think we just did," said Brian.

The prosecutor told Kinnick that Dean Burris's trial would probably not begin for at least a year. He'd hired a "constitutional lawyer" out of Michigan who planned to challenge every aspect of the case, beginning with the long-shot theory that the state had no standing to prosecute him for using his Second Amendment–guaranteed gun rights, and arguing that Dean had essentially acted in self-defense against Shane, a man who had asked for Dean's help in retrieving his wayward wife from a psychedelic music festival in the woods, and then went into a rage, and started attacking him for it. Dean's lawyer even wanted to depose Bethany about Doug and her past drug use.

"But that won't work, right?" Kinnick asked. "Blaming the victim?"

"Oh, no, I strongly doubt it," the prosecutor said. He explained that they were holding accessory charges over Bobby's head, hoping he'd testify against Dean. "But in these rural communities," the prosecutor said, "in this atmosphere, you just never know."

In a photo from the arraignment, which Kinnick looked at over and over, on his new iPhone, Burris looked thin and wan, his suit sleeve pinned to his shoulder where what was left of his right arm had been amputated.

It was one of the hardest adjustments for Kinnick, owning a cell phone again. It was like a nosy neighbor with a constant supply of scary news, a pocketful of drip-drip dread and festering fear. He was glad to be able to call and text Bethany, but the thing was a constant delivery system for terrifying developments from all over the country, from around an overheated, overpopulated planet. Technology, as he saw it, had finally succeeded in shrinking the globe, so much so that every news story felt dangerous and personal, every war a threat to his family, every firestorm, hurricane, and melting ice cap a local disaster, the seas boiling up around them, every cynical political and legal maneuver part of the same rotten fabric—and half the country somehow seeing it exactly the opposite way. He tried *not* reading the news on his phone, but after so long away, it was impossible, like he'd spent seven years quitting booze and then someone had assigned him his own, pocket-size twenty-four-hour bartender. Carrying around this little harbinger of doom, Kinnick was constantly reminded of the cold epiphany he'd had about the eternal nature of cruelty.

Shane's funeral was unbearably sad, held near his family's home in Salem. His parents wanted him buried in the family plot, next to his brother, who had overdosed after two tours in Afghanistan. Bethany, who didn't have the money for a proper funeral, hadn't argued with this. During the service, Shane's parents and his two sisters wouldn't even look at Bethany, and she suspected they blamed *her* for his death, for running off like she had. And sometimes, she told her father, she feared that she *was* to blame. ("You know that's not true," he told her.) Bethany was a wreck leading up to the service, but after getting the cold shoulder from Shane's family, Kinnick noticed, his daughter's back stiffened and she concentrated on consoling the children. Leah cried in short jags, but then would compose herself, pulling away from any arm that settled on her shoulder, including Sluggish Doug, who surprised everyone by coming to the funeral, and promising to be more involved in Leah's life. Asher cried less than his sister and was happy to have his mother's arms around him. He had a thousand questions for Kinnick—*Do they ever dig up the caskets and use them again? Have they ever accidentally buried someone alive? What will they do when they run out of places to put people?*

For months afterward, though, Asher was besieged by nightmares: his ghostly father calling out to him, various monsters and villains chasing him through the woods. He kept asking Kinnick to tell him "exactly what happened" that day, and he said he would never understand why his dad's friend would just up and shoot him like that. And why bad things had to happen to people anyway.

Bethany told him that bad things didn't *have* to happen, and that most of the time, Asher would find, they didn't. But when times got tough, like now . . . "Well, that's when we need to be strong. And to take care of each other." Asher said he would try.

Watching this conversation at the house in West Central Spokane that Kinnick had rented for himself, Bethany, and the kids, Rhys thought his daughter might be the best parent he'd ever seen.

For a while, Leah went into adolescent shutdown mode, just as Bethany had feared, sulking and keeping to herself. She continued her email correspondence with David Jr., with the blessing of Bethany, who thought that since they'd been through this ordeal together, writing to Davy might help her process it. She even agreed that Leah could get a phone on her fourteenth birthday. Things had cooled between Leah and Davy, who talked his parents out of conversion therapy. He and Leah agreed to postpone their betrothal while Davy took a year off school to "figure out who I am."

Davy's dad, Leah said, was greatly disturbed by what had happened but was refusing to completely cut ties with the Army of the Lord. In fact, the publicity had only increased church attendance, and, it turned out, people were writing from all over the country to inquire about the Rampart.

Leah refused to go to family therapy with her mom and her brother. "He wasn't my dad," she said, adding, "that's y'all's grief," part of a strange new way she'd begun speaking after only two weeks at her new public middle school. One day, not long after that, she told Bethany that she would never go to church ever again.

"I don't know if I believe in God," she told her mother.

"Well, that's understandable," Bethany said. "But if He does exist, I hope you know that He'll continue to believe in you."

Leah rolled her eyes, said, "*Ew*," and went to her bedroom to read.

If there was anyone Leah *could* talk to, it was her grandfather, so long as they stuck to conversations about books. That summer, she helped him get rid of hundreds of his old hardcovers, trading them in at a used bookstore downtown for newer titles, and helping him sort through the dozens of notebooks and journals that he hauled out of the little cinder block house in the woods. At one point, surrounded by the open notebooks, filled with years of his scribblings, Kinnick looked over the rim of his reading glasses and said to Leah, "I don't think there's a book here at all."

"Well," she said, "maybe there's a different book."

This made him smile. "About what?"

"I don't know," she said. "Maybe about what to do when the world seems like it's gone crazy."

"I'd read that book," Kinnick said.

A few weeks later, Leah burst through the door and asked Bethany, "Where's Grandpa?" The Honors English reading list had been handed out at school that day, and she and Rhys spent an hour bent over it, like two old men over a racing form, circling the horses that looked promising.

Kinnick required two surgeries to reconstruct his battered face. His jaw was wired shut for four weeks, and the doctors said that his right eye would forever sag over its repaired socket. He really liked his occupational therapist, though, who shared hilarious TikToks and Instagram posts, insisting that laughter was the best exercise for strengthening facial muscles. Here was the only proper use for this terrible pocket-size anxiety-dealing bartender, Kinnick decided, and he raced home to share the appropriate videos with the kids on his iPhone. "Watch this dog sing 'Happy Birthday'!"

One day, after dinner, while the kids cleared the table, Bethany put her hand out and touched Rhys's stitched, stapled, and resculpted face.

"I kind of like it," she said. "You're softer now."

"Like an old catcher's mitt," he said.

"Like a pillow," she said.

"Like mashed potatoes."

"Like soft-serve ice cream."

Some nights, he could hear Bethany crying in her bedroom, but he wasn't sure if he should say anything. The distance between them had narrowed, but he was still conscious of it being there, of her not quite trusting him. And why would she? At night, Bethany went for walks alone along the river. She and Anna took a yoga class together, and she got a part-time job teaching English as a Second Language. Bethany had decided to stay in Spokane, at least for the time being, and she planned to send her résumé out, in the hopes of getting on full-time with the school district. For her birthday, Kinnick bought Bethany an expensive spa day with Anna, including a bottle of champagne.

The easiest decision—and, in some ways, the hardest—was putting the failed Kinnick family sheep ranch up for sale. Of course, the place had gone seventy-five years without hosting an actual sheep, and it felt more like a crime scene than a ranch now, but Kinnick couldn't help but feel the loss of it in his bones. He had rebuilt himself up there, following the hardest season of his life—at least until now. There were trees he would miss like old friends, and cloudless night skies, and surreal dawn light, and the tracks of visitors in the fresh snow. His biggest regret was not sharing it sooner with his family; imagine the bends in the creek he and Asher could've explored, the autumn colors Leah might have named. But he got a good price for it in the end, though he surely would've gotten more had he not insisted on carrying the contract, so that he could stipulate that the land not be subdivided or clear-cut. He got rid of the ancient Audi, too, and bought a used Outback like Brian and Joanie's. He found a job as a starter at a golf course along the river, telling foursomes of old, retired guys when to tee off, when to "pick up the pace," and reminding them to not leave empty beer bottles on the tee boxes. These are also trees, he tried to tell himself on the golf course, when he felt the loss of his forest refuge. This is also water.

He had coffee a few times with Lucy, who had managed to explain to Chuck why she couldn't be his little buddy anymore. "He's doing great," she said, "fully recovered, back to work at the law firm, dating some woman he met when he returned her stolen jewelry box a few years back. He says he likes her because she's not as complicated as I am. I said, 'Damn right she's not!'"

One time at coffee with Lucy, Kinnick broached the subject of the two of them "you know, um, maybe, I mean, if you wanted to, perhaps seeing each other again, you know, in a more, well, romantic way," Lucy doing him the favor of not bursting into laughter once he'd stammered all of this out.

Instead, she seemed to really consider it for a moment, before finally saying: "Rhys, you know how, sometimes, you'll be in the kitchen, and you'll decide you need a glass of wine, but you can't find the fucking corkscrew? So, you try the usual drawers. And it's like you're gonna die if you don't get this fucking wine bottle open, so you just keep opening the same two kitchen drawers, moving around peelers and graters and the can opener, because that's where you *usually* keep the fucking corkscrew, and you're sure you put it there, even though it's pretty fucking clear by now that the corkscrew is not in those fucking drawers, but you just keep trying them anyway?

"Well," she said, "I think it might be time for me to try a different drawer."

Kinnick worked at the golf course from dawn to 3 p.m. so he could pick the kids up after school. He took Asher to his monthly junior chess club tournaments at the Episcopal Church in their new neighborhood, where the former boxer Brandon had officially made Reverend. At the first tournament, he introduced Asher to a recent Syrian immigrant named Abdel, who was eight, and whose English wasn't great, but who had studied the game as intently as Asher had, and who played three strong games against him, winning two and drawing the third. Kinnick worried that his grandson would be discouraged, losing to a boy younger than him, but he wasn't at all. "Did you see that? He opened with Ruy-Lopez, but he didn't even do it right! Plus, his people invented chess. And I almost beat him in the third game! I'm getting better!"

Unlike his sister, Asher found he *did* want to keep going to church—he suddenly had a million questions about good and evil, about what happened to your soul after you died, about whether he would see his father again someday—and so Bethany began taking him on Sundays to her mother's old Unitarian services, which, she admitted, were a bit bland and "woo-woo," but, at least, she told her father at dinner one night, "no one is packing heat."

One Saturday, the whole family went to see Cortland at the nursing home, but he was so far gone, the only person he seemed to recognize was Kinnick, who he mistook for his father.

"I'm sorry, Dad," Cortland said.

Kinnick patted the old man's wrinkled hand. "It's okay," he said. "You did your best."

The next afternoon, a breezy October Sunday, Bethany offered to take Rhys to the place where she had scattered Celia's remains.

He quickly agreed, and they went for a walk down a paved trail into the Spokane River gorge, then turned onto a dirt path that led to a small clearing alongside the river. Bethany said that because her mother had died so early in the spring, she hadn't realized that this little meadow and beach often became a homeless encampment during the summer. That's why, she explained to her father, she always brought a garbage bag, and used it to pick up the empty beer cans and drug foils, macaroni boxes and candy wrappers.

On that day, there was only a little bit of garbage, which they quickly gathered up, Bethany handing Rhys the mostly empty garbage sack and saying, "Give me a minute?"

"Of course," he said, and she wandered away from him, toward the river's edge, where she crouched down, and seemed to talk to herself for a few minutes. Rhys felt like he should give her some privacy, so he wandered downstream fifty feet. He stood there, listening to the water babble over ancient, exposed boulders. The river was incredibly low that fall, rocks and rebar and rounded old bricks emerging in the shallows, like prehistoric bones rising from the deep. Up along the canyon walls, sunlight made clouds of late-hatching caddis flies glow like lit candles above the treetops.

What a lovely spot, Rhys thought. Celia would've liked it here.

After a few minutes, Bethany stepped up beside him. "I come down here and talk to her sometimes," she said, "catch her up on what's going on."

"I'll bet she appreciates that," Kinnick said. He wanted to tell his daughter that he wouldn't mind having his own ashes scattered here, too, one day, but it seemed somehow presumptuous of him.

"Do you want to know what I said to her today?" Bethany asked. Kinnick nodded and she reached out and took her father's hand. "I told her not to worry. You were home now."

Acknowledgments

I have somehow been publishing books with HarperCollins for half my life. I am endlessly grateful for the talented people I get to work with there. This time out, thank you to my editor, Millicent Bennett, and to Liz Velez, Jonathan Burnham, Milan Bozic, Maya Baran, Tom Hopke, Zaynah Ahmed, Amy Baker, Doug Jones, Shelly Perron, Joseph Jasco, Nikki Baldauf, and others.

As always, I am indebted to my agent and friend, Warren Frazier, and to everyone at John Hawkins and Associates.

Thanks to Kyle Baird for his tour of proper off-the-grid living (unlike my fictional version), and to the Salish School of Spokane, whose commitment to keeping the Interior Salish languages alive and vibrant I am honored to share (SalishSchoolofSpokane.org).

My deep gratitude to the family and friends who helped with this book, during such a difficult season. Alec, Ava, Brooklyn, Miky, and Anne—you provided great love, support, and inspiration. Anne also broke out her fine editing chops, and Brooklyn and Miky shared their keen insights to help me invent a music festival.

Finally, a special thank you to some great writer friends who read versions of this book along the way, and who shared both their artistry and their camaraderie: Katy Sewall, Jim Lynch, Mark Steilen, and Amy Grace Loyd.

About the Author

JESS WALTER is the author of seven previous novels, including the best-sellers *The Cold Millions* and *Beautiful Ruins*, the National Book Award Finalist *The Zero*, and *Citizen Vince*, winner of the Edgar Award for best novel. His short fiction, collected in *The Angel of Rome* and *We Live in Water*, has won the O. Henry Prize, the Pushcart Prize, and appeared three times in Best American Short Stories. He lives in his hometown of Spokane, Washington.